The Place Reader of Annanbourne

Tiggy Greenwood

MEADOWELL

Published in Great Britain in 2015
by Meadowell
Meyden Revel, Cheselbourne, Dorset DT2 7NP

A CIP catalogue record for this book is available from the
British Library.

Printed in Great Britain by Berforts Information Press,
Stevenage, SB1 2BH

ISBN: 978-0-99326-251-7

Paper used in the production of this book is a natural, recyclable
product made from wood grown in sustainable forests.

www.meadowell.com

Have you ever walked into somewhere and IMMEDIATELY felt good about it? You may not have seen him, but that's the Holder you're sensing. Every property ever built has one. You've always known it really.

And if you feel the place strongly; if you think you can, in your mind's eye, see what a house was like in years gone by, then you might a Place Reader. The best ones seem to glimpse the former Dwellers too. Maybe that's where people's mistaken idea about ghosts comes from...

The Place Reader of Annanbourne continues the story of Mossy, its Holder, but in it the Place Reader emerges ever more clearly. And he's not just any Place Reader. On the one hand he's just a child. But his gift is strong, and there's something very special about him. Mossy can't understand it at first. Could this be the boy he's been hoping to meet for centuries now?

Read more about Place Readers at
www.annanbourne.com

To Jay, Rosie and Tom,
my living dreams

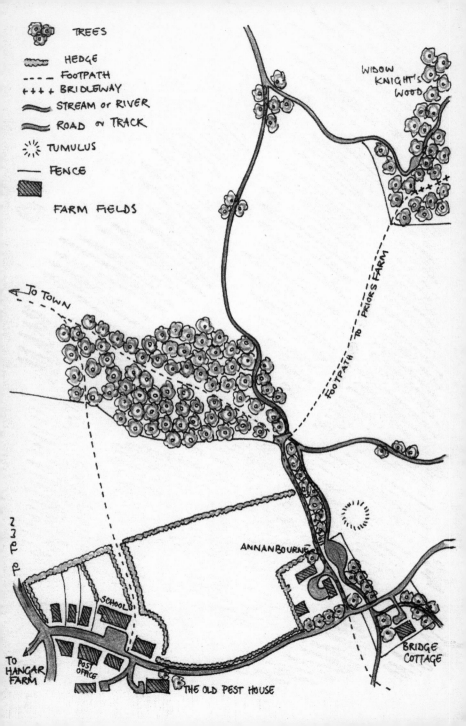

Chapter 1

What Have I Done?

Mossy sat on his Starting Stone in Annanbourne and rubbed his hands against the smooth surface. How could he have made such a stupid mistake? For centuries he had remained safely out of sight, as good as invisible to his Dwellers, but now he had been seen.

Until the Breeze family had arrived, none of his Dwellers had ever known he was there. He had been able to look after them secretly. All people had ever said was that 'the house felt good'.

It had been a bit of a struggle bringing this family through their difficulties. Dodging Rollo, with all his special skills as a Place Reader, only made it harder. Not only had Rollo sensed Annanbourne's past stories, but he had soon latched onto Mossy's presence.

Pleased that he had finally solved their problems, he relaxed, and in that unguarded moment, as he fell from the roof after being dive-bombed by the sparrowhawk, he had forgotten to keep himself properly out of sight.

Part of him was glad that he had been safely caught, kept from crashing to the ground and causing terrible damage to his beloved Annanbourne. But at what price ?! Rollo had not simply spotted him. They had spoken, shaken hands. A human knew who he was. A Dweller knew a Holder.

'What's done is done,' he sighed for the umpteenth time in the last few weeks. 'I'll just have to cope and keep out of his way.'

And yet deep inside there was a warmth. Rollo seemed so pleased, so sure.

'I always knew you were there somewhere,' he'd said. 'I could feel you looking after us, and I knew you were more than just a feeling in my bones. It's as if you are someone I've known all my life, even though I've only just met you.'

Is that it? Mossy asked himself. Is this when it all began...**how** it all began? He scratched his head, a frown settling over his shining blue eyes.

Whatever it might be, he decided, I'm not saying any more till I'm sure. He stretched his legs across the familiar stone, relaxing onto its comforting surface. Take it slowly, he reminded himself, you've all the time there is. No need to jump to conclusions. He smiled. It was jumping about that caused him no end of troubles, always tripping over himself.

'Don't jump with your feet any more than with your mind,' he muttered to himself. 'But maybe I should just find out what, exactly, a Place Reader can do.' He'd noticed how well the boy understood the needs of a building and picked up on the people who had lived there before. What other hidden skill might he have?

Rollo kept his side of the agreement. He gave no sign that he knew when Mossy was near, only ever looking when he was sure he was alone.

But then, one night not long after, Mossy felt a tingle; Rollo wanting to get in touch... Mossy normally lurked in the darkest shadows, sitting curled in corners, well out of the way. It made no difference.

'Goodnight, Mossy,' Rollo murmured as he closed his book and turned out the light.

'Oh... Um... Mmm... G'night,' muttered Annanbourne's Holder in response, ducking his head into his hands and rubbing his fingers through his hair. What had he let himself in for?

He found out a few weeks later. Instead of turning over and pulling the duvet round his shoulders when he closed his book, Rollo sat up in bed.

'Mossy?' Mossy stuck his head round the corner of the chest of drawers. 'May I ask you something?' He kept stock still.

'It would help if I could see you,' Rollo added.

'Oh well. In for a penny, in for a pound,' sighed Mossy. 'I suppose if you know I'm here, you might as well see me too.' He edged forward, shimmering into visibility as he leaned against the bookshelf. A smile spread across Rollo's face.

'What is it?' asked Mossy.

'Did you hear Mum talking about the changes that she wants to make to her studio?' Mossy nodded his head.

'What do *you* think?' Rollo continued. 'Does it matter if she adds new bits?'

Mossy's eyes gradually shifted from blue to green as he pondered. He'd never been asked about changes to the buildings before; he'd just had to cope with the consequences. Maybe being able to talk directly to one of his Dwellers could be useful.

'They're only changes in the granary,' he replied, folding his arms over his chest. 'It's not the main Holding, so I won't be affected too much, and generally it should only make us stronger,' he explained.

'So it *was* a granary!' exclaimed Rollo. 'I thought so,' he grinned. 'I remember we noticed something when she first started using it. Cissy said it smelled like beer. It must have been the grain!'

The granary smelled of oil paint and turpentine now. Mossy smiled as he recalled the energy that Annie had brought to the building through her work there, and then he remembered a strange tickle he'd been feeling on the bottom of his left foot.

'You might warn her about the floor at the back. I think some of the boards might have woodworm.'

'OK. I'll let her know,' said Rollo, reaching for his book again.

'How will you do that without her finding out who told you?' asked Mossy, his ears twitching in alarm.

'Don't worry,' smiled Rollo. 'I'll think of something.'

In fact it was Cissy and JJ who helped them find a way that weekend.

'Mum!' called JJ, running into the studio where Mossy

was watching Rollo help his mother move some paintings.

'Dad says we have to ask you if we can all go to the film in town this evening,' added Cissy, arriving hot on his heels.

'Hey, look! Isn't that that place we found when we went on the bike ride last weekend?' JJ asked, as he ran to the back of the studio to examine a painting that stood drying on the easel. 'I like the way the light shines through the wool caught on the fence.'

Me too, Mossy agreed silently.

'Have you noticed that the floor's squashy over here?' said Cissy as she twirled past the shelves to join him.

'Squashy?' echoed Annie, her brow creasing as she shifted another painting. 'That's not what a floor should be.'

'Have you ever thought about getting this place checked for woodworm?' threw in Rollo. 'It is old, and if you're going to be doing improvements, maybe you should check it out first?'

'Trust you to be thinking about worms!' laughed Cissy. She wriggled across the room like a vertical wave. 'Worms wiggle, bugs jiggle,' she chanted.

But Rollo had sown a seed, and Mossy was delighted when someone came to inspect the old granary.

'We'll need to treat this section,' she said. 'And while we're about it I'd recommend...' But Mossy wasn't really listening. What mattered was that the tickle in his foot would be resolved without having to wait until someone fell through the floor.

'There may be advantages to talking to a Dweller,' he told Puddle, the Holder of Bridge Cottage and his nearest neighbour, when he saw him a few days later, 'but I don't intend to make a habit of it.'

The following Saturday Jon, one of Puddle's Dwellers, came over after lunch.

'We'll be back well before teatime,' Rollo assured his mother.

'Just keep an eye on JJ,' Annie reminded him.

'I'm nine now. I don't need an eye kept on me,' complained JJ as he stuffed an arm down the sleeve of his jacket. Cissy pulled on her wellies.

'So no one needs to point out that you've just put your coat on inside out?' she laughed.

I'll be there anyway, decided Mossy, slipping through the door behind them.

The air was still warm, even though leaves were already scattering the ground with the reds and golds of autumn. Swallows swooped through the afternoon breeze, grabbing beakfuls of bugs, stocking up on food in preparation for the long flight south, their sharp cries ringing through the blue sky.

'It's just a walk,' Mossy told them as he ducked under the step of the stile. 'Nothing like the kind of trek you make.'

'Did you get the part you wanted in the play?' asked Jon.

'No,' Cissy frowned. 'I have to be one of the courtiers, and I only have one line. "My Lord, he left yesterday."' She bowed with a flamboyant flourish. 'I still think I could be Lady Chorlton better than Sophie Eggars.'

'One line is better than nothing,' Rollo pointed out as he

climbed over the stile to join them.

'And Sophie **is** in Year 11,' Jon reminded her. 'It's rare for a Year 7 to get any speaking part. You must've been good.'

'Leapfrog?' called JJ, running to catch up. Rollo bent forward, gripping his knees as Jon and Cissy ran ahead. Mossy smiled. Dwellers may change, he thought, and names may change, but the games stay much the same.

Rollo went flying as JJ's leg caught against his back.

'Whoops!' he laughed, disentangling himself.

'Anything broken?' checked Cissy, hopefully, as he waggled his feet.

'A bit lower?' suggested JJ, dusting himself down. Cissy bent her knees to make it easier for him to jump over her, disappointment forgotten as she watched him run up.

'*Tuck your head in,*' projected Mossy.

On the far side of the field the path wound its way steeply up through the wood as the ground rose towards the downs.

'How come there's a great wide track here?' asked JJ, peering at the tangled growth beyond the bank beside the path. 'There's no path in the field at all.'

'And how come the sign says it's a footpath across the field to here, and now it turns into a bridleway? No other path has joined it,' Jon pointed out. Cissy stopped still, staring at the sign.

'So if you've galloped down the track to here, you have to get off, leave your horse and walk. It doesn't make sense.'

Ah, but it used to, thought Mossy. There was a place where you could leave your horse, though not many did. He stood on the top of the bank, peering between the trees at the rough ground. No hint of anything now; no path, no yard, just a slight unevenness in the abandoned wood.

No loss, he thought.

No one seemed to care for the wood any longer, though once it had been a productive and useful place, even if it had never been popular. It was as if the misery of that lost house had spread far beyond its boundaries. Not surprising really; Tannor had been a bad Holder, and his Holding and all those that lived there had suffered. Mossy shuddered at the memory. He had never understood what made him like that.

The children were rounding the corner, climbing upwards out of sight, as he turned back to the path. Running to catch up, a smooth pebble shot out from under his foot, rattling down the rough track. Flinging himself to one side, he grabbed a sapling to stop himself from slipping. The slender growth snapped, a loud crack jarring the air, and he fell anyway.

'What was that?' asked Cissy sharply, her eyes darting back. 'Who's following us?'

Rollo glanced over his shoulder to where Mossy lay sprawled in a patch of mud at the edge of the track. They can't see me, Mossy told himself as he checked that the ground was still clearly visible through the hand he held in front of his eyes. But a smile of understanding flashed across the boy's face, and he winked in Mossy's direction.

'It's nothing, Cissy,' he reassured her. 'Things are always falling off trees.'

'Not true,' grimaced Jon, his arms rising in the air, his fingers stretched out over her head. 'It's me, the Ghost of

Widow Knight, come out of the wood, to gobble you up!' His hollow laugh echoed off the trees.

Cissy's yelp, and the laughter of the others, covered up the squelch of Mossy pulling himself free, and no one noticed as he rubbed himself clean with a bunch of grass and flung it into the undergrowth.

By the time he caught up they had reached the top of the hill.

'Hello, there.' A burly man emerged from between rows of vines, his big hands grimy with dirt, and Mossy braced himself in case he needed to protect his Dwellers.

'Hi there, Mr Barker.' Cissy waved a hand cheerily, and Mossy relaxed again. No help was needed if they were already friends.

'Mum said we should ask if you still want some help with picking the grapes,' said Rollo.

'Are they proper grapes? Ones we can eat?' JJ was examining the vines.

'A bit small for eating really, but fine for wine-making,' Mr Barker replied, rubbing dirt from his hands onto his trousers. Mossy joined JJ examining the vines that curled about the wire frames. They had made all sorts of things here in the past, he thought, but never wine. He looked about for Denny, the Holder of Prior's Farm.

'Can we taste some?' JJ carried on.

'They'll be a bit sour yet,' chuckled the man. Mossy rested against the old oak tree at the corner of the field. 'Harvest won't be for a while yet; we need to wait for the first frost, probably at the end of your half term. Tell your Mum and Dad I'll call as soon as we know when it'll be.'

'They said if it's a weekend we'll all come,' added Cissy.

'That's good to know. And what about you, Jon? Will you be bringing your family too?' Mr Barker turned to him. 'The more helpers we have the quicker we can do it, and the sooner we get to enjoy Marie's harvest lunch.'

'If we can't all make it, maybe I can come with the Breezes,' Jon replied.

It sounds like the old days I remember, thought Mossy, when all these farms helped each other out. It was only Tannor's Holding that never joined in.

CHAPTER 2

In The Wood

'See you for the harvest then,' said Mr Barker from the farmyard gate. 'I'll be in touch. If you're going through the wood, watch out under foot. All sorts of stuff has been dumped in there over the years, and we've rather left it to go wild. It can get quite dangerous once autumn comes.'

Mossy swung on the gate, jumping off as it clanged shut.

'So how come it's called Widow Knight's Wood?' asked Jon. 'I thought the Barker's family had been there for donkey's years. Who d'you think she was?'

'Not a ghost,' laughed Cissy. 'So don't try that one on me again!'

'I wonder,' muttered Rollo.

I remember her well, thought Mossy; a tough old lady, who had worked hard to make a living from the wood, regardless of the rumour and gossip still attached to the area. She had built the original farm and raised her five daughters there after her husband died. She'd been well respected by everybody, and it was her eldest daughter who had married Solomon Barker, nephew of the Prior of an abbey. They had renamed the farm in thanks for help he had given them. But the memory of her lived on in the wood.

'She must have been there before the Barkers arrived. But I guess she was quite someone if the wood was named after her,' he added. Mossy shook his head. It was as if Rollo could read his mind sometimes.

As the track dropped to the left JJ peered over the edge.

'Look down there.' He pointed to where the ground dipped between the trees. 'See?'

'It's almost like a path,' agreed Cissy, clambering over the bank and heading down the slope towards it.

'Fungi,' Jon pointed off to the left. Mossy was impressed. Most people would have thought they were mushrooms, but these were the dangerous ones.

'I don't think those are safe for eating,' said Rollo. Mossy's eyebrows raised in surprise. That boy was catching every thought!

'Poisonous?' asked Cissy, pulling a face. 'One sniff and you curl up and die?' Not quite that bad, thought Mossy, but they'd give you quite a tummy ache.

The dip in the ground widened as it grew deeper, a trickle of water gathering as the slope dropped away.

'It's a stream starting!' exclaimed Cissy, forgetting about poisons as she stepped around the glistening mud.

'It must join the one that goes past home,' said Rollo.

'Watch out, it's getting really boggy.' There was a squelch as JJ struggled in the ooze. The others were ahead now, Jon giving Cissy a hand to pull her up beside him on a fern-covered tree trunk that spanned the gap. Mossy lingered by JJ.

'Hang on!' called the boy. 'I've got my foot, but I've lost my boot.'

'Dappy daftie!' shouted Cissy, jumping down on the far side of the tree as Rollo came running.

By the time JJ, his boots and the mud were all back in their proper places, Cissy and Jon were nowhere to be seen.

'Hey! You two!' Rollo's voice rang through the wood. Mossy strained his ears to catch any sound that would show them where the others had gone, but apart from the twittering of birds and the scuffle of rabbits behind brambles, all was quiet.

'Cissy!' Rollo's voice was louder now.

'Is she lost?' asked JJ. There was a crashing noise of broken twigs, and Jon's face emerged from beyond the fallen tree.

'Where's Cissy?' asked Rollo.

'We've found a huge old tank. She's keeping guard. This way,' beamed Jon. Mossy wasn't quite so pleased and a frown furrowed his forehead. Tanks didn't belong in the wood, and children didn't belong inside them. What if they got stuck there? There'd been stories of lost children in the past. He didn't want that happening again.

He climbed the tree bridge and scanned the terrain that spread out below them. With many leaves already fallen from the trees, and the undergrowth beginning to die back, he could see quite clearly ahead. There was Cissy, beside a rusty block that jutted out of the ground. Rollo, Jon and JJ were hurrying to join her, pushing old brambles out of the way, clambering over fallen branches and rotting vegetation.

'Listen!' she called, thumping a clenched fist against the metal. A dull note, like a half-forgotten gong, boomed around them. JJ arrived and banged both hands against the red-stained wall. A double beat thrummed inside the tank.

'And what's more, there's a hole in the other side. We can get in!' exclaimed Jon.

No! cautioned Mossy.

'Rollo!' he projected. *'Not inside the tank!'* But this time Rollo didn't want to catch his message. Maybe I'm too far away, Mossy decided, and he jumped down from his viewing point and broke into a run.

'Let me go first. I can check that it's safe,' Rollo decided, pushing aside a vine that draped over the corner.

By the time Mossy arrived, Rollo was out of sight.

'What can you see?' Jon called.

'Not much, it's rather dark.' Rollo's voice rumbled inside the tank. 'And it stinks in here.'

'What does it stink of?' asked Cissy.

'I've got matches,' called Jon, digging a hand into his pocket and working his way to the jagged hole. 'That should help you see, even if it's a bit brief.'

'It might not be the kind of brief you're thinking,' fretted Mossy, his nose quivering as he breathed in the air from the tank. It was the kind of smell he'd caught seeping out of rotting plants or buried rubbish, the kind that led to surprise fires and sudden explosions.

'I want to see,' protested JJ.

'I found it first,' Cissy retorted.

Rollo's face appeared from the gloom.

'Plenty of space,' he grinned, 'but you'll have to come in one at a time.'

'*Not matches,*' pleaded Mossy silently. He hurried to Rollo's side, softly laying a hand against his knee. '*Rollo, no matches, please. Think about why it smells.*'

Jon ducked his head into the space.

'What makes it stink like that?' Rollo asked. Jon backed out.

'Rotting vegetation makes… um… gasses.' He scratched a hand through his hair. 'Not sure exactly which, but maybe it wouldn't be such a good idea to light a match.' He stuffed the matches back into his pocket. 'What we need is a torch.' Mossy heaved a sigh of relief.

Now it was Cissy who thrust herself into the darkness, quickly swallowed by the blackness inside.

'Yuk, it's all slimy,' her voice echoed. 'But it's worth it for the sound effects.' A mournful roar was quickly followed by a whoop, a howl and then a shriek that sent shivers down Mossy's spine. It reminded him of something. He wrinkled his nose, checking the vibrations in the air. Was there a stranger lurking?

'Is that you Cissy?' asked JJ, peering into the black cavern.

'Come and see for yourself, little boy,' came a strange voice, far deeper than Mossy had ever heard Cissy produce. What if there was someone else in there, someone the others hadn't seen in the darkness? Mossy stepped forward as JJ hesitated at the entrance.

'Go on JJ, she's just fooling you,' laughed Jon.

'D'you want me to come with you?' asked Rollo. JJ waved a hand, pushing him away.

'No, I'm not scared,' he said, but he seemed unable to take another step.

'Whoa-ha-ha-ha-ha!' laughed the voice in the tank. 'I like eating little boys.' JJ took a step backwards, reaching behind him for the comfort of his brother.

'And she complained that I wasn't to tell her ghost stories,' laughed Jon.

'Come on out of there!' Rollo shouted towards the tank as he ruffled JJ's hair.

''S just me.' Cissy's grinning face appeared in the opening. 'Did I scare you?'

''Course not,' protested JJ, but Mossy noticed he no longer wanted to explore.

'We'll come back with a torch,' Rollo reassured him. 'Then you'll see it's fine.'

Mossy was relieved when the children abandoned the tank and returned to following the trail of the growing stream.

'D'you think this is how the Amazon starts?' asked Cissy, bending to dip a hand into the clear water. 'I could be Stanlietta Livingstone.'

'Where does the Amazon start?' added JJ, balancing on a stone.

'I know where the Nile starts,' suggested Jon, unhelpfully.

'Wrong continent and wrong person for the Amazon,' Rollo reminded them. 'Bramble,' he added, pointing it out. Mossy caught the jagged growth springing up from under Cissy's foot, successfully stopping it from whacking JJ in the face.

The trickle of water now flowed over a gravel bed between

banks overhung with grass and the last of the summer's dying flowers. Mossy spotted the entrance to a water vole's home. The roots of an alder stretched into the water, forcing it to curl around the trunk before it dropped over a rock.

'Look, it's made a little pond all of its own!' exclaimed JJ, peering over the edge.

'I'll test it. I've got wellies on,' announced Cissy as she lowered herself into the water. 'It's not too deep,' she called over her shoulder. Her arms suddenly shot out sideways. 'Eeer, euch!' She pulled a face. 'Yes it is. Much deeper than I thought, actually... Oh yuk!' She reached a hand up to Rollo, who was laughing. 'Gimme a tug, will you?'

'Now who's a dappy daftie?' said JJ as she sat on the bank to pull off her boot and pour out the water.

'OK, fair comment,' Cissy agreed, stripping off a muddy sock as well.

Mossy took advantage of the pause to look around him. There was nothing familiar. He hadn't been in Widow Knight's Wood for ages, and markers that he'd used to guide him in the past had disappeared. Since his last visit, forgotten seedlings had become wide, spreading trees that arched branches above their heads. Even the track had changed, the banks to either side seeming to rise more steeply than before. Or maybe the path had sunk?

When the children set off again, one of Cissy's feet squelched. The stream continued its descent through the wood, dropping through several more little falls. As the ground levelled out, the trees thinned, opening to a view of a valley that fell away beyond the bank of the stream. Here the water ran more slowly, lingering in a pool already scattered with brown leaves, before it found a split between two boulders and burst tumbling over rocks to the fields below. Mossy glanced around him. It was strangely quiet.

JJ gazed thoughtfully across the water and then looked up at the oak tree that reached over it.

'See that branch?' He pointed overhead. 'If we tied a rope on that we could swing right over the water.'

'And if you let go...' added Cissy, her eyes lighting up at the thought.

'Sploosh!' JJ clapped his hands.

'Good idea,' laughed Rollo. 'Though I'd have thought you two were soggy enough already.'

'We've got plenty of rope at home,' Cissy reminded the others. 'All that stuff left over from when Dad helped us make the rope ladder?'

'Could you climb up there to attach it?' JJ asked.

'What d'you think, Jon?' countered Rollo.

'Piece of cake,' Jon nodded his head. Not so sure about that, thought Mossy, though he could imagine that a rope swing would be fun. He wouldn't mind a go either, sweeping over the water; it'd be like flying. Mind you, he frowned, you'd have to make sure you held on tight or you'd sail over the stream to where the ground fell away, and then it would be a long, hard fall.

Cissy rummaged through broken wood on the ground while Jon and Rollo examined the base of the oak tree, looking for handholds to help them climb. JJ picked up a stone and threw it across the stream.

Mossy shivered. Had a cold breeze blown through the wood? Suddenly he felt a sharp burst of pain, like a burning coal between his shoulder blades. He spun round to search the undergrowth. Nothing moved.

Rollo rolled his shoulders, easing them as he, too, looked around.

'You know, we ought to be getting home. We told Mum we'd be back by teatime, and it's five already.'

'I saw a fence over there,' said Jon, pointing through the trees. That's right, thought Mossy, time to move on. I don't like the feeling here. Something's wrong. He scanned all around them, but still saw nothing out of the ordinary, nothing that explained the way his skin prickled.

'We'll have to find our way back to the track. It can't be far,' said Rollo.

'It should be this way,' Cissy agreed, launching off to the left.

'But we can come back another time,' insisted JJ, 'can't we?'

'Sure,' agreed Rollo. 'It's not long till half term. We'll do it then.'

'Look, there's the weird signpost, the bridleway/footpath one. That bank must be the edge of the track,' called Cissy.

Mossy stood on the banked side of the path and looked back to where they had been. The stream was no longer visible, the ground mostly level with a few dips, hollows and bumps. Then it hit him. They had just crossed the ground where Tannery Cottage used to be.

Again a shiver ran through him. It was uncanny the way a bad feeling could linger so long after the house and all its inhabitants had disappeared.

A flicker of movement in the undergrowth caught his eye.

Mossy stared hard. Low under the scrub of a bramble thicket he saw two dark red pinpricks glowing in the shadows. They blinked. I knew it, thought Mossy, something had been watching them. What animal could it be? Maybe he should warn Rollo before they came back?

CHAPTER 3

By The Beacon

Acouple of weeks later they were in the kitchen after breakfast.

'Make sure you've got gloves and hats. You can always take them off later, but it'll be chill on the top of the downs,' Jack reminded everybody. Mossy tucked his toes out of the way as Rollo dumped a pile of plates on the dresser.

'Is it true that we'll be able to see some of the other beacons as well?' asked JJ.

'Not now, during the day, but tonight we should,' Annie told him, handing him the knives.

'Imagine it, lines of beacons passing a message. It must have been so exciting.' Cissy waved a tea towel over her head.

'It depends how exciting you thought it might be to be under attack,' Rollo reminded her. 'It wasn't just any old message.'

'But this time it's just for the festival. That'll be fun,' countered Cissy.

It was a long time since Mossy had been up to visit the beacon on the top of the down, and he decided to go with them. How would they be travelling?

'Bung your wellies into the back of the car in case we need them,' Annie said. 'It shouldn't be wet, but you never know.'

Ah, thought Mossy, the car. He missed the days of travelling by horse. It had always been easy to cadge a lift then. You could talk to horses, but cars were full of problems. He prepared to slip through the door with the first person out.

'Mum, have you seen my other glove?' shouted JJ as he burrowed about in a heap of clothes.

'Where did you leave it?' asked Annie, zipping her coat. Cissy grabbed her boots.

Could I ride in them? wondered Mossy, but he changed his mind when he saw Cissy sling them into the back of the car and slam the door shut. There had to be a more comfortable way.

Jack reversed the car out of the barn.

'Rollo, can you help me hitch up the trailer?' Mossy looked over to where it stood, heaped high with hedge trimmings and fallen leaves.

That was his answer. A bit breezy, maybe, but easy to jump into, no door to trap him inside or out, and well-cushioned at the moment. Running ahead of Rollo, he quickly clambered in and perched himself on the top of the heap. Rollo grabbed the hitch and pulled the trailer round as his father reversed towards them. Some of the clippings shifted, slipping to one side and tumbling Mossy onto his back. Whoops! He grabbed at the edge.

'Mossy?' Rollo's voice was hardly even a whisper. 'I hadn't realised you were there. You OK?' Mossy glanced about him. There was no one else around, just the approaching car.

'Fine,' he replied. It seemed rude to keep quiet when he had been directly addressed.

'Are you coming with us?' Rollo continued, a smile spreading across his face.

'I thought it would be good to see the beacon,' Mossy answered.

'Are you OK there?' I can't see you. I just heard you fall and...'

'D'you want a hand?' called Cissy, running to join them.

'Just help me hitch it onto the tow bar,' Rollo told her. 'It's easier with two.' Cissy looked up as the connector clunked into place, saw JJ running towards them and abandoned Rollo.

'Bags I the window seat,' she shouted, as she grabbed the door handle.

'If you'd prefer, you can have a lift in my coat pocket.' Rollo's voice had slipped back to a low whisper.

'Kind of you to offer,' Mossy replied, knowing that Rollo meant well. Quite frankly he could think of little worse than travelling in a pocket. He had noticed that boys had a tendency to stuff them with all sorts of rubbish. 'I fancy a bit of fresh air,' he added, to ensure that Rollo didn't try to change his mind.

'Everything alright?' asked Jack, joining them. Rollo stepped away from the trailer.

'Yup, fine,' he said. 'I was just attaching the wires for the lights.'

In no time the trailer was bouncing behind the car on the steep lane to the top of the down. Ahead, the car swerved to avoid a pothole, but the trailer wheel jolted into it. Clippings slithered down to the back corner, taking Mossy with them. He tucked his toes under the rim to make sure he wasn't flipped over the side. This wasn't as easy as he remembered.

A sharp twig sprang loose, and a shower of greenery leapt into the air. Mossy shifted his legs to avoid being spiked as another sprightly branch made a bid for freedom.

'Oh, no you don't,' he muttered, pulling it back down. 'And you're not taking me with you either,' he added, as it pressed against his back. He wriggled round, unhooked some leaves from his ear and crawled back to the top of the pile.

He was just beginning to enjoy the ride when the car turned onto a rough track. The trailer lurched sideways, more clippings tumbled over the edge and this time, as Mossy grabbed for the frame, he felt it slip between his fingers. Springy grass cushioned his fall, but he still hit the ground with a hearty whack. He struggled to his feet, rubbing his hip as he watched the trailer bounce cheerily across the top of the down. He knew the way to the beacon however, and set off on foot, following the line of the fence.

Two sheep grazing on the other side lifted their heads from the close-cropped grass. They paused in their chewing, one bleating at him.

'Didn't see any sheepdogs,' he reassured her. 'But if they're making a fire I expect they will move you.' She bit the head off an old plantain and blinked at him mournfully.

'Keep to the middle of the flock,' he advised, 'and then they can't possibly nip your heels.' Who'd be a sheep? he thought as he hurried on; always worried about something.

He soon spotted his Dwellers, their car parked beside the fence. JJ was playing tag with another boy, and Cissy was propped against a wide gate, chatting to two girls. Rollo was inspecting the trailer, while Jack and Annie talked to some other adults.

The sound of an engine drew his attention. It looked as if he'd been reassuring the sheep too soon. A sharply pointed, black-and-white nose thrust over the shoulder of Will Earp, their neighbouring farmer, as he steered the quad bike past him. Mossy hurried after it.

'Thanks for waiting,' Will called, jumping off. 'Don't want the sheep spooked tonight, and we'll have them out in a jiffy.' He unlatched the gate.

'Where are you taking them?' asked Rollo.

'Down to the fields near you, actually,' he replied. 'They've finished the grass up here, and I want them closer before the rams join them. By the way, Jack, that manure you were asking about is ready.'

'Oh good!' exclaimed Cissy, breaking off from her conversation to join her parents.

Mossy arrived as the dog thrust its head through the wire fence, enthusiastically inspecting the sheep.

'Any chance you could go easy on them, Meg?' Mossy projected. A short yip made him step back as the dog turned sharp eyes on him.

'No, of course I don't want to teach my grandmother to suck eggs,' Mossy apologised quickly. *'You do as you think best.'*

'If you could wait here 'til we've brought them through the gate...' said Will, jumping back onto his bike and speeding off in one direction as the dog circled off in another. Mossy saw the sheep scatter, breaking into a nervous trot, their heads held high, as they spotted Meg. A long whistle brought the dog streaking low over the grass towards them, darting first to one side, then another, gathering the sheep together, collecting them into a herd.

In no time the woolly mass tumbled towards them. Mossy stepped behind the shelter of the gatepost as the leaders hurtled past, bleating crossly.

'I wasn't lying,' he protested. 'I had no idea they were coming.'

'If you could shut the gate when you've finished,' shouted Will over the noise, chasing his flock, the collie slipping through to remind stragglers who thought they might stop for a quick bite to eat, that lunch was still a long way off.

As the cars started off across the abandoned field, Mossy was just in time to grab the back of the trailer. JJ swung on on the gate as it closed, jumping off when it clanged shut, and running to catch up with the others as they followed the cars.

'What were you looking for in there?' Cissy asked Rollo. Mossy felt a twig of evergreen tickle the back of his neck.

'It looked like some stuff had dropped off,' Rollo replied. 'I just wondered if it was anything important.'

''S only bits and pieces. None of that's important anyway,' Cissy pointed out, waving a hand in Mossy's direction. Mossy smiled. He knew what Rollo had been looking for, and was surprised how good it felt.

A large pile of old timber, and other dry, burnable stuff was already heaped on the grass. Mossy inspected it carefully.

'We're going to build the bonfire over there,' announced a tall, bearded man, pointing to a pyramid of timbers that pointed towards the sky. 'All help welcome.'

'We'll leave our stuff in the trailer until the end,' decided Annie. 'Then we can put it directly into place.'

'No point in shifting it twice,' agreed Jack.

Coats were stripped off, hats and gloves abandoned, as everybody worked together. Mossy kept an eye on JJ, though these days he hardly needed it any longer.

'Hang on, I'm putting my gloves back on,' he said, before picking up the splintered end of a plank.

Mossy did his own bit of clearing too.

'Keep well away,' he told some rabbits who peered out at him through the dry grass. They twitched their noses and folded their ears back.

'Just tonight. You'll be fine again tomorrow, but there won't be much grass left round here anyway. Stick to Grandfather's Bottom, if I were you, hardly any Dwellers go up through there these days.'

'Bonfire and fireworks,' he warned some field mice.

Two earlier arrivals left, taking the children's friends with them.

'See you later,' called Cissy. Another car rumbled across the field towards them, a big trailer groaning behind it, laden with more fuel for the fire.

'Wow! It's going to be massive,' exclaimed JJ.

'Were the beacon fires always so big?' asked Cissy. 'Is that why there're no trees up here?'

Rollo stared around him. *'Go to the beacon,'* projected Mossy. *'You'll feel the answer there.'*

'D'you still need us here?' Rollo asked Jack.

'Nearly finished,' his father replied. 'Why?'

'I just wanted to check out the beacon.'

'That's fine,' called Annie. 'We'll call when we're getting ready to go.' I'll be listening, decided Mossy.

Over by the beacon, JJ turned to Rollo.

'Give me a leg up, would you?' he asked, reaching his hands towards the top of the plinth. Soon all three were standing on the top of the concrete beacon marker, the wind buffeting against them, tugging at their hair.

'I can't see home.' Cissy pushed the hair out of her eyes. 'It's behind the shoulder of the hill, though I can see where the path comes up.'

'I can see the sea, the Isle of Wight and all along the coast towards those spiky things over there,' added JJ.

'That's the oil refinery. That's why they made the beacon here,' explained Rollo.

'Because of the oil refinery?' JJ looked puzzled. Rollo smiled.

'No, because they could see the sea, and the harbour and the channel. They could see if anyone was coming to attack.'

'And then they lit this beacon?' JJ asked. This time Rollo nodded. Mossy leaned back against the smooth concrete.

'Tell them,' he projected. *'Tell them what you can feel.'*

'Imagine it, all cold and dark, the wind whistling over the down, and then you spot the enemy sailing up the channel,' started Cissy.

'How did they spot them in the dark?' asked JJ. 'Did they have lights on?'

'Good one,' Rollo laughed, sitting down on the plinth, his legs hanging over the edge as he stared out to sea. 'No, it was daytime. But they'd been waiting for ages.'

'It must have been lonely up here, just waiting.'

'I bet it was,' agreed Cissy.

'Someone from Annanbourne,' Rollo's voice spoke softly now, as if he was searching for a memory.

'That's it,' agreed Mossy. *'I remember it well.'* He shut his eyes, cast his mind back.

'Taking turns with others to keep guard up here,' Rollo continued, 'aware that the enemy was coming, but never sure when. Knowing that they had to keep the fuel dry, ready at a moment's notice.' He looked around him. 'Over there,' he pointed at the far horizon. 'And there too.' He swung to point in another direction. 'Constantly searching for the spark of light from another beacon.'

Mossy saw it vividly in his mind's eye; Thomas standing there, wrapped against a chill wind.

'One of the girls brought up something for him to eat,' Rollo continued, almost as if he was describing the scene that Mossy had watched with his own eyes. 'They stood together.' Mossy looked up at Cissy and JJ staring out towards the sea.

'Suddenly they saw a speck on the horizon. 'What's that?' she asked, and then they saw them; the beacons lighting. 'The Warning,' she called. 'The Warning of The Armada."

Mossy shivered. It was uncanny the way Rollo could see it so clearly. Mossy had been there when it had happened.

Listening had brought it all back to him, as clearly as if it were happening afresh.

Now Cissy was pointing out towards the horizon. JJ shielded his eyes against the sun.

'Look,' she whispered.

'I can see it too,' JJ nodded his head. Mossy searched the sea. What was he seeing there? A sail in the far distance? Surely... He searched around him. Over by the bonfire Annie and Jack were unloading the trailer, raising the stack higher. He almost believed that he had slipped back to that day when...

"Raise the alarm!" called Rollo. "Fetch the tinder box!' They had to find the dry lint to light the beacon.' And then? thought Mossy. Do you know? He watched Rollo intently.

'He dropped the tinderbox.' Rollo's face paled as he spoke, his eyes closing as if he couldn't bear to see the sight of it. 'Don't let the side down. Find the flint.'

Mossy smiled. *'I kicked it free, remember?'*

'Got it.' Rollo's voice had dropped until it was barely above a whisper. 'Light the torch and lift it high. Fan the flames and bring the dry faggots.' Now his voice rose again. 'There she goes, and there's the flash of the fire on Beacon Down to the left. They've seen it too. Turn round.' Cissy and JJ spun to face the hills behind them. 'There it goes!' Now his voice sounded triumphant. 'The message is passing down the line. There's the spark from the beacon up by the Hog's Back. In no time the Queen will know in London, and the message will be passed to all the commanders of the Navy. We've done our bit to defend our country. We've passed the message through.' Rollo heaved a huge sigh.

'Wow, Rollo!' Cissy's eyes shone. 'That was amazing. It was almost as if we were there. Like you were describing it in real life.'

'And see,' added JJ. 'There **is** the Armada.' He pointed down to where, far away on the sea, two yachts battled the choppy sea as they struggled towards a safe harbour.

'I don't think it's quite an Armada,' laughed Rollo. 'But you're right, we can see the boats really clearly.'

Annie was heading in their direction.

'We're finished,' she announced. 'There's more stuff coming later, but we've done our bit for now.'

'Rollo's been making up a story about the beacon,' JJ told her, as Cissy lowered herself over the side. 'And then we spotted the Armada coming to attack. Watch out, I'm going to jump.'

'From up there?' Annie looked alarmed. Mossy laid a restraining finger against the side of her leg.

'*Trust him,*' he projected. '*He's thought it through.*'

'Pwagh!' grinned JJ, as he dusted the earth off his hands. 'That was a big one.'

'You OK there, Rollo?' Annie looped an arm over his shoulder on the way back to the car.

'Yeah, fine,' he replied. 'It's amazing up here. I can't wait 'til this evening; I'm really looking forward to seeing the beacons light up. You said that there'll be fires on four that we can see from here.'

'That's right, apparently,' agreed Jack. 'But we've got another job to do first. All aboard.'

Mossy hooked a leg over the back of the trailer. No need to worry now, he grinned to himself as he settled into the corner. Nothing to bounce him out this time. That didn't mean he didn't get fairly thrown about as they rattled back towards the lane.

I wonder? he thought. That was quite some Place Reading Rollo had done. Right in every detail, even down to dropping the tinderbox and lighting the beacon at the same time as the one on Beacon Hill.

Then a more worrying thought entered his mind. What had Jack meant by 'another job to do first'?

CHAPTER 4

A Tricky Choice

Mossy gripped the side of the trailer, the wind buffeting him as the hedgerows flashed by. Sometimes a particularly hearty bounce jolted him, but it was fun, and he laughed as he spread his feet wide for stability. A sharp cry rang through the rushing of the wind, and he looked up to see two buzzards cruising on a thermal between the clouds.

A flash of brown on the verge caught his eye and he staggered to the back of the trailer.

'Buzzards!' he called, cupping his hand round his mouth to send the warning further. The rabbits ducked into the shelter of the hedge, flapping their ears.

'You're welcome!' he called, as the trailer swung round a corner. The road down to Annanbourne disappeared to the left behind them. Mossy stared after it. Where were they going now?

The car slowed, and Mossy read a sign announcing Aller Farm as they turned onto a rough track. A pothole flung him from one side of the trailer to the other, landing him on his back. He had just staggered up onto his feet when the car stopped by a low brick wall.

'Can I ring the bell?' asked JJ, heading for the house.

'Morning, Jenny,' Cissy greeted the woman who answered the door.

'We met Will up by the beacon,' Annie explained.

'Collecting the sheep,' JJ added.

'And he mentioned the manure,' finished Jack.

Mossy looked around him. Manure? What manure?

'Of course,' smiled Jenny. 'It's over there, behind the barn. I'll get the boys to give you a hand. I'm glad to see you, Annie, because I wanted to ask you about...' The two women disappeared into the house.

Mossy's heart sank as his transport was reversed round to the back of the barn. This didn't look good.

'Hi there,' said the two boys who appeared with a couple of pitchforks. 'Mum says the pile to the left is the best rotted.'

'It's pretty stinky,' grumbled JJ.

'That's the fresh bit, where we dumped the stuff from the pig pen after they got turned into sausages.'

'D'you turn the whole pig into sausages, Andy?' asked JJ, turning to the older of the two boys.

'How can you eat a pig you've given a name to?' added Cissy.

'Piece of cake!' laughed Andy's brother. 'Get Mum to cook it and it tastes yummy!'

'The roast pork we had last weekend was from here,' Jack reminded her. Mossy chuckled as Cissy clapped a hand to her mouth.

'Oh no, I was eating someone who's back I might have scratched!'

'Even though it wasn't sausages,' joined in JJ.

'But it was delicious,' Rollo mused. Mossy nodded his head. He'd enjoyed it too.

'Come on, Rollo,' interrupted Jack. 'Grab a pitchfork. We can't let Andy and Nick do all the work.'

Mossy's heart sank further as he dived off the trailer, tumbling onto a soft patch of grass near the base of the pile. He leaned back against the wall of the barn, watching Rollo approach the dark heap.

'D'you want to come and see the new pigs?' asked Andy. 'They're in the field.'

'Can I give them apples like we did last time?' JJ cheerfully turned his back on the manure.

'I'll help Dad first, and then I'll come and find you,' said Rollo.

'Looks like you're going to have a bit of a mucky ride home,' said a soft voice by Mossy's shoulder. He turned to find a Holder beside him.

'Albi!' he smiled in greeting. 'If I'd known they were going to do this,' he waved a hand at the activity, 'I wouldn't have hitched a ride.' He thrust both hands deep into his pockets as Jack dumped the first load of manure into his trailer.

'At least it's not the fresh stuff,' Albi pointed out, trying to cheer him up. 'Why not travel in the car? There's a window open.'

'It'll be full of Dwellers, and keeping out of the way will be tricky. Anyway, I got locked in it a few months ago, and I'm not keen on a repeat performance.'

'What brought you up anyway?'

As Mossy explained, the heap in the trailer spread until every corner was filled. Then it grew higher and higher.

Albi decided he'd join his Dwellers at the Beacon that night.

'Long time since I've seen the beacon lit. Last time they were worried about the invasion.' Mossy nodded his head. Albi was nearly as old as him, and they'd helped each other out in the past on more than one occasion.

'Phew, hot work,' said Rollo, stripping off his jersey and flinging it through the window to join his jacket on the back seat.

A slurp of manure rolled to the edge of the trailer, paused and then splatted onto the ground.

'I think that's about it,' decided Jack, scooping it up and putting it back in place.

'Leave the pitchforks here,' said Nick, sticking his in the ground by the heap. 'Mum said she wanted some taken to the veg patch for her, too. Come on Rollo, let's find the others. They'll still be in the field, I reckon.'

Mossy and Albi followed the trailer as Jack drove the car round to the front of the house and disappeared inside.

'You could always walk,' suggested Albi. Mossy nodded.

'You're right. But in that case I'd better set off now.' He had already turned towards the lane, when the sound of running feet stopped him in his tracks.

'I just want to get my jersey,' Rollo yelled back to the others, who were still out of sight. He arrived at the car. 'Mossy?' he asked urgently in a horse whisper, searching around. 'Mossy, are you there?'

'He knows your name?' Albi turned incredulous eyes on him.

'Long story; he's a Place Reader and I finally had to give in. But he's OK.'

'You know, he reminds me of someone. Your friend... thingummy... You know.'

'Mmm.' Mossy deliberately didn't answer. 'Stay there,' he instructed Albi, 'and keep well out of the way. I wouldn't be surprised if he could spot you too.' He ambled over to Rollo's side, briefly shimmering into visibility as he arrived.

'What is it? A problem?'

'I was thinking of you,' said Rollo, bending down to untie his shoelace. 'How are you going to get home if the trailer's full of manure?' He retied the lace and immediately undid it again. 'I know you weren't very keen on the idea, but I wondered if you might want to change your mind about a ride in my pocket?'

'What's the matter with your shoelace?' asked Mossy, slipping back out of sight. 'That's the third time you've untied it.'

'If I stand up normally and talk to you, everybody will hear me. If I just crouch down and whisper and anyone sees me, they'll think I've gone barmy. I'm just trying to look normal.' Mossy laughed quietly as Rollo reknotted his lace and then slipped it loose once more.

'Good idea,' he admitted.

'Rollo!' Cissy's voice called. Rollo glanced over his shoulder.

'I've got to go. Andy's going to show us how the new tractor works. Tell you what. I'll leave my jacket on this bench. If you want a lift, you can get in the pocket. Otherwise, I'll see you at home sometime, and I'll just hold my nose if you smell terrible. Maybe we all will!' he laughed, as he tied his shoelace one final time and stood up.

'Rollo, you coming or what?' Nick shouted as the others came into sight from the far side of the yard.

Before Mossy could respond, Rollo had grabbed his jacket, flung it onto the bench and, still pulling his jersey over his head, ran off to join the others as they headed into the tractor shed.

'You could knock me down with a feather,' laughed Albi, once the children were out of sight. 'Talking to a Dweller, cool as a cucumber. But, you know, it's not a bad idea.'

'Travelling in a pocket?' protested Mossy. 'It's so undignified.'

'Better than smelling of pig manure and easier on the feet than walking,' Albi pointed out. 'It's not as if he doesn't know that you're there anyway, by the look of things.'

The roar of a tractor engine shook the air.

'How old's that boy?' asked Mossy in alarm, as Andy drove the tractor out into the yard. The Breeze chikdren were crammed into the cab beside him.

'Sixteen next week,' replied Albi proudly. 'Been driving tractors since he was ten, only on the farm mind, but he's coming along a treat. Did a great job clearing out the lambing sheds last spring.' Nick opened the gate, letting the tractor rumble and bounce into the field, before he turned to smile at the parents who had emerged from the house.

'We're just taking them to collect that trailer of hay bales Dad loaded this morning,' he told them.

'Don't worry, they're perfectly safe with him,' Jenny reassured them too.

'I just wish our lot would let us know sometimes before they rush off to do these things.'

'Don't worry, they can't blow anything up on the tractor,' laughed Nick.

'Ah, so you heard about that, did you?' Annie blushed. Mossy remembered that explosion well.

'We all heard about that.' Nick was still laughing as he turned and ran after the disappearing tractor. 'I wish I'd been there too!'

The parents were joking about blasts from the past as they went into the house, leaving Mossy and Albi by the car.

'So, to pocket or not to pocket? That is the question,' grinned Albi. A splot of rain hit Mossy's nose. That did it.

'Give me a leg up?' he asked, reaching for the seat of the bench.

He had just tucked himself into place when the clouds opened and torrential rain stormed down on them. Albi ducked low, spread his hands over his head in place of an umbrella, and ran across the yard. He nipped past Annie's legs as she burst through the door and raced in the opposite direction towards the car. Mossy folded his legs and slid into the depths of the pocket, tucking his ears and nose safely out of harm's way. There was a sudden jolt as she grabbed the jacket, then turned and fled for the shelter of the porch again.

'Daft boy,' she laughed, flinging it down on a chair in the hall. Mossy landed with a thump, the back of his chin whacking against something hard. He winced. 'He'd leave his head behind if it wasn't growing on his shoulders. I can't think why he took it off in the first place.'

'I thought he'd left it in the car,' came Jack's voice. 'It's a good thing you saw it.' Mossy reorganised his limbs, straightened his left ear and pulled his nose into line. Now he was there, he'd better make the best of it.

'At least I'm dry,' he thought.

He was beginning to feel quite cosy in the pocket by the time he heard the door fling open again.

'...'f you ask my Dad.' The children's feet rattled across the stone floor.

'What's it like having a Dad who's a teacher?'

'Better than having one who's always away on business.'

'And Mum likes it better now too,' added JJ.

'Mum? Dad? Have you seen my jacket? I left it on the bench,' Rollo called. The footsteps headed further into the house.

'I hope I haven't just made a terrible mistake,' Mossy sighed.

CHAPTER 5

A Place Reader At Work

Mossy felt himself being swung into the air and then swirled round. There were unexpected hazards to this pocket travel, but things calmed down quickly and he felt an arm brush softly past the outside of the pocket.

'*Whatever you do, don't stick a hand in and feel me,*' he projected.

'*As if!*' He could even hear the chuckle in Rollo's response.

'I'm sitting by the window,' he heard him announce.

'Bags I the other one.'

'How come I always have to sit in the middle?' grumbled JJ.

'You don't,' Rollo pointed out. 'I was in the middle on the way here. Come on JJ; fair's fair.' Mossy felt the space around him as the car door slammed shut.

'Hey, budge over, Rollo,' complained JJ. 'I'm all squashed up against Cissy.' Mossy felt himself shifted about, but when he peered out of the pocket he noticed that Rollo had created a gap by resting an arm against the door. Rain drummed against the window, drops racing each other down the glass. He smiled. Maybe there were upsides to knowing a Dweller well enough to cadge a ride; at least he was warm and dry and someone was going to make sure he found a way out of the car.

'So, Rollo? When you said they kept watch up by the beacon,' came Cissy's voice. 'Did the girls join in as much as the boys?' Mossy pricked up his ears, wriggling higher to hear clearly. How would Rollo answer that? These days girls did pretty much the same as boys, but back then...

'It was different in those days,' replied Rollo. 'Girls weren't allowed to do half the things that you do now. Stuck in a long dress, even you would've found it tricky to tramp about all over the place. It would have been mostly men who kept watch. Still, if the father of the family had been up all night and there was no one else to do it, then that's when one of the boys would have been asked to help out.'

Mossy squirmed round in the pocket and looked up at Rollo, his nose twitching in excitement. How come he knew the precise reason why Thomas had been asked to take over the watch? His father had been exhausted after a tricky night calving. Albi's Dwellers were ill, struck down with fever, and Denny's lot busy in town on business. No one had even thought to ask Tannor's Dwellers to help, and many of the other houses nearby now hadn't even been built then.

'But you mentioned a girl,' Cissy pointed out.

'You aren't the first troublesome girl,' Rollo chuckled. Mossy grinned. That was just how Mary Rose's father had referred to her, 'Trouble in Petticoats', but he'd always smiled as he said it.

'So she would have been there too.' Cissy sounded pleased. 'Helping to light the beacon.'

'Wrapped up in a blanket against the chill of the night and alone in the darkness, straining your eyes against the black to search for the faintest light.' Once again Rollo's voice sounded as if he was describing something familiar. 'They knew that trouble might come, but not from which direction.'

'But how could they tell the difference between lights from the towns, from travellers, an approaching ship or another of the beacons?' chipped in JJ.

'It wasn't like now. In those days there were no lights in the streets. At night it would have been pitch dark, and during the day there was nothing else like the light from one of the beacons.'

Mossy listened enraptured as Rollo launched into stories about the beacon watches; about a girl who helped her brother spot the warning beacons that flashed along the coast and carried the message up to London to tell the Queen that the King of Spain's armies were sailing in attack. They helped make sure the whole nation was ready to defend themselves in time.

'This girl… What was she like?' asked Cissy. Mossy's eyes widened in amazement at Rollo's reply.

'Not like you, always in jeans and a T-shirt. She had dark eyes and a big smile; freckles like JJ's.'

'Oh come off it,' laughed Cissy. 'You don't know about the freckles.' But Mossy nodded his head. Mary Rose had indeed been freckled.

'She climbed these hills in a long skirt and never cared if

she had to walk miles,' Rollo continued, as if he was describing a friend that he knew well.

'Looks like the rain's stopping,' Jack interrupted them finally. 'All this talk of lighting things has reminded me that we need to chop some wood. Are you up for giving me a hand?'

'I'll help,' volunteered JJ.

'Not with an axe, you won't,' Annie reminded him. 'You can help me and Cissy build the wood stack in the barn. I can't let it be thought that we wouldn't join in and do our bit after all you've been telling us. I don't know where you get your imagination from Rollo, conjuring up these pictures of the past, but they certainly make me feel almost as if you'd been there.'

Mossy nodded his head in agreement. He'd been there, and it was uncanny the way Rollo had read the beacon site. Was there more to Place Readers than he'd heard? More than simply understanding the feeling of a place? Maybe it was time to check, and as he felt Rollo turn to get out of the car he tucked himself well out of sight, flattened against the wall of the pocket.

Rollo abandoned his jacket, hanging it over the end of the wood pile so that Mossy had an opportunity to ease himself out and slip away unobserved in the noise and activity.

He paused, watching as Rollo picked up the axe and listened to Jack's instructions. He looked just like any other boy, absorbed in his own world, doing the sort of things that all boys enjoyed, testing his strength and learning new skills. A crunch at his back made him turn to find Cissy bearing down on him with JJ riding in a wheelbarrow. Quickly he dived into the damp undergrowth, where a shower of small drops cascaded onto him from the dripping leaves.

An annoyed nose twitched at him, and two small eyes glared from beneath the damp undergrowth.

'Oops, sorry,' Mossy apologised, avoiding the sharp prickles and edging to one side as he sat up. 'No, not trouble exactly. You don't happen to know anything about Place Readers, do you?' The hedgehog flicked its whiskers.

'So who would you ask?' The hedgehog turned sideways and pulled the leaves a little closer.

'Really?' Mossy was surprised. 'I haven't seen him in years, hadn't realised he was still around. But won't he be hibernating?' This time the hedgehog turned his back, burrowing his head under the darkness of the heap of dead leaves.

'Ah, yes. Point taken.' Mossy blushed in embarrassment. 'I suppose you were sort of, but it wasn't **deep** sleep was it? And if you don't mind me saying, it might be better further into the copse. They build bonfires here.' The hedgehog turned round to look at him again, his eyes blinking sleepily.

'Tell you what,' decided Mossy. 'To make up for breaking your sleep like that, I'll help you find a better spot where no one will disturb you. And gather some padding to keep you warm. In return, if you can think where I might find him, maybe you could let me know?'

With a loud crack a log split apart as the axe thumped through it.

'Well done, Rollo!'

'Wa-hey!' chorused Cissy and Jack.

'We'll put more ready for you,' called JJ. Their

enthusiastic voices faded as Mossy and the hedgehog crept away.

Once a safe winter lodging had been comfortably settled into, Mossy turned his energies to finding others who might help him.

'What exactly do you think a Place Reader can do?' he asked the rabbits as he passed their burrow.

'Apart from seeing me,' he pointed out as they disappeared into the darkness.

'Any suggestions?' he asked a couple of mice, their cheeks stuffed with the last grains of maize that had been left for the pheasants. One wiped a paw over her whiskers, while the other washed his ears.

'Thanks, but I think I'd already worked out that they 'know stuff'.'

A rook cawed loudly in reply, and various other birds twittered frivolous responses, but Mossy wasn't as amused by their jokes as they were.

Finally he found him, buried under a pile of leaves in the hollow trunk of the old oak tree whose leafless branches reached up to the clouds that scudded by overhead. He tapped discretely at the shell and coughed. Nothing stirred. The hedgehog had mentioned apples, he remembered. He hurried off in search of a particularly sweet one. When he returned, everything remained still. He hoped he wasn't too late. He knocked again, stepped back and then knelt down to hold out his offering.

'I wondered if you would like a last bite of apple?' Silence. Mossy stood up again and tossed the apple from one hand to the other. It smelled good. His nose wriggled in pleasure as he lifted the apple closer. He was just about to take a bite when there was a grunt from under the patterned dome.

'No, of course I wasn't going to eat it myself,' he protested, almost dropping it in his haste to distance it from his mouth. Slowly a creased face emerged, from which two sharp eyes peered blearily out at him, but Mossy wasn't fooled. Those eyes saw through most things, and Mossy stood still as he was inspected from head to toe.

'Glad to see you looking so good too,' he replied politely. 'It's been a long time.' The sharp jaws bit into the juicy flesh of the apple, and still Mossy waited for permission to ask his question.

The apple was half eaten before there was a pause that invited him to speak.

'It's about Place Readers,' he explained. 'You may have heard that one of our Dwellers is one, and I wondered if you knew any more about them than I do.' Slowly the wizened head swayed from side to side.

'Oh,' said Mossy at one point.

'Right.' He nodded his head. But the next comment made him step back in surprise.

'Really? Are you sure?' he checked. 'You're not just pulling my leg?' There was a sharp grunt as the head snapped back under its shell again.

'No! No!' exclaimed Mossy. 'That's not what I meant. It's just that... What I mean is... Are you really suggesting that it could actually be him?'

The dull drip of old rain falling from empty twigs was the only reply. Mossy's shoulders slumped. He felt confused. Maybe he hadn't heard correctly, but he knew better than to try asking again. Disturbing a tortoise was bad enough, but a grumpy old one, interrupted at the start of hibernation, was never going to give him a second chance.

'I'm sorry,' he apologised. 'And I wish you a safe, calm winter and a warm spring to follow,' he finished, using the traditional autumn farewell.

As he headed back towards his house, his head was in a whirl. Alright, so the tortoise was well known for his delight in telling tall stories, and it wouldn't be the first time that Mossy had listened in amazement only to find out that the wizened old fellow was laughing at him behind his back. A couple of decades ago he had been enthralled by a story about the stars being holes carved into the curved dome of the sky, almost believing that they really were tiny windows letting through the bright light of a vast night sun.

He shook his head, reluctant to be fooled again. There was one other person he could try. It might mean that he had to miss the lighting of the beacons, but maybe then at least he'd know.

CHAPTER 6

In Time, Or Too Late?

Mossy stayed up on the roof long after the Barn Owl had left. For the first time since he had known her she had no clear answer. She neither confirmed, nor denied the tortoise's suggestion, insisting instead that this was something he had to work out for himself. He had to watch and listen and think.

What she had made clear, however, was that he owed Rollo 'a debt of gratitude'. He tapped his toes on the roof tiles in frustration. OK, so he had yet to thank him for getting him home safely, but that was an easy one to put right. However, deep inside, a lingering feeling niggled at him that this 'debt' was something more than a ride in a pocket.

And then there was that warning. He shivered as dark clouds blocked out the light of the moon. 'Take care what trouble your feet lead you into.' Had she, in fact, been warning him of troubles ahead? Trouble for him rather than his Dwellers this time? He couldn't think of anything that could go wrong now that his Holding and his Dwellers seemed so settled. He stopped tapping his feet.

Bright lights crested the hill and then swooped down towards Annanbourne. In no time car doors were slamming, and Cissy's voice rang through the chill night air.

'And the beacon on the Hog's Back. I never thought we could see so far!'

'Whoosh! Zoom!' JJ flung his arms up towards the darkness. 'If I were a Buddhist I think I'd like to come back as a firework.'

'Really?' laughed Annie. 'Are you sure? It's a short life.'

'But think, Mum. All those people saying Oooooh, and watching, and being excited when you go off, ker-bam, bright lights everywhere. Think of all the people you make feel happy. When's Bonfire Night? I can't wait.'

'Half term,' said Jack, as Mossy felt, rather than saw, him slip the key into the heavy lock of the front door. Smiling, he stood up, one arm resting along the top of the chimney as he prepared to climb back down to settle his Dwellers into his home for another night. Then he caught a glimpse of the perfect thank you to Rollo, wafting its way towards the house.

JJ was soon curled into a lively dream of flying sparks and swirling flashes of light. Cissy was sailing on the high seas, a cutlass gripped between her teeth as she boarded a pirate ship in search of glittering treasure. Downstairs, Jack and Annie were talking quietly as Rollo read in bed. He looked up as Mossy slipped silently into the room, his face breaking into a broad smile as the Holder shimmered gently into visibility.

'You missed a sight tonight,' he said, closing his book and dropping it to the floor by his bed. 'We beat the beacon on Harting Down by a millisecond, but Cissy spotted the one on the Hog's Back and there was hardly time to turn round and we could already see the spark on Beacon Hill. There were so many people too.'

'Not the first time there have been celebrations on the hill,' grinned Mossy.

'I'd give almost anything to have been there the first time they were lit,' sighed Rollo, his face taking on a dreamy look.

'I could tell you about it,' suggested Mossy, tentatively. 'I was there then.' Now Rollo was all attention, his eyes sparkling. Mossy felt a ripple of excitement run through him. Was this what friendship with a Dweller could bring? A chance to share some of those times with him, relive them in his mind? Was that what the tortoise had meant?

'You were? Wow, that would be almost as good.' Rollo sat up in his bed, arms wrapped round his knees.

Outside in the corridor, footsteps approached. Mossy dived under the corner of the duvet as Annie stuck her head round the door.

'I thought I heard voices,' she said, smiling as she crossed to the bed. Mossy pulled his toes in a little closer and hoped that the duvet was rumpled enough for no lumps or bumps to give him away. 'Please don't tell me you've taken to talking to yourself?'

'No Mum, nothing to worry about,' grinned Rollo. 'Not unless you're hearing strange voices coming out of thin air.'

'Time to settle down anyway. School tomorrow, remember,' added Jack. Mossy shifted sideways, flattening himself against the edge of the mattress, as Rollo pulled the duvet over his shoulder.

'See you in the morning,' he mumbled, his hand reaching for the bedside light.

The darkness wrapped itself tightly around them as Annie and Jack departed for their own room, their voices gently rising and falling, punctuated by the occasional burst of soft laughter. Mossy didn't dare speak or move, lest something alert them to his presence. If he could hear them, then they might still hear him talking to Rollo. He'd just have to wait.

Rollo's breathing came steady and low.

'*Wait*,' Mossy projected, hoping it wasn't too late already. The instructions, if they were to be trusted, had been quite clear. He had to wait until Rollo was really tired, but once he was asleep it was no good.

Gradually silence wrapped itself around the house. Mossy eased himself out from under the duvet. A thin beam of light seeped around the edge of the door, just enough for him to see the dream he had spotted earlier lurking in the far corner of the room; billowing sails, creaking wooden hulls, straining wet ropes – it looked like the sort of thing Rollo would enjoy. As Mossy slipped silently to the floor the last light disappeared.

'Rollo?' he whispered. Rollo turned over, a soft sigh of sleep telling Mossy that he had missed his chance.

Never mind, he thought, and he stepped out of the way, beckoning the dream over and inviting it to do its work.

'*Thank you Rollo*,' he projected. '*Thank you for the safe ride home.*'

Captain Drake and Walter Raleigh, potatoes, cloaks, saltwater and … Hang on! Mossy pulled himself upright. What was that he'd caught a glimpse of? Thomas and Mary Rose? Where had they sprung from?

Carefully he repositioned himself, climbing up to the top of the bed, gently placing his hands either side of Rollo's sleeping head. A smile flitted across the boy's face, and Mossy could see why. This was a vision of Annanbourne a long time ago, a Place Reader's dream.

Mossy knew many of the people that Rollo was meeting in his sleep, old Dwellers of his, long since gone, children grown up, married and moved on. He remembered those celebrations at the end of harvest, celebrations that included a thanksgiving for the new young Queen who promised an end to the terrible religious persecutions. Had the Travelling Holder visited then? Other Holders had come with their Dwellers for sure, but he didn't remember the Travelling Holder coming while that particular set had been with him. That wasn't until years later, at the time of the beacons. And anyway, he chuckled to himself, Sir Walter and Captain Drake had never come to Annanbourne.

This was just a dream; a good one, but nothing more than that. Maybe this was what he had to understand: this was how Place Readers worked, not those tall tales that the tortoise had spun him. He should have known better than to have let himself be hoodwinked. Still, at least he'd done as the Barn Owl had reminded him and found a way to say a proper 'thank you'.

CHAPTER 7

Friendship

Heavy rain pounded down on Annanbourne on the first day of half term.

'It's like being a prisoner,' moaned Cissy. She glared at it bouncing off the stone path. 'Stuck indoors all day.'

'You can go out and get wet if you want to,' JJ pointed out.

'Can I go round to Bella's?' asked Cissy, her face brightening at the idea. 'We need to get together to write our drama thingy for the Christmas Show.'

When Rollo disappeared off to Jon's house, Mossy spent the morning with JJ and Annie in her studio. The energy of their painting fairly zinged around the room, and he smiled in delight as JJ called his mother over to admire his work.

'Wow, JJ, that's brilliant! Why don't we get it framed, and you can give it to Dad for Christmas?'

After lunch, Mossy joined Jack in his study. He stretched his legs across the top of the books, rested his head on a copy of Treasure Island and watched Jack humming quietly to himself as he leafed through some books before settling down to draw a huge map. Mossy smiled. His Dwellers were all happy and fine. Life was good.

'And if there's time can we go the Natural History Museum, too?' asked JJ the next morning, racing Rollo for a seat in the car.

Mossy didn't catch Jack's reply, but he was glad to let them go on their own. He had things to attend to.

The constant rain had brought the level of the stream rather high, and he wanted to warn Will's sheep in the meadow about a possible dousing. He looked at his home and smiled. Thank goodness we're on higher ground than the fields.

Rain plastered his hair against his head, dripping from the tips of his ears and nose, shrink-wrapping his clothes against his body. A duck quacked loudly as it paddled frantically against the rush of water.

'Should be fine if you can get there,' agreed Mossy. 'Good luck!'

Water was already tugging at the base of the bridge. Mossy laid a finger on the moss-covered wood. He felt it straining, but he could also feel its strength.

'Just stay put,' he muttered encouragingly as a twig pirouetted towards him. It caught against one of the struts, creating an eddy of rushing water.

'Not you,' he said, hooking a long finger under it and setting it on its heady journey once again. 'I was talking to the bridge. You need to aim for the sea.' The twig twirled into the heaving water of the pond, made a quick circuit and then headed on to shoot the rapids as it hurtled towards the woods. This was getting serious.

'Head for higher ground,' Mossy kept repeating to all the creatures he met. 'Water's rising. Higher up a blade of grass won't help,' he warned a spider. 'Go and find a tree.'

A deep roar greeted him at the foot of the old willow, where the stream dropped over a series of boulders into a pool of water. Now it buffeted against the worn wood, curling into its hollow trunk before leaping and battering against the roots, tickling the earth and stones from their place. The branches creaked and groaned. Mossy brushed the rain from his face, shook the drips off his fingers and placed a hand on the shuddering wood.

'At least it's been a good, long life,' he sighed, 'and I've seen you rise from batterings like this before.'

He ducked under the fence, heading into the meadow with his warning. A crack of lightning was followed almost instantly by a rumbling roll of thunder. Glancing up at the heavy grey clouds that dragged across the sky, Mossy felt the rain slicing into him as the grass bowed under its battering.

Another flash of lightning rent the grey, and he looked anxiously at the trees surrounding the meadow. Many still had leaves, though the rising wind was snatching them, flinging them in handfuls across the sky. If it grew much stronger it would bring further trouble. Beneath them he saw the sheep in a damp huddle.

'You need to get to higher ground!' he called. One of the ewes butted her neighbour.

'Climb onto the tumulus.' Two more sheep turned their backs on him and another bleated crossly.

'I didn't lie to you that time, and I'm not lying now either. I really didn't know that they were coming, but this time I do.

And it's not collies, it's water, lots of it.'

A quick check of the stream confirmed his fears; it rushed by, lapping at the top of the bank. He broke into a run and cupped his hands around his mouth.

'Flood!' he called. The water snaked its fingers into the meadow, flattening the grass before it, darting through the dips and hollows, washing everything out of its path. The sheep skittered sideways, bleating anxiously and then running in front of the water.

'Not that way, you idiots,' shouted Mossy and broke into a sprint. What was it the dogs did? He grabbed a handful of soggy wool on the leader's back leg and tugged hard. Then he ran round to another and did it again. The sheep split into two groups, one half jostling each other as they struggled towards the tumulus, the rest staggering through the heavy grass and aiming for a rise at the far end of the field.

'Stay there!' he called, the wind whipping the words from his mouth and throwing them out of earshot. Now he needed to get himself to somewhere safer. He turned and ran towards the tumulus, where the sheep stood looking at him, water dripping from the tips of their ears.

'I'm coming to join you,' he called.

Suddenly he came up short. A tough old bindweed had twisted itself around his ankle. He turned, stooping to unwind it, his eyes flickering over to the fast approaching water. Another tendril seemed to grab his wrist. Mossy grimaced, lifted his right foot and then stamped it down again as a loop ensnared the toes on his left.

'Keep calm,' he reminded himself, checking the oncoming flood. Over by the stream there was a loud crack as the willow gave way, collapsing into the stream and smashing the bank.

'Oh no,' Mossy groaned, his fingers battling with the rubbery coils. Water leapt at the fallen trunk, then surged into the meadow. His fingers worked frantically, but each time he released one fetter, another wrapped him in its embrace. Twisting round to check on the water, Mossy saw a wall of foaming white racing towards him. He stumbled back, feet still tied in place, tripped in the wet and crashed to the ground. Up on the tumulus the sheep blinked rain from their eyes. One bleated.

'No, no,' called Mossy. 'Don't even think about it.'

A loud squeak made him look down. Two small black eyes peered up at him from the grass.

'I'm sorry,' he gasped, snapping his foot away from the mouse's tail as his eyes lit up. 'You couldn't just...?' The whiskers twitched as teeth were bared.

'Promise I'll keep still.'

Small teeth made short work of the bindweed, snapping through the stems as Mossy struggled to his feet and shook off the last shreds. He ran beside the small brown body, inches ahead of the water that gurgled as it grabbed at their heels. A dock leaf flapped heavily down across their path.

'Come on,' he called, scooping the mouse into his arms. 'No time to ask if you mind,' he muttered. He heaved the mouse onto the sloping side of the tumulus and scrambled after him. The sheep stepped aside to make space.

As the water surged around the base of the mound Mossy sat, his elbows on his knees, his head in his hands, surveying the chaos around them. The fallen willow now diverted the floodwater into the meadow, where it was turning a shallow dip into a churning pond, beyond which it hunted for a new route across the grass on its way to join the old streambed further down. Beyond it, the rest of the flock stared back at him through the sheets of steel grey rain.

'Goodness only knows what would have happened if you hadn't poled up in time,' he said, turning to the mouse that now sheltered under a sheep. 'If I'd been washed away I dread to think what would have happened to Annanbourne.' He shuddered at the thought. 'I'll see if I can find some food as a 'thank you'. Pasta OK? By the back door? It won't be until after my Dwellers get back, but I think I know a way to avoid mouse traps being set.'

A coot and two ducks splashed down beside them.

'I'm glad you're pleased,' chuckled Mossy, 'but I can feel a strange trickle down the back of my neck which tells me it's time I went to check on my house.' He turned for home and then remembered one last warning he needed to deliver.

'Don't be surprised if some collies do turn up.' The sheep hung their heads, water dripping off their noses.

By the time Mossy had hauled soggy leaves out of the gutter, so that water slipped down the pipe rather than splashing down the wall, the rain had eased to a steady downfall, and the wind had settled into playful gusts.

He and Annanbourne were still fine. Maybe the Barn Owl had been warning him unnecessarily. Birds feel the weather more than we do, he reminded himself. And it was his feet that had got him into trouble. He let himself into the house via the chimney and headed to the airing cupboard to dry out.

Mossy could still hear the steady drum of the rain against the darkened windows when his Dwellers finally arrived home.

'Did you see the stream?' asked Rollo as they hung wet jackets to dry.

'It was really high,' JJ added.

'Do you think we'll be flooded?' fretted Cissy. Mossy saw Rollo shake his head.

'The water would go out across the meadow before it came up to the house,' he said.

'I wouldn't count on it,' added Annie, looking anxious. Ah, but you can, thought Mossy. He's right; he knows. But, just to be on the safe side, he laid a finger on her arm to help her relax.

Mossy trailed after Rollo, watching for a quiet moment when he could talk to him on his own, finally catching him as he went to get an extra jersey. He shimmered into visibility as soon as Rollo's head burst through, one arm still battling to find its way down the sleeve.

'Hello there,' grunted Rollo. 'Something up?'

'Nothing serious, but you need to let your friend Will know that his sheep need help. Flood water in the meadow.'

'That's not serious?' asked Rollo, running for the door.

'Not serious for me or the house,' shrugged Mossy, as Rollo hurtled down the stairs.

'Thanks for the warning,' said Will, with Andy at his side, once the sheep had been shifted to a dry field further from the stream. 'And for the help too.'

'I'm not sure what made so much water flood in there, but we'll have a look in the morning and let you know,' Jack assured him. Time enough for that, thought Mossy, knowing that he still had another favour to ask of Rollo before the morning came.

He waited till late supper was done with and the children had gone to their rooms. Rollo looked up from the book he was reading and raised an eyebrow when he noticed Mossy appear by his bedside light.

'Thanks for that,' he said. 'They did look wet. And Will said they'd be all too likely to do something daft if they were left all night. It was fun shifting them.'

Mossy crossed his legs once, then uncrossed them and crossed them the other way.

'Is there something else?' asked Rollo.

'It's more that I need to ask a favour.' Rollo said nothing, just relaxed against the pillows and watched Mossy. 'You see, someone gave me a hand today, well, a tooth to be precise. I sort of owe him. You couldn't put a handful of dried pasta in the shelter of that pot by the back door, could you? I promised him some food in thanks. It's just that if I help myself...'

'No problem,' grinned Rollo, flinging back the duvet and heading for the stairs.

Mossy faded out of sight and followed him softly down.

'Hello there!' Jack and Annie looked surprised as Rollo and Mossy entered the kitchen. 'Problem?'

'Just peckish. D'you mind if I get something to eat?'

'After that huge supper?!' exclaimed Annie.

'Boys his age have hollow legs,' Jack reminded her, rising to his feet. 'There's plenty of fruit.' Mossy wasn't sure the mouse would go a wow on fruit.

'I was going to take it up to bed, and fruit will make a mess of the duvet,' Rollo pointed out. 'Any chance of some dried pasta? Fewer crumbs than biscuits,' he added.

'Dried pasta?' Annie looked puzzled, but Jack was already reaching into the larder.

'Help yourself,' he said, passing the packet to Rollo.

'How many are you planning to feed?' asked Annie as Rollo scooped a double handful. 'Are you lot up to something? Should I be worried?'

'No, Mum,' laughed Rollo as he headed for the back door. Mossy watched with growing admiration.

'Where are you going now?' Annie looked even more puzzled. 'Your bed's upstairs, not outside.'

'Just checking the rain,' explained Rollo, grinning broadly as he returned, his hands considerably less burdened with pasta. He planted a kiss on his mother's cheek. 'I reckon we'll need to check the stream and the meadow tomorrow, don't you?' He glanced over at Jack and headed back towards the stairs.

Mossy could have laughed out loud as he turned to follow his friend.

'What is it with teenage sons?' Annie asked Jack. 'I could have sworn there was something else going on there, other than a hungry boy. Something, but I've no idea what,' she admitted.

Upstairs, Rollo dived back under the duvet and turned a cheerful face to Mossy as soon as he appeared.

'Even if they do look, I don't think they'll see it. I shoved the pasta right behind that pot. Here...' He held out a dry spiral to Mossy. 'D'you want some?'

Mossy's eyes sparkled a mischievous yellow as he remembered an old trick he'd seen previous Dwellers play. He took the pasta and put it into his mouth before placing hands on either side of his head. He winked at Rollo and bit down firmly as he gave his head a sharp twist to the left. A loud crunch cracked through the quiet room.

'Good grief!' Rollo lurched bolt upright in his bed, wide-eyed in shock. 'Was that your neck? You alright?'

By the time all the pasta had been finished, Rollo could crackle his neck as loudly as the delighted Holder. 'Make sure you're there when I show the others tomorrow,' he laughed.

Mossy's eyes had turned to a soft, turquoise blue.

'I'd never realised that having a Dweller as a friend could be so much fun,' he admitted. 'Let alone be helpful as well.'

CHAPTER 8

Cracking On

Mossy watched as Rollo pulled on his waterproofs and headed over to the barn to collect his bike for the paper round the next morning. It was strange, this feeling of having a friend at hand. Someone living in his Holding who knew he was there and seemed to like him.

Cissy rushed into the kitchen when Rollo arrived home.

'The pond is about to overflow,' she announced. Mossy looked out of the window again. Surely the water couldn't have risen that high so quickly? The rain had almost stopped.

'It's not the pond, so much as the stream,' Rollo told them. 'You can't get to the little bridge any longer, but that's only the beginning. Further down the track you can see ducks swimming about where the sheep were.'

JJ was all for abandoning breakfast and rushing out immediately.

'See! I told you! We're going to be flooded.' Cissy was only briefly glum. 'D'you think they'll send a helicopter to rescue us?' Mossy felt the tingle of her excitement.

'The bridge is in a dip,' Jack reminded her, 'and the ground slopes down from the house to the stream, so the meadow is lower than us.'

Mossy inspected the flood damage beside his Dwellers.

'Wow!' JJ admired the expanse of new water. 'It doesn't look like it could ever have had sheep in it at all!'

'And here's Will back. I hope there weren't any left behind last night,' said Jack, pulling on a waterproof and going out to join him.

Mossy followed them into the garden.

'Can we help?' called Rollo.

'Dad spotted a tree down,' shouted Andy over the noise of the engine. 'Although the water is going out into the meadow, it's backing up around Bridge Cottage. Jon and Sophie'll be flooded soon if we aren't careful.'

Mossy looked up the track to see Puddle heading their way.

'It's OK,' he reassured him. 'They're going to clear it.'

'I've come to help too!' shouted Jon, running to join them.

'D'you remember what it was like organising help in the past?' Mossy asked Puddle as they sat on a branch of an alder, watching the tractor winch the heavy trunk away from the stream.

'And how the horses got stuck in the mud?' added Puddle. Rollo, Jon and Cissy squelched about in the sludge of the broken bank, whilst JJ grinned down at them from his perch in the tractor cab.

'It can still be difficult with some of the new Holders and their Dwellers,' Puddle reminded him as the grown-ups set to work with spades.

'There have always been Holders who can't be bothered or

who have trouble built into them,' Mossy agreed. 'It's not just the new ones.'

By lunchtime the stream had returned to its usual route, though the new 'lake' still lingered in the meadow. Seagulls had joined the ducks, shouting raucously when anyone came near. At the pond by the house Mossy was pleased to see that water levels were already dropping, despite the wooden bridge still swimming in its personal swirl of water. Sticks and other debris stranded on the bank showed how high the water had risen.

'At least you don't need to worry about being flooded any longer,' Mossy reassured Puddle as they said goodbye.

'Thanks again,' grinned his neighbour. 'It was a close run thing.'

As his Dwellers laid the table for lunch, Mossy noticed Rollo diving into the larder.

'JJ, if you can let Mum know that lunch is on the table, we're all ready,' said Jack. Rollo lingered by the cooker while the last things were put out, bending to fiddle with his shoe as they seated themselves.

'Are you skipping lunch today?' Cissy asked. Mossy wasn't the only one looking at Rollo when he straightened up, a loud, grinding crack clearly audible as he rubbed at his back. Annie was on her feet immediately.

'Rollo!' She rushed to his side. 'What on earth have you done?'

'Was that your neck, or your back?'

'I'm going to have a wheelchair-bound brother!' announced Cissy, striking her forehead dramatically.

Rollo grinned, and Mossy clapped a hand over his mouth

to stifle a laugh.

'What was that you put in your mouth?' asked JJ.

'Well spotted,' laughed Rollo, flinging a handful of dried pasta onto the table. Annie cuffed his shoulder gently.

'So that's what you were up to last night,' she laughed. 'Pretending you were hungry, practising to give us heart attacks.'

By the time lunch was over, joints were creaking and cracking all around the table. The dry pasta had been raided several more times, and Cissy was looking forward to giving her friend a surprise when they met up at the cinema.

Mossy was even more impressed. By settling his parent's minds about what he'd been doing last night Rollo had covered his tracks without giving away the real reason for wanting the pasta.

'Was it Jon that showed you?' asked JJ, crunching down on a final piece and adjusting his elbow dramatically.

'No,' admitted Rollo. Mossy narrowed his eyes. Once again he'd taken things for granted when it was too early to be sure. How difficult would it make things if Rollo did tell them? One Dweller knowing about him was manageable, but if they all did, how was he supposed to look after them properly?

'No, it was someone else.'

'Who?' quizzed Cissy, scrubbing the table.

'No one you know,' muttered Rollo. 'Just a friend.' Mossy felt a glow of warmth course through him, his ears twitching in delight. He was surprised how pleased he felt that Rollo described him as a friend. Cissy paused.

'Just a friend?' she echoed, a cheeky light shining in her

eyes. 'I know all your friends at school. Which one?'

'Not from school,' Rollo admitted.

'Got it!' grinned JJ, winking at Cissy. 'It's a girlfriend,' he decided. 'Mum! Dad! Rollo's got a girlfriend!' Now it was Rollo's turn to round on his brother and sister, glaring at them.

'He's certainly not a girl, he's…' He paused, sighed. 'It's just someone local. I do know one or two people you haven't met, you know.' Mossy had never realised that keeping his existence hidden might cause Rollo problems.

'*Tree swing,*' he projected, sending the idea spinning into the room.

'D'you still want me to help you build that swing in the woods?' Rollo asked JJ.

'Across the stream? Oh yes!' JJ's attention was caught afresh.

'Not today,' interrupted Annie. 'I think you've had enough wet outside for one day, and I promised Mrs Adlington we'd help her sort out the stuff for the Bonfire Night barbeque. Tomorrow should be drier. If you're going to be doing things in the wood, tomorrow will be better.'

'And I'll be able to help too,' announced Cissy, flinging her cloth into the sink.

Mossy smiled to himself. Well done, Rollo. He'd successfully kept his existence a secret and distracted the others from their teasing. Now it was time to leave them to their own devices, he decided, and slipped quietly from the room, heading for the door to the garden to check if all the pasta offering had been found.

CHAPTER 9

Swinging Out

The following morning the sun shone on a sodden world. The meadow was still far too soggy for the sheep to return, and although the stream was back within its banks, it still hurtled by at a ferocious speed. A blackbird searched among the tangled driftwood for interesting titbits as a duck sailed backwards past them, dragged by the flow.

'See you down in the woods,' called Mossy.

Rollo emerged from the barn with a long coil of rope slung over one shoulder.

'We can find all the rest of the stuff we need down there, I reckon.'

'Look after each other,' called Annie, waving them off. 'See you at lunchtime!'

JJ ran ahead, jumping in puddles all the way down the track. Mossy, now mud-splattered, hung back by Cissy, who was keeping out of the way. As the path began to rise, Rollo launched into the woods.

'This is the place!' announced JJ as they came into the

clearing. 'See that bank?'

Mossy looked around him. He still didn't feel comfortable here, even though there was no sign of the old buildings. He felt a shiver go through him. What was it that he'd seen last time? He racked his memory, but couldn't remember quite what it was that had so unsettled him.

Pools of light glistened on the wet ground. Mossy shook himself.

'Don't be silly,' he muttered. 'Any kind of trouble is long since gone.' He forced himself to look through fresh eyes. It wasn't surprising that JJ liked it. There was lots that was perfect. A big oak stretched out across the stream that tumbled energetically past them. The water widened to a calmer pool before turning to splash noisily round some rocks and drop down to the valley beyond. Vegetation was dying back.

'If we make the swing there,' JJ pointed to a thick branch that hung high over the water, 'and launch ourselves from that mound,' he pointed to a hummock beyond the trunk of the tree, 'we'll swing right over the water, and high over the valley too.'

'We'll need a stone or something to weight the rope. Then I can throw it over the branch, climb up and tie it in place,' decided Rollo. 'Anyone see anything?'

They scattered into the wood, searching through the undergrowth.

'How's this?' suggested Cissy, waving a long, sturdy bit of wood. 'If we prop it against the trunk it'll help you start climbing.'

'Hey! Look!' Now JJ was waving something. Mossy

edged closer to see what he was holding. 'This bit of wood is completely round. Would that do instead of a stone?'

'It almost looks like a door knob,' said Cissy, hurrying over. Mossy peered round her leg.

'Don't be daft,' called Rollo. 'You don't get door knobs in the middle of a wood. And anyway, I need something heavier.'

Mossy was puzzled. You could find all sorts of things if there used to be a house in the middle of the wood, he thought. In fact it wasn't a door knob. It felt more like the roundel off the top of a post.

He looked at Rollo. How come the Place Reader hadn't felt the lost house that had once stood there? He frowned and scouted around him. What other bits and pieces might they find?

'This'll do,' said Rollo, holding up a rough flint about the size of a tennis ball. Cissy abandoned her search to help him tie the rope around it.

Mossy stepped back as Rollo eyed up the branch, took aim and threw hard. The stone soared through the air, falling back to the ground with a thump.

'Nearly!' shouted JJ. A couple of throws later it thudded against the branch.

'Watch out!' called Cissy, diving to one side as it bounced back at them. She grabbed JJ and pulled him out of the way as the flint glanced against his shoulder.

'Ow!' he yelped, giving it a rub. That shouldn't have bounced over to there, thought Mossy, his eyes wide in surprise. It was almost as if the branch had thrown it back at them.

'Stand a bit further away,' called Rollo, preparing to throw again. Finally the stone sailed over the branch. Its rope snagged on the rough bark and slowly came to rest, dangling down, the end swinging like a pendulum.

'That'll do,' decided Rollo. 'All we need now is to climb up and tie it in place.'

Mossy kept well out of the way as Cissy and JJ gave Rollo a leg up into the lower branches.

'Mind my shoulder,' grunted JJ, when Rollo's foot slipped.

'Grab that bit,' instructed Cissy. 'Not my hair, that branch up there.'

'I'm not touching your hair,' he protested, hooking his leg over a branch and waving at them cheerily. 'I'll be OK from here. See if you can find something to use as a seat.'

Cissy and JJ returned to their hunting about.

'There's a whole heap of stones here,' called JJ.

'We need something wooden this time,' replied Cissy. 'Not a stone seat; it'll be too heavy.' Above them a twig snapped as Rollo climbed higher. Mossy glanced up. A small movement caught his attention and he scrunched his eyes, trying to see beyond the mesh of twigs. What was it?

'Look! I've found a handle off something now!' announced JJ. Mossy stopped searching the tree; nothing so hard to see as a bird that doesn't want to be spotted. A clumsy pigeon battled through the dark twigs, sending a shower of leaves spiralling earthwards, its soft coo shooting a shiver down his spine.

'*I **am** watching out for them,*' he projected. '*Are you telling me there's something in particular I should be looking for?*' There was no reply beyond the rattle of departing wings.

'No, we need a bit of branch,' Cissy told JJ. Mossy looked back at them.

'Yeah, but it's weird. First that door knob and now this handle thingy,' muttered JJ, balancing his finds on a fallen log. 'And look, this rock here; it's got a carved edge!'

Above them a sharp crack was followed by a yelp from Rollo. Mossy felt another shiver rattle down his spine as a cascade of twigs fell on his head.

'Rollo!' shouted Cissy, waving her hands upwards as if trying to reach him.

'It's OK,' he called back, 'my foot slipped, but I'm fine. I've just got to edge a bit further along this... Ow!' He lifted a hand from the branch he was holding.

'Wassup?' Everyone on the ground strained to see him, but yellow leaves obscured their vision.

'Owch!' shouted Rollo again. Mossy headed for the tree. If Rollo was in trouble, it was time he got up there. 'It's like a wasp sting, but I can't see the wasp.'

Wasps in October? thought the puzzled Holder. It's too late for wasps. Tucking his thin fingers into the rough bark, he followed Rollo into the tree. Soon he was at the first branch. He ducked his head this way and that, searching for his friend, until he caught sight of a pair of feet.

'I think I'm there,' called Rollo, his voice sounding calmer again. 'JJ, this is where you meant, isn't it?' Mossy arrived to find him sitting astride the branch, his feet dangling down on either side. Hanging back by the trunk, so as not to distract him, Mossy looked around. No sign of any stinging insects.

'Yup.'

'That looks good,' the others shouted up.

'And there's plenty of rope to wrap round.' Having wound it into place, Rollo tied the rope firmly. Mossy nodded in approval; the knots were sound and tight.

He smiled down at the two faces peering up from the floor of the wood. How different it all looked from here, he thought, catching sight of a pattern half hidden beneath the fallen leaves and rotting wood. Something made him wonder... And then suddenly... Paving! He saw it quite clearly. Slabs he had once walked across. JJ kicked at some fallen acorns, scuffing dead leaves to one side with his foot. He bent to push the debris away with his hands.

'Hey, Cissy! Come and look!' he exclaimed, bending closer. 'It's like a floor!' Cissy was down on her hands and knees beside him.

'And here's more!'

Before they had time to go further in their explorations Rollo and Mossy were back at their sides.

'OK?' checked Rollo, pointing at the dangling rope.

JJ abandoned his scrabbling.

'I'll say,' he grinned, as Cissy held up a length of timber. Mossy took a step back. Where had she found that?

'And this should make a pretty good seat. See? It's rock hard, even though it's old.' She whacked it against the ground. Tiptoeing to her side, Mossy placed a long finger on the end of the wood. A tingle of recognition shot through him. Just as he'd suspected, part of a roof beam.

He walked away, racking his brains.

He hadn't been there the night of the fire, but he'd seen the blackened ruins. No Dwellers remained after that, and no one visited. His own Dwellers at the time had talked about it, but even they had been unsure how it had started. He never knew quite what had happened, but they all assumed that the lonely man living there had fled, and he'd certainly never been seen since. No one had wanted to visit after that; it had been an unpopular place anyway, with its terrible stench of dead things and the revolting smells of the liquids they had used.

The passing centuries had finished the work that had begun that night, until almost all traces had vanished. He had never been back to see what had happened to Tannor. It would have been like checking that he was gone, and that felt cruel. Now, however, it looked as if not quite everything had disappeared.

'Right!' Rollo's voice called him back to the present. 'It's your swing, JJ. D'you want first go?'

The younger boy took the wooden strut in his hand and, pulling it back, climbed up the slope, stretching the line tight. He hooked a leg over the strut, holding tightly to the rope above his head. As his other foot left the ground he swung out, across the stream, the pool, and into the open space beyond.

'Wa-hey!' he called, his voice ringing clearly through the trees. Mossy could feel his excitement sparkling in the air, shattering his black thoughts and filling him with the thrill of the moment.

'You go next,' Rollo told Cissy, when JJ arrived back by his starting point and stumbled off his perch.

'You hold me from going,' Cissy instructed Rollo. 'I want to get both legs in place.'

'OK, then?' he checked. 'Go!' And he launched Cissy to spiral off through the air. The rope creaked and Mossy glanced upwards at a flicker of movement. There was definitely something up there, up by the rope.

'Watch out!' Cissy warned as she swung backwards towards them. 'You'll have to catch me!' The boys reached out to grab her, and Mossy stopped trying to make out what was going on up above him. A mouse maybe, probably looking for food, and anyway, his Dwellers were down here, not up there.

The children took turns, daring each other with different methods of flight.

'Try standing up on it!' JJ suggested breathlessly. 'It's ace!'

'We'll have to bring Jon to have a go soon,' panted Rollo, passing the swing to Cissy again.

'Did you see what we found?' asked JJ, when Rollo jumped down from the seat several turns later.

'Hmm?' Rollo was examining the rope above them. 'Hang on Cissy, something felt weird just then and I want to check it. It looks different, not the way I tied it.'

'You just want another turn without letting me have a go,' she complained.

Now they were all looking upwards, including Mossy.

'Oh no,' groaned Rollo. 'The knot's slipped. How did that happen? I know I did it OK.'

'You're just trying to stop us having fun,' protested JJ. But Rollo headed back to the trunk and started to climb.

Mossy wasn't so sure. He'd checked the knot before he and Rollo came down. It had been a firm double half-hitch with a long tail that hung down. Now he could see quite clearly that half of it had come undone. He scanned the branch. Knots don't undo themselves. He knew that perfectly well. Maybe he had seen something up there, after all. He gave himself a shake. What was he thinking? Why conjure up trouble where there isn't any? he reminded himself.

Whilst Rollo and Mossy inspected knots up the tree, Cissy and JJ continued exploring the ground around the clearing. Mossy caught snatches of conversation.

'...'ver here...'

'... worn into a dip...'

'This one's broken.'

'...like it was drilled...'

He decided to shimmer into visibility.

'Oh! You're here!' exclaimed Rollo.

''Course we're still here!' Cissy shouted up to them. Mossy put a finger to his lips.

'D'you mind if I look at that?' he whispered.

'I can't think what happened,' Rollo complained. 'I know I tied it properly.'

'What was that?' shouted JJ. 'Is it OK?'

'It will be!' Rollo called back. Mossy frowned as he turned the rope over in his hands.

'It hasn't been chewed, and I agree; you tied it fine. I was watching.'

'So how did it happen? How could it have worked loose?'

'I don't know.' Mossy shrugged his shoulders, holding his hands wide. 'There's something here that doesn't feel right.'

'You coming?' called Cissy. 'We've got something to show you.'

'It's OK now,' announced Rollo when he dropped back to the ground again.

Mossy, safely invisible again, returned via another route, landing in a heap as he dropped from a low-hanging twig that almost reached the ground. He scurried behind the children as they examined Cissy and JJ's discoveries.

'And here's the best bit,' declared Cissy with a flourish, presenting something which she held up for Rollo's inspection. 'Isn't it hideous?'

JJ was tugging at the seat of the swing, pulling it back to the top of the mound behind the oak.

'Last go,' said Rollo. 'We promised Mum we'd be back by lunchtime.'

'That's not fair,' grumbled Cissy. 'You deliberately went back up the tree again, so we'd run out of time.'

'I ran out of time as much as you,' Rollo reminded her. 'Tell you what, we'll get Jon to come back with us this afternoon.'

'And you can have first turn,' panted JJ, leaping from the swing and rolling to the ground, wrapping himself in moss, dead leaves and small twigs.

Mossy watched as JJ picked up the gargoyle.

'Are you sure you want that?' asked Cissy. 'It's really ugly.'

'They were supposed to scare off evil spirits,' Rollo told her.

'It'd certainly scare me off,' agreed Cissy.

But it didn't work here, Mossy remembered. How could it, when the trouble here was partly the Holder himself? He was glad to be leaving, but knew he'd have to come back again if the children returned. He hunched his shoulders and then shook them free as he followed Cissy towards the main path.

Turning a corner, he looked back. That was a good swing they'd made, he reminded himself. Maybe if they came here and had fun, played games, laughed, they would finally shift all the stored unhappiness of the place. It was about time. It's always possible to heal, he reminded himself.

'D'you need a hand with that?' Rollo asked JJ.

Mossy hurried to catch up and then he felt it again. A hot, burning sensation hit him between the shoulder blades. He spun round. Finally he remembered what it was he'd seen last time.

His eyes searched the undergrowth. Nothing moved. Nothing blinked this time. He reached a long arm over his shoulder and rubbed at the spot. Maybe he'd just pulled a muscle.

CHAPTER 10

Return Visit

Jon was keen to come with them that afternoon, and Mossy followed the chattering group as they set off down the lane. He'd had no opportunity to warn Rollo about his worries.

You're going soft, he told himself. You've never directly warned your Dwellers in the past, but you've always managed to look after them, all the same.

'You can stand on the seat if you grab the rope in both hands,' JJ assured Jon.

'Or we hold it still while you get on it,' added Cissy.

'Or both,' finished Rollo.

'And there's all sorts of stuff there, too,' added JJ. 'I found a gargle.'

'We've put it by the front door,' Cissy told him, sticking out her tongue, rolling her eyes and pulling her mouth wide. 'To thcare away ve waddies.'

'Well, if it looks like you, it'll just make them fall over with laughter,' teased Jon.

Huh, thought Mossy, shoving his hands deep into his pockets as he walked along beside them. I've never needed any gargoyles on my house. We've always been fine. He shrugged his shoulders. I'm not convinced that they do any good anyway. Looking after the Dwellers and keeping trouble at bay is the Holder's job.

'It's weird though,' JJ reminded them. 'It almost looks as though someone made a paved area. Why'd someone do that in the middle of a wood?'

As they turned off the track onto the newly trampled path their feet were making, Jon pointed to the signpost he'd noticed before.

'Maybe that's got something to do with your paved bit. What if people rode down to here because there used to be something that they were coming to visit? That would mean that the bridleway stopped here because they didn't need to go further,' he suggested.

'Not just a pretty face,' said Rollo, clapping his friend on the back. Mossy was impressed too. Jon had worked it out before Rollo this time. 'You might have a point there.'

'Ta-daa!' announced JJ, spreading his arms wide to indicate the swing.

'And I'll show you how it's done,' said Cissy, grabbing the rope.

As she prepared to launch herself, JJ took Jon and Rollo to admire his collection of findings. After a quick glance at the knot to check it was still firm, Mossy followed them. Rollo was bent over the paving, his fingers resting lightly on the surface. JJ held up his treasure piece by piece.

'A bit of curly metal, and this looks like a handle off a jug, though I can't see any jug to go with it.'

'No one would have made a paved area out in the woods,' murmured Rollo. 'But it's by the stream, and there's that pool of water there too.' He scrubbed a hand through his hair and looked around him. Mossy felt a tingle of excitement shiver along his fingers. This was more like it.

'*Go on Place Reader,*' he projected, his hands clenched in anticipation.

'The ground here is level, when all around it slopes,' muttered Rollo.

'And then there's this thing which I think is a lever, but Cissy says she's positive it's a window latch,' JJ rattled on.

'And that hump there, where we launch ourselves, what made that? It could be where the root from a fallen tree has grown over with vegetation, but it could be...'

'What are you on about?' asked Cissy, running over to them, as Jon took his turn. 'Has JJ shown you the bit of glass I found?'

Rollo was still scanning the terrain when JJ abandoned him to greet Jon back off the swing.

'It's brilliant!' enthused Jon.

'Watch this!' called JJ, hooking his leg over the swing seat and sailing out into the open.

'And what's this?' mused Rollo, as he headed across the clearing towards a small dip in the ground.

'Aren't you going to have your turn?' called Cissy, when JJ landed with a whoop and tumbled down to the foot of the oak tree.

Rollo shook his head and, finding a strong stick, scratched at the ground, shifting old, dead leaves and damp earth. Mossy watched eagerly and was delighted when some coarse stonework emerged. He'd completely forgotten the pits, though seeing them brought back the smell that had lingered around the cottage. His nose wrinkled at the memory... It had been one of the worst smells he knew, enough to make you sick, were it not for the bunches of mint visitors could hold to their noses to block the stench.

Now he was the one searching for a sign of past activities. Did mint still grow at this time of year?

'What have you found?' Jon joined Rollo.

'See?' Rollo pointed at the underground wall he was beginning to expose, showing where it disappeared into the ground. 'I think there was some kind of pit here. Could be circular. And see that dip? I reckon that's another. I think there must have been a building here once, and these are signs of other workings nearby. That mound, where we've been launching ourselves, could be part of it too.'

'So that would fit in with my suggestion about the bridleway/footpath thing.' Jon looked pleased.

'Wheeeeee!' called Cissy and JJ, flying in tandem past their shoulders.

'Pond, water, buildings,' Rollo ticked off the ideas on his fingers. 'Hammer ponds?'

'What? Some kind of engineering?' asked Jon. 'Out here? All in the wild woods?'

'No, no, no. *You're barking up the wrong tree'.*

'Tree,' echoed Rollo. He rubbed the back of his neck as he looked around them again. 'Hmm, bark.' He frowned in concentration. 'Cissy?' he called.

'Want your turn at last?' Cissy turned a grinning face to him.

'That's an oak,' said Rollo, 'but I'm not sure about these other trees. You're the one who knows about that sort of thing.'

'Um… Lots more oaks, some fir over there, which is odd in a wood that's as old as this one. Down by the stream there are some alders, and over there are willows. They're really unusual to find in a wood, come to think of it, and those look like they were pollarded some time donkey's years ago. But I'll tell you the weirdest bit. I found some mint over there.' She waved a hand at a bit of ground beyond Mossy. 'That doesn't usually grow wild in woods. It's more of a garden thing.'

'Got it!' Rollo grinned. 'It's not hammer ponds; it's tanning. Oak, willow, plenty of water, away from other people who would have hated the smell. I'll bet this was a tannery once. Those could have been tanning pits!'

Mossy had to clasp his hands together to stop himself from clapping in delight.

'*Well done Rollo,*' he projected. '*Spot on.*'

'Hated the smell?' echoed Jon, frowning. 'Tanning… That's leather, right? Leather doesn't smell bad.'

'No, but making it did back then. Imagine it: skins of dead animals, often not very well cleaned when they first arrived. And they used pee to help make the leather soft too.'

'Pee?' Jon wrinkled his nose in distaste.

'Horse pee, human pee, almost any kind of pee. People used to collect it and bring it to tanneries. I bet you're right about that path, but it must have been a ghastly place to come to.'

'Well you'd never know now, thank goodness.' Jon's frown disappeared as he turned back towards the others.

'But I tell you what; there's something sad about this place,' Rollo added. Mossy nodded his head in agreement, not surprised that The Place Reader could feel it.

'What d'you mean?' Jon looked at Rollo. 'It's fine. A bit soggy from all that rain, but look at the way the sun's lighting up the trees. And if there used to be a house here, then it must have been quite a while ago. See that tree there, the one growing up with the paving around it that Cissy said you all thought was some old floor? If that was part of a floor once, then this tree has grown up since the house fell down, which must've been some time ago, because it would have been in the middle of a room otherwise. And that's one big tree. It must be at least a hundred years old, if not older.' Leaning against the bark of the trunk, Mossy nodded his head in agreement. It felt more like a two hundred year old tree to him.

'I dunno.' Rollo shrugged his shoulders. 'It just feels like there's something unfinished here, a sadness.' He sat down on the old floor, his hands resting on the smooth damp stone. Suddenly a shiver shook him.

'You're having me on,' laughed Jon. 'You're trying to get at me with your 'Widow Knight' story again. Just because I spooked Cissy that time.' Out of sight Mossy shook his head. Rollo was right, he felt it too.

'No,' said Rollo, his voice firmer. 'Something went wrong here, something that needs to be put right.' This time Mossy was surprised. What did he mean about putting something right?

'*You can't change the past. If it was wrong,*' and he had to admit that much had been wrong here in the past, '*then wrong it will stay.*'

The sombre feeling was shattered as the others bounced over.

'What's with the long faces?' demanded Cissy.

'Aren't you ever going to have a go again?' asked JJ. 'Don't tell me you're going to do a Dad and say that you're 'too old for that'. Even he'd like to have a go one day. He said so at lunch.'

'Nothing the matter,' Rollo assured them, getting to his feet, brushing bits of dead leaf off his hands, and winking at Jon.

'And what's that winking about?' quizzed Cissy. 'What are you two up to?'

'Nothing.' Rollo grinned at her. 'I was just saying to Jon that what with your paving, and those bits and pieces you found, I'll bet there was once a house here.' He paused. 'Right! I think it's my turn next, isn't it?'

Cissy and Jon held the seat still as Rollo climbed onto it, gripping the rope firmly and placing both feet on the wood.

'Ready?'

'You bet,' replied Rollo, letting go with one hand as he swung into the open air.

'And don't think you can have all your 'catch-ups' in one fell swoop,' shouted JJ after him.

As the children continued to take turns, Mossy examined their findings. The paving was definitely an old floor, but little remained. At the edge he found a thicker, worn slab that broke the regular pattern, but it had cracked and the ground was scuffed beside it.

Was something missing? If so, it looked as if it had only disappeared recently. Maybe that's where JJ had found the gargoyle, he told himself. Gently he laid a hand on the worn stone. He felt the passing of feet, faint now from the centuries since anyone had crossed it. Ah, he thought, the old threshold stone, an entrance to the lost house. He turned to JJ's heap of treasure.

Careful not to disturb anything, he examined the collection. The 'lever' was an old scraper for cleaning hides. The jug handle was just that. Another bit of twisted metal felt like something from a door, or was it a window? A curved piece of glass had grains of earth nestled in it where once there had been wine, and the shells were oysters, cheap food in hungry times. Plenty there to help Rollo find out more about the place, but nothing crucial.

An uncomfortable feeling, as if he was being watched, made him turn around. The children were looking the other way, engrossed in the swing. Who was it? Maybe there was something more important that he needed to check. With bits of the house left lying about, he needed to check what had happened to the most important stone in the place.

Carefully he inspected the ground. Would he be able to spot it, and avoid the shock of accidentally touching it? Holders know their own Starting Stone, but spotting another's was much harder, even more so when the house had more or less gone and it had lost its zing. In fact the likelihood of finding it was pretty low, he had to admit.

If it were still there, then the house could still rise again. But then if it were still there, he'd have seen Tannor by now, surely?

Mossy was so engrossed in his search that Jon's shout shot through him like an electric shock. He hurtled back to the oak tree to find Rollo, Cissy and JJ clustered around Jon, who lay groaning on the ground. His leg was twisted under him.

'Can you still breathe?' asked Cissy, collapsing to her knees at his side.

''Course he can.' Rollo's voice was sharp with anxiety. 'Even you couldn't make that kind of noise without breathing.'

'No blood,' announced JJ, cheerily.

'Oooarw,' groaned Jon. 'My leg.'

'His leg,' repeated Cissy. 'Oh no. His leg.' She abandoned the hand she had grasped, glared briefly at his leg, and then collected his hand again. 'It's OK, we won't leave you out here to be eaten by wolves. We'll get you home somehow, even if it takes all night.'

'It's not teatime yet,' JJ reminded her. 'And I'm not missing that.'

'Oh, and I helped make apple cake, so you'd better not die before you've had some of that,' decided Cissy, brightening briefly before gripping his hand even more tightly when another groan creaked out of Jon. Even though he wasn't one of his own Dwellers, Mossy slipped a finger onto his ankle. Hmm, nothing broken, but a fair bit of damage, he realised.

'Cissy, if you carry on mangling his hand he won't be able to use that either,' Rollo reminded her. She stepped away. 'Can you move your leg at all?'

Carefully Jon rolled onto his side, gently easing his leg out from under him now that he had the use of both hands. Another moan of pain had Cissy diving to his side as Rollo gently pulled him into a sitting position.

'It's doesn't feel like my leg at all.'

'No bones sticking out though,' said JJ matter-of-factly. 'So it can't be too bad.'

'What happened?' asked Rollo.

'What happened?' repeated Cissy, rounding on her brother. 'It's your rotten knot-tying. That's what happened.' She waved wildly at the rope, which no longer hung from the branch but snaked its way through a prickly bramble beside them.

A shower of leaves scattered through the still air as Mossy scanned the trees overhead. Seeing a movement, his eyes turned a sharp yellow. Was that the flicker of a tail? A shadow of some small creature? He narrowed his eyes, scouring, searching. Suddenly the hairs on the back of his neck stiffened. Nothing moved. Not a bird, mouse, beetle: even the ground under his feet was still. No wood was ever naturally this deserted. Lifting his nose he took a deep, slow breath.

There it was. This time he recognised it; faint but unforgettable, a hint of tannin. His nose twitched, wrinkled. Decay. Death. But how could that be?

'That knot was fine,' protested Rollo. 'I checked it twice. It's been fine all afternoon. If it was a manky knot, we'd have known long ago. It would have slipped or something.'

'Oh, so you're saying that the rope untied itself.' Cissy stood with her hands on her hips, glaring at Rollo.

'It's OK,' Jon reassured them. 'It's just my leg. Gi' me a hand and I'll be able to hop about the place.'

'It's not a matter of hopping about,' insisted Cissy. 'Everybody always thinks that Rollo does everything perfectly, and this just shows. What if you'd been way out over there when his perfect knot failed?' Her voice was heavy with sarcasm as she flung an arm in the direction of the open space where the valley fell away beyond the stream.

Mossy groaned. She was right. If the rope had fallen loose when one of them had been out at full swing, it wouldn't be a hurt leg that they'd be worrying about. Then whoever it was would have been dangerously hurt, if not killed. He racked his brains. Had that knot been right? It had looked right, but was he an expert?

'Yes, but I wasn't way out over there,' Jon reminded her gently.

'He was here,' added JJ, cheerfully, pointing to where he still sat.

'But you're right. I tied that knot and, however it happened, it isn't tied now,' Rollo admitted. 'It's my fault and I'm really sorry.'

'Well, like Grandma says, 'Sorry's all very well, but you shouldn't have done the wrong thing in the first place'.' Cissy still frowned at Rollo.

'Actually what Grandma says is 'putting it right is what matters' and 'learn from your mistakes'. She said it to me last time we went over to her house, and I broke that flower pot,' JJ reminded them all.

'Huh,' huffed Cissy.

'And 'bygones should be bygones', added JJ. 'And 'all's well that ends well.''

'You're just as bad as Rollo,' shouted Cissy. 'Mr Know-It-all!' JJ flushed red.

Now Mossy turned to inspect her. This wasn't the familiar Cissy he knew. Drama Queen she might be, and ready to see trouble long before it arrived, but she was always fair. He let one long finger slip against the side of her foot, and even as he watched her, her shoulders relaxed, and she smiled at Jon.

'Come on, getting cross isn't going to get you home. And I guess, if you're anything like JJ, what you need is one of Mum's sort outs.'

'Hold on,' said Rollo, stretching an arm round his friend, pulling him to a standing position. Jon gasped, his eyes clamping shut as pain shot through him again.

'Cissy, you go the other side. Jon, put an arm round her shoulders. She's stronger than you think.' Now Cissy smiled in pleasure.

'We'll go slowly,' she reassured him, 'and if it hurts too much, say so, and we'll stop for a bit.'

Jon nodded his head, wincing as he took a tentative step with his sound foot. He rested heavily on Rollo and Cissy, holding his injured leg carefully off the ground. JJ shot over to one side and rummaged about in the undergrowth, before re-joining them as they set off.

'Here, I'll hold that bramble back,' he volunteered, reaching round to pull a tendril out of the way.

Mossy watched until they disappeared out of sight onto

the main path, and then he turned to the paved slabs. He pulled his shoulders back, his ears twitching in anticipation, and took a deep breath.

'OK,' he said, his voice firm and low. 'Where are you hiding?'

Chapter 11

Found You

Mossy looked around. Damp leaves glistened in the soft light that found its way through the branches. A light breeze gently shifted them so that they sparkled, but nothing else moved. No one flittered through the twigs above him, nothing scrabbled in the undergrowth. The only sound was the burble of the stream tumbling over rocks that protected the bank. I should have realised that this place was still being avoided, he chided himself.

'Tannor!' he called, his nose twitching as he caught the familiar smell again. 'I know you're here somewhere. You can't hide for ever, even if you've been out of sight so far.'

'I'm not hiding,' hissed a soft voice close behind his shoulder.

Mossy spun round, his hand snagging on a sharp blackthorn spur as he heard the low hiccup that he recognised, even after all this time, as Tannor's version of laughter.

'Good grief,' Mossy staggered back, aghast at the sight of

the Holder he saw standing before him. Holder of a small Holding – Tannery Cottage had never had more than a couple of rooms – he'd always been short, but now he had undergone terrible changes.

'What on earth has happened to you?' No wonder Tannor had been hard to see, he thought. This was the shadow of a Holder, as if someone had tried to grate him out of existence, to scrub him from this life. These were the last wisps of a charred spirit.

'As if you care,' spat Tannor, his sunken eyes shooting a charcoal stare, one scrawny hand lifted, a claw-like finger pointed at Mossy's chest. 'Bringing your happy bunch of cheerful Dwellers to break my silence. How dare you?' He glared ferociously.

Mossy shrank back. If I'd known, I wouldn't have dared, he admitted to himself. Neither would they.

'I never thought…' He struggled to find words.

'You never did,' snarled Tannor, shrugging a hollow shoulder, turning his back on him and taking a couple of stumbling steps in the direction of the far pit.

'But what happened to your hands?' Mossy managed at last. 'And your foot? How long has your leg been broken?'

'Since the night of the fire,' Tannor replied. 'You know as well as I do that when your Holding falls apart, so do you. They burned us down, didn't they? Didn't see you here then. No one here to help us then, was there?' Tannor leaned against the base of the oak tree, panting from the effort of talking. 'This leg, missing fingers, a cracked face, what do you expect?'

'But I thought… I thought the Holding was gone.' This

time Tannor's hiccup broke into a cough.

'You mean you **hoped** it was gone.' Tannor's head slumped forward, his rasping breaths making his thin chest heave. 'You thought that if they burned us down that would be an end to it. But my Starting Stone never broke, even when everything around it went up in flames. And more to the point, you never knew I had something to keep me here. No one did.' Tannor jerked a twisted thumb over his shoulder. 'Never found, was it? But it's kept me trapped in this abandoned place that no one dares visit any longer.'

'The threshold?' murmured Mossy, more to himself than Tannor. He racked his brain, desperately trying to see it in his memory. Surely it had been broken, hadn't it? And then he remembered. The threshold had been cracked, with something missing from beside it.

'As if that could be my Starting Stone,' cackled Tannor. 'You'll never find it, especially not now.'

'You've hidden your Starting Stone?' Mossy was shocked. How could that be possible? No Holder would ever think of doing such a thing. More than that, how could Tannor have managed it? He remembered how he curled up to sleep on the lovely, warm hearth that was his own Starting Stone at Annanbourne. But move it? That was impossible. Move that and you moved everything. Mossy shook himself to knock the idea away. It didn't bear thinking about.

'It was **you**, wasn't it?' he challenged Tannor, changing the subject. 'Cissy was right; ropes don't untie themselves. No other creatures dare come here, so it must have been you. Why?' He frowned in confusion. 'Why would you do that? What could my Dwellers have done that would make you want to hurt them?'

'You don't get it, do you?' Tannor's words split the air. His eyes glowed a dull red. 'You bring them here, all laughter and games. I hate games. I hate their happiness.' He spat at the ground.

'Pwah. You think that's what feeds you – happiness, love, kindness, laughter, all that rubbish. But I tell you; I found another way.' He rapped a clenched fist against his chest, making a strange, empty, thumping noise. 'Make their lives hell, make them hurt. OK, so it's no easy life, but there's a raw energy to it like nothing else. Anyway, why should I be the only one to bear the pain?'

'But that's not what Holders do.' Mossy shook his head in bewilderment. 'We're here to look after our Dwellers, to protect the Holding. I know there are some who are lazy, who can't be bothered. But they suffer for it. And there are new Holders who take time to learn the skills, but I've never met one who wanted to hurt his Dwellers before. What went wrong? What changed you?'

Tannor struggled to his feet. He lurched towards Mossy, his nose pointing sharply at him as he lifted a hand to Mossy's face.

'Wouldn't you so like to know?' Tannor bunched his fingers together, then suddenly jerked them out, flicking them against Mossy's chest.

A sharp pain zapped through him, a pain so sudden, so strong, it took his breath away. He clutched at the place where Tannor's fingers had struck, struggling for air as he staggered back. 'Admit it.' Tannor thrust his head towards him. 'Wouldn't you like the power to do that to someone?'

Mossy realised with dawning horror that the stretched lips leering up at him from Tannor's damaged face were supposed to be smiling. He shook his head.

'No,' he said. 'No. Never.'

Tannor spun on his heel and turned his back on Mossy.

'Pathetic,' he spat. Then he lifted his head, opened his mouth and let out a cackle of broken hiccups, a peel of crazed laughter.

Mossy took advantage of Tannor's distraction to examine him. He needed to look beyond what he could see with his eyes, and reached out with all his senses. There was more to this than just the damage that had been inflicted by the fire, the breaking down of the building. He knew how severely he would suffer if anything happened to Annanbourne, could remember hard times in his own Holding.

Watching now, he could see that somehow Tannor had gained some strange kind of strength from the hurt he had inflicted. But as he listened, his ears tingled with understanding. Under that terrible laughter lurked a sob of utter anguish, of heartbroken pain and loss, of abandonment. His nose twitched at the smell of a deep, grinding hurt at the core of the Holder in front of him. From deep inside himself Mossy felt an ache of sympathy. Tannor was a broken Holder. He reached out a hand towards the stiffened back.

'Don't you dare to feel sorry for me.' Tannor glowered over his shoulder at Mossy. 'And don't even think of bringing those horrible creatures back here. You let them come this way and next time my timing will be better. That boy wasn't supposed to fall on this soft ground. I meant him to fall out there.' He waved a hand at the stream as it tumbled over the rocks to the lower valley. 'He'd have fallen really badly – just the way that girl imagined.'

Again a cackle of hiccups broke across the clearing, shivering through to the tips of Mossy's fingers, making his skin shrink tightly in fear. Tannor turned to look at him, his empty eyes a dull grey now. 'She may be your Dweller, but I can work with her. Did you notice?'

Mossy understood then where Cissy's crossness had come from, that strange flash of harshness and temper. Somehow Tannor had put some of his anger into her. Thank goodness they had gone home quickly.

'D'you follow?' Tannor's voice broke through his thoughts. 'Keep them away from here, or next time it won't just be a few bruised muscles. Get it?'

Mossy nodded his head. But at the same time another thought came to him.

'Tannor, you know, it doesn't **have** to be like this. You don't have to hurt them…' he started.

'I know,' leered Tannor. 'But I'm not going to wimp out like you. You still don't understand, do you? I rather like it. I **like** hurting them. So what if I suffer? I always have. Every time they opened that door, I suffered. This is my revenge, and now I have the opportunity to do it afresh. You can hurry home if you like, but remember that I'm here. I'm not far away, and where you go, I can follow.'

Mossy shuddered at the menace in Tannor's voice. His words cut the air, stripping all warmth from the sun. They seemed to turn shimmering sunlight into shards of ice that stabbed through the chill of the autumn afternoon.

Suddenly all Mossy wanted was to get away. Turning his back, he broke into a run, tracing the children's footsteps to the track. He ducked under a low bramble stretched across the path and jumped over a fallen piece of wood. His heart beat a thundering message in time with his feet.

Warn...The...Chil...Dren...Warn...The...Chil... Suddenly a smile broke across his face.

This time he could! He actually could warn one of them. He could talk to Rollo.

Throwing caution to the wind, he lifted his arms in celebration. A briar rose sprang free of a bramble and snagged his trouser leg. But now nothing held him back.

We'll be safe in Annanbourne, he told himself, looking ahead to where the tall signpost on the track pointed towards home.

Glad at last to be heading into safer territory, away from the grim misery of Tannery Cottage, he didn't notice the draping strand of ivy until it had wrapped a tendril round his neck, stopped him in his tracks and thrown him onto his back in the muddy earth.

'Oouf!' he grunted, wondering where his breath had gone. He rolled onto one side, coating himself in more mud, and struggled over to drier ground.

'Even the plants are against us,' he grumbled to a passing stag beetle as he scraped the worst of the mud off his elbows and knees. The beetle stopped in its tracks, waving its antennae at him.

'Of course,' Mossy agreed. 'You're right. You wouldn't be here if it was his territory, but it certainly felt as if he was reaching out to get at me still,' he muttered. The beetle rubbed its front legs together.

'Really?' Mossy smiled. 'Actually on our side?' he paused thoughtfully. 'I suppose that makes sense. I can ask the natural forces to help, but I can't make them do something. And the plants are rooted in the earth, and nurtured by light.' His eye caught sight of a splash of red spotted with white. 'Although our friend over there is pretty poisonous.'

The beetle took its time polishing its armour, and Mossy listened attentively.

'Hmm. I'll bear that in mind. It could be helpful if I ever have to come back. Though I have every intention of keeping away.' A shiver ran down Mossy's spine, and he looked back over his shoulder to where he could still see a branch of the tall oak tree where the children had made their swing. Beyond it the crisp blue of a clear afternoon sky lifted his heart, promising good things ahead.

'You're right, time and nature heal everything in the end. And they're doing a pretty good job there, even when Tannor is fighting against it as hard as he is. If he'd had his way, the children wouldn't have had any fun at all. And Jon's injury will heal.'

A scuffling sound above them raised Mossy's gaze in time to see a squirrel run nimbly down a slender branch. It kept drooping further until he was nearly down to ground level. The squirrel rubbed a paw across his nose. Mossy nodded his head in agreement.

'Absolutely – and the sooner I pass on the message the better.' He got to his feet again, brushed the last of the mud off his hands, ignored a smudge on his nose and set off for Annanbourne with a cheery whistle.

CHAPTER 12

A Chill In The Night

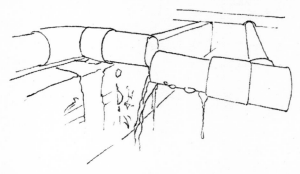

When Mossy slipped, panting, into the kitchen, he found the children ranged in front of their parents and Jon nowhere to be seen.

'We just can't take that kind of risk again,' Jack was insisting.

'If you're making something like that, another time you must ask Dad or me to check that it's done properly,' agreed Annie.

'Mum, I know I did it right. I checked it twice,' protested Rollo. It was nothing to do with knot checking, thought Mossy, positioning himself between Jack and Annie, a long finger resting on each of the adults.

'*They did their best,*' he projected softly.

'And we'd played on it for hours,' JJ carried on. 'It was absolutely fine until right up to 'Kerbang!' I remember seeing the tail end bouncing about all on its own every time we launched.'

'I wrapped it round the branch twice and used a double

knot. You know, same as those ones you used when you made the rope ladder.' Rollo rubbed the back of his head. 'And I left a whole lot hanging spare so that we'd notice even if it did slip. How come it went all at once without any warning?'

'Well, there was a warning, sort of,' Cissy pointed out. 'Remember when you made us stop before lunch; when you said it felt weird.'

'She's right,' sighed Rollo, 'and that time half the knot had come undone.'

Jack raised an eyebrow at Rollo.

'Knots don't undo themselves, you know. Maybe you just hadn't done it quite as well as you thought. Anyway, half term's nearly over and we're going to be busy helping the Barkers harvest their grapes tomorrow. You're not to go back there without Mum or me checking it first. Understood?'

'It could have been so much worse. Jon was lucky to only sprain his knee,' added Annie. Mossy felt anxiety ripple through her. 'Though I doubt he thinks he's lucky right now. Thank goodness his Mum was at home. Even she thought it looked serious, and she's used to seeing really bad things in A&E. I reckon he'll be using crutches for quite some time.'

'That's what Cissy said,' JJ reminded them. 'Not the crutches bit, but the something worse bit. She was even crosser than you.' He pulled a face at her. 'All shouty and horrid.'

'I just kept seeing images of Jon all bloody and injured.' Cissy's face blanched at the memory. Mossy scowled.

Tannor had clearly been able to plant worries into Cissy more easily than he'd thought possible. 'I knew he wasn't that badly hurt, but it felt as if he were.' Mossy shook his head, creeping round to her side now and placing a calming finger on the tip of her foot. At least with Jack and Annie feeling the way they did, it shouldn't be too hard to keep the children away from Tannor in the future.

'But you said you wanted a go at some stage, remember?' butted in JJ. 'So we'll have to get it sorted, and you know you'll be able to make it right, don't you?'

'It **was** brilliant,' admitted Cissy with a grin. 'Flying through the air.' She spread her arms wide.

'Until then,' added Rollo, who still looked dejected.

'We'll see,' finished Jack.

'Huh. 'We'll see' is what you say when you mean 'no',' muttered Cissy.

'Who's going to help make supper?' Annie briskly interrupted.

It was only once the children were in their beds that Mossy dared to present himself to Rollo.

'Mossy, you were there.' Rollo said, as soon as he shimmered into visibility. 'Did you see what went wrong?'

'Don't worry, you tied that knot fine,' Mossy reassured him.

'You mean it wasn't my fault that Jon was hurt?' Rollo looked so relieved, Mossy was glad that for once he was able to tell one of his Dwellers something directly. 'So how on earth did it happen?'

'Well, it's a long story,' started Mossy as he settled down to explain. 'And I don't know all of it...'

'But I thought you Holders only did good,' exclaimed Rollo at the end of his tale.

'If we surround ourselves with happiness and love, then we live well and comfortably. For most Holders, and I'm one of them, that is reason enough to keep things running smoothly. It's as much for us as for you,' he admitted. 'Sometimes a Holder may be lazy or not bother, and the house can feel sad and neglected. Sometimes Dwellers damage a place, and then the Holder can seriously struggle to do his job. I've never heard of any other Holder like Tannor.

'My guess is that something went seriously wrong right at the beginning. Something to do with the building of the house must have damaged him. I have never known a Holder who wanted to hurt a Dweller before. Something he said makes me wonder if he might even have done something worse than he did to Jon. That's why it's so important that you understand. You have to keep the others away from his Holding. He threatened terrible things if you go back.'

Mossy shivered. Outside he could hear a cold wind beating against the window, but right then he felt as if it had wrapped its arms around him.

'You OK?' checked Rollo.

'Fine,' Mossy assured him, but he wasn't so sure. His mind was fogged, and a tiredness dragged at him so that he felt as if he were swimming in treacle.

'Time for me to be on my way,' he said, setting off on a

patrol of his house, checking each room in turn, and all of his Dwellers, before he settled down to sleep beside the embers on his warm hearth.

The headache and general tiredness lasted through the next two days. Even his Dwellers' enjoyment of the grape harvest and the last days of their half-term break gave him no respite. He kept himself well out of sight, keeping close to the hearthstone for comfort, resting whenever possible. Maybe he'd been daft to think that he could chat away with one of his Dwellers and not suffer from it.

Mossy leapt from a restless sleep with a jolt, his ears stiff with fear. Although his face was dry, he felt chilled, as if splashed with icy water.

Something was wrong somewhere. He tiptoed across the floor to the stairs and peered up into the darkness. Everything was still. No movement anywhere.

There it was again! A dripping sound. Ah! He shrugged his shoulders; it wouldn't be the first time that someone had left a tap dripping. They would find it in the morning.

Yawning, he turned back to his hearth, but the warmth of the cinders was gone and the coldness persisted. He turned onto his back and wrapped his arms around himself. Briefly the image of Tannor's damaged face floated above him as if the other Holder was looking down at him. Mossy closed his eyes firmly.

'Stop imagining things. You're just spooked by the recent events,' he muttered to himself. Nearby something hiccupped softly. Mossy's eyes sprung open again, searching the empty darkness. He sighed. Now he **was** hearing things. He turned onto his side, wriggling into the reassuring comfort of the stone.

But still the iciness persisted.

'Who am I kidding?' Mossy asked a spider who crept softly across his hand. He sat up, ears twitching. He could still sense the dripping.

He sniffed the air, then shook his head to clear it. He should have noticed before. Now that he was properly awake he realised that it smelled like quite a bit of water.

Upstairs he checked the bedrooms. Sleeping children were surrounded by happy dreams. The bathrooms were still. Mossy frowned. If the taps weren't dripping in the bathrooms, then where was it happening? It was up there somewhere.

As he walked along the landing towards Jack and Annie's bedroom his feet sunk into damp carpet. He stopped in his tracks, peering up through the gloom at the ceiling, frowning, as his eyes turned a curious green.

There it was, a growing patch of gathering wetness that released a drip to splash on his forehead. Mossy brushed it away with the back of his hand, sharpened his vision and stared intently upwards. The ceiling was beginning to swell and bulge. If he left it until his Dwellers woke in the morning they would be too late to save the ceiling. It might even be at risk right now.

'Mu-um!' he called softly. He paused, listening.

It worked.

'I'll go,' he heard Annie's sleepy voice, and as the duvet rustled he stepped to one side, hiding behind a bookcase.

Annie emerged, heading towards JJ's bedroom. As soon as her bare feet hit the wet patch, everything changed.

'Jack!' she called. 'Come quickly. Something's wrong!' Jack was at her side in a flash.

'Who is it?' he demanded, flicking on a light.

'Not who, what?' She pointed at the carpet. 'It's soaking. You check that while I go to sort out whoever called.'

She soon returned. 'I must've imagined it, they're all asleep,' she reported.

'Not so good here,' Jack informed her.

'Dad?' Rollo was rubbing the sleep from his eyes. 'Mum?'

'Fetch some towels from the bathroom,' Jack told him. Cissy popped her head round her door.

'Party time?' she grinned. 'Oh my goodness,' she clapped her hands to the sides of her face. 'Look at the ceiling. It's about to explode.'

Annie grabbed a torch and climbed a ladder into the roof space. Mossy was close on her heels. The beam of light lit up battered cardboard boxes, stored camping equipment and the underside of the roof. Then it shone on a small metal tank out of which water poured in a steady stream. Mossy skipped nimbly over sodden bits and pieces as Annie crept round low-slung trusses and stepped carefully over ancient beams. He knew what this tank did; it filled all the other tanks in the house, constantly topping up so that there was always plenty of water when his Dwellers needed it.

'I've found it!' called Annie. 'It's the header tank. It's overflowing.' I'll say, thought Mossy, and by then he could see why. A short spar of wood was wedged so that the lever, which should have cut off the flow of water when the tank was full, couldn't work. In no time Annie had flicked it out of the way, but the damage was already done. It had clearly been flooding the attic for several hours.

While his Dwellers organised a rescue operation for their holiday equipment, Mossy inspected the piece of wood. Where had it come from? To get stuck there it had to have fallen from the roof above, in which case he needed to check it thoroughly. Wood falling out of roof beams indicated serious trouble, but he had felt nothing to indicate anything like that, no sudden headache, not even a twinge of one. Carefully he started inspecting the rafters, ducking out of the way as Annie passed another soggy sleeping bag to Jack.

'That bulge in the ceiling is getting bigger,' Cissy informed them. 'And it's not dripping any longer; it's a steady trickle now.'

'I'm putting this stuff in the bath,' Rollo informed them.

'Don't worry. We'll wring it all out in the morning,' Jack shouted back.

'I'll need wringing out before then,' giggled Cissy.

'Along with the tent,' came JJ's voice, indicating that he, too, had joined in the activity.

Annie crawled back to the open hatchway.

'Cissy?' she called. 'Move away from under the wet patch!' Good idea, thought Mossy. He rubbed his neck, to ease an ache in it.

'*The stopcock!*' Mossy projected, wondering if Rollo could hear him through all the chaos. '*You need to stop the water. Find the main water pipe and turn it off.*'

'Just do as I say, please, and quickly.' Annie's voice sounded unusually harsh. Mossy felt a strange dragging feeling in his throat as if someone was trying to pull him down. He lifted a hand.

'Annie!' Jack sounded anxious. 'Come back down here! Annie!' His voice was tense. 'I can see a split appearing!'

'There are still the other two sleeping bags and the camping stove,' protested Annie, looking back to where Mossy stood, clutching the side of the tank, a choking sensation in his throat. He tried to swallow, but it was as if something was stuck there, a huge, great, bulging blockage.

Annie reached towards the sack that lay between them.

'Annie! No! Forget it!' Now Jack's voice was sharp. 'Cissy! Get out of the way!'

'Muuum!' JJ's voice was almost a wail.

'*Go!*' projected Mossy. '*Go now while there's still a chance.*' Annie's face disappeared.

The soaked wadding beneath Mossy's feet lurched. There was a terrible rending sound. The tank at his side slipped towards him, as if someone had pushed it, dousing him in water. Mossy grabbed it to steady himself, but the floor disappeared from under his feet. His throat clenched tighter, and then suddenly it felt as if someone had ripped it out of him. As he lifted a frantic hand to check, Mossy was flung forward. Something hard and metallic bashed his head. Dust and water clouded about him as he spiralled downwards, hands flailing, desperately trying to find something, anything, that might break his fall.

He landed on his back, all breath beaten out. Plaster, dust, shards of wood and showers of water cascaded on top of him. Through one battered eye he saw a great gaping hole that led up into the black roof space beyond. A final piece of plaster, that had been dangling on a thin strand above them, gave up waiting and fell, landing on his left foot.

'Is that it?' asked Cissy. I jolly well hope so, thought Mossy, as the water trickled to a stop.

'Did you turn off the water?' Jack asked as Rollo came back up the stairs.

'I couldn't think of anything else I could do to help,' he replied.

'What a mess,' sighed Annie, brushing some dirt off her face.

'Still, no one's hurt,' Jack pointed out as he balanced a bucket beside Mossy to catch the remaining drops of water that still fell slowly from above. 'Though it was a close call with you and Mum.' He gave Cissy a hug. 'You only just got out of the way in time.'

'Strange as it might seem,' added Annie, 'I suggest we all find dry night clothes and try to get a few more hours of sleep. There's nothing much we can do right now that won't wait until morning.'

Good idea, agreed Mossy, and then I can sort myself out too. Footsteps and voices scattered. Mossy lay still. Water trickled round his neck. He sighed. His throat was still desperately sore, and his head ached even more.

'And here are fresh pyjamas,' came Annie's voice at one point. A piece of plaster tickled Mossy's armpit.

'No, no. We'll do it in the morning,' he heard Jack telling JJ.

That's what I thought at the start of all this, he reminded himself. I should have known. How come I didn't realise there was a problem sooner? His head throbbed. I've been too wrapped up in myself, he realised, to notice what's been going on around me.

'If this were termtime, would we get the day off for flooding?' asked Cissy. 'Maybe we should take Monday off anyway to help with tidying up?' she added hopefully.

'We'll be fine by Monday, don't you worry,' Annie reassured her. She skirted round Mossy and the soggy heap of debris, flicked off the landing light and headed for bed herself.

The house fell still and mostly quiet. Mossy could hear water seeping through the carpet, spreading itself a little further. Another droplet plopped into the bucket. Slowly he sat up. Damp plaster stuck to his clothes and face, and his hair stood up in spikes. His back was stiff; there was a scratch across the back of his hand. A small bit of rubble rolled down the heap and onto the carpet.

Above him the yawning hole where the ceiling had collapsed stared blackly down. I never did find where that spur of wood came from, he thought. Better start looking.

CHAPTER 13

Consequences

It was hard work getting back up into the roof space. The loft ladder had collapsed along with the hatch and the ceiling and now lay sideways along the base of the wall. Mossy had had to climb the outside of the house and wriggle his way through a gap where the roof hung over the walls. The bluetits who had used it for access to a nest had long since left, but their entrance remained.

The first glimmerings of dawn were streaking the sky silver as he crawled stiffly along the beam that spanned the house. Gently he tapped the wood. It rang softly in response to his touch. It was all sound. The water hadn't damaged the walls, or any of the joints, just the ceiling.

He edged his way gingerly past the chimney, taking care to avoid the soft insulation between the beams, feeling the way with his hands. A shaft of light filtering softly upwards indicated the hole. Mossy smiled. That would help with his inspection.

The dripping had stopped, but the chaos of damage was

still evident. Twisted pipework led to the header tank which now tipped to one side, a small puddle of water lurking in the lowest corner. Round the edge of the hole, broken laths were stained with damp. Crumbled plaster waited for a chance to drop on any unsuspecting head that might be wandering beneath.

Mossy balanced himself astride two beams, his bottom resting against the side of the tank. He now stood exactly where it had been before. Looking upwards, he scanned the rafters. Then he scanned them again. Everything was fine. He shook his head, sighing with relief. His headache must be something to do with the damage of the hole rather than the roof.

Then he frowned. Hang on... If the roof was fine and nothing was missing, where had that shard of wood come from? He folded his arms across his chest. Could it have bounced?! He examined the roof further from him, but that too rose strong and solid.

Suddenly he spotted the spike of wood that had caused all the trouble. It was resting against the broken pipe. He picked it up and examined it closely. Frowning, he could see that it was nothing to do with his Holding. There was lichen and moss on this wood. One end was starting to rot.

Yes, it had come from a Holding somewhere, he could feel that quite clearly, but not from Annanbourne. It had been outside, exposed to the weather for a long time. In that case, how had it got there? The wood had been wedged so firmly under the rim of the tank, over the lever and then tucked under the far side. It almost looked as if it had been put there on purpose.

Mossy's eyes darted around the dark space, coming to rest on two bats hanging neatly upside down near the top. He whistled softly. One of the bats turned his head, his ears quivering. Mossy opened his mouth to speak, but no proper words came out. Instead his voice grated hoarsely; the words were broken, the pain in his throat terrible. His shoulders slumped. The damage to his Holding was too recent; he would have to get their attention in another way.

Abandoning speech, he tapped instead on the side of the tank. Both bats were now cocking their ears in his direction. He held up the wood.

'Stuck,' he croaked. 'How?' Each word burned like fire in his throat. The first bat stretched his leather wings and drifted silently down to the edge of the tank, catching the rim and hanging again, upside down, this time with his wings spread loosely about him. He wriggled his nose at Mossy.

Mossy frowned. Last night? But he hadn't been anywhere near the loft for ages, not since his Dwellers had done all the repairs when they first arrived.

'Sure?' he checked, his throat tightening in an agonising spasm. His question was greeted with a barrage of squeaks. The other bat swooped down to join them.

Mossy took a step backwards. Of course he hadn't meant anything bad about their sight. He knew they lived by their hearing, often seeing with their ears things that others missed with their eyes. He held up his hands in apology. How to check when each word he uttered split his throat like knives? He tapped his chest.

'Sure? Me?' he whispered. He listened attentively to the

114

twitter of squeaks that responded. Bats often spoke so fast it was hard to follow them. When they argued it was twice as difficult. But it certainly gave him food for thought.

Finally he waved goodbye, bowing in thanks as they flew back to their daytime sleeping posts. Even if they couldn't agree it was him they had seen yesterday evening, they had still convinced him that they had definitely seen someone. And that comment at the end – not as solid as me, he pondered. What did they mean by that?

Below him sounds of stirring were leading to activity. Annie's voice drifted up through the hole.

'… start with getting rid of this lot.' Peering down over the edge, Mossy saw the tousled top of Cissy's head pass under.

'D'you think any more ceilings are going to come down? This carpet is still pretty soggy.'

Oh, I hope not, thought Mossy, tenderly stroking his throat. One was bad enough. And if just one had already taken his voice with it, what else might he suffer if another went?

It took all morning for the family to clear up the mess. Mossy shivered as the carpet was pulled up, leaving sharp tacks sticking up at the sides of the landing and down the stairs. Better watch out for them, he thought, seeing JJ pad along to his room in bare feet.

'We can take it all to the dump on our way into town,' said Annie as she loaded the final bag of rubbish into the back of the car.

'And it's Bonfire Night at last,' announced JJ as he rubbed the dirt off his hands onto his jeans.

'I'm helping Dad build it,' said Rollo. 'Jon and Rajesh were coming too, but Sue says he's not better enough yet.'

'But surely he'll be able to come to the fireworks?' checked Cissy.

'I think it's a 'we'll see' thing,' admitted Rollo.

'I bet you feel gutted that it's all your fault he might miss it,' Cissy rattled on.

'It's not all my fault,' protested Rollo. 'It… The rope…' His voiced faded. He sighed. 'If he can't go, then I'll stay and keep him company.'

'That's a good idea,' agreed Jack. 'But meanwhile we have other promises to keep.'

The younger ones went with Annie, while Rollo and Jack set off on their bikes. Mossy watched them go and then to headed up the stairs. He had jobs of his own to see to.

If those bats had been so sure there had been someone in the loft the night before, it was down to him to check things out. He stood on the bare landing and stared up at the hole. A long ladder was propped up where Jack had used it to reach all the last bits of loose plaster. Its top disappeared into the dark emptiness beyond.

Mossy reached out a hand and grasped one side. He rolled his shoulders to ease them. He seemed to be stiff all over; his back ached and his head still throbbed.

'No one hurt,' he sighed.

'Not this time, though I nearly caught her too,' chuckled a voice in Mossy's ear. Mossy closed his eyes. His hand dropped to his side. The soft tones made his skin creep. Slowly he forced himself to turn round. Now the bats' last words made sense.

'Tannor,' he breathed, his eyes turning an icy blue.

'You thought you'd left me behind, didn't you?' leered Tannor. His pale lips stretched tight over broken teeth as he squinted up and pushed his face close to Mossy's chin. 'You never listen to anything I say. I told you I could follow you, and here I am.' There was something about the way he spread his arms wide in the greeting gesture that made Mossy's heart sink into his boots.

Mossy waved a hand in the direction of the small tank which had been roughly set back in place. He rubbed the other over his face as if trying to scrub the sight of Tannor from his eyes.

'I thought I should let you know I'd arrived,' Tannor replied. 'It took me a while to work out this piped water business, but now that I have, I can do it again if you like. That should keep them entertained, make them thirsty.' Mossy shook his head. How could this be happening?

'Got a bit of a problem with your voice have you?' Tannor's strange laugh hiccupped, sounding even more hollow than usual as it bounced off the bare boards of the landing.

'No' poss-ble.' Mossy could barely get the words out.

'Oh, but it is.' Tannor pressed his hands together and then pointed both his forefingers at Mossy. 'I know what you're thinking; no Holder can tamper in another Holder's Holding. But I'm not doing that. You see…' He paused, winking one dark eye at Mossy. 'I've come to join you.'

Mossy felt as if steel bands had clamped round his chest. His breath came in short bursts. His face drained of all colour.

'H... H...' he panted.

'Don't worry.' Tannor sounded almost pleased. 'It's quite alright. If you're not happy, you can always leave. I'm sure I can arrange for an accident to happen to your Starting Stone. So convenient, a hearthstone, at the bottom of a tall chimney. It wouldn't be the first time that a brick has worked loose and fallen down to break a hearth. Fatal for you, but it doesn't matter any longer. I'm here, in place, ready to take over.'

Tannor lifted his good foot and then stamped the heel hard on Mossy's toes. As Mossy hopped back, cradling his injured foot in both hands, he saw the rogue Holder bunch his three fingers together and lift them towards him. He ducked out of the way in the nick of time, just before Tannor's fingers flicked out.

Mossy staggered backwards for a few steps and then turned and ran, his feet making a hollow beat on the bare wood. He needed time to think. What Tannor was saying didn't make sense. No Holder could take over another's Holding. Tannor couldn't stay there without a Starting Stone of his own. And no Holder could move a Starting Stone. It simply wasn't possible.

CHAPTER 14

Defence and Attack

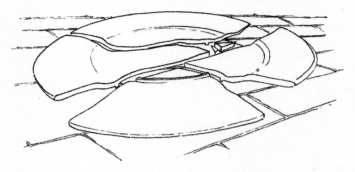

M ossy took refuge in the chimney. Tannor's threat had shaken him, even though he knew Tannor couldn't directly touch the hearthstone. Despite his warped pleasure in hurting others, he wouldn't be able to bear the agony of touching another Holder's Starting Stone. Mossy thought back to visits from friends. The only Holder he'd ever known to be able to touch his hearth was the Travelling Holder, and there was not even the remotest connection between him and Tannor. Even so he wasn't prepared to risk allowing Tannor access to the structure above it.

Carefully he checked every stone and brick, each joint between them. He heard the family return, clattering about, and hoped that Tannor was keeping to himself. With a bit of luck, he'd be working out how things had changed since he had last been with Dwellers. He had all sorts of things to learn about; piped water was only a beginning. Mossy chuckled to himself. Carpets, heating and cookers would give him plenty to trip over. He was pretty sure Tannor had never learned to read, and computers should tie him in knots. Mind you, he reminded himself, Tannor had already caused quite enough trouble, and nothing seemed to have slowed him down yet.

Once he had noted any possible cracks, Mossy went in search of help. Two big house spiders slipped down from resting places, unravelling silk behind them. Explaining what he needed by knitting his fingers into a mesh, he pointed them at the places that he needed marked. The spiders quickly spun a fine web across each vulnerable spot. Now Mossy would be able to see if anyone tampered with anything.

Finally he pointed at the wide opening across the base of the chimney.

'*Fireproof?*' he checked. The spiders' legs danced, and they set off again, this time with a thicker thread. Mossy felt relieved. They were as keen as he to keep the house safe, and soon the space above the hearth was draped with a wide mesh. Smoke could pass through, but anyone trying to climb up would leave a clearly visible trail. The spiders set off for the top of the chimney to repeat their work up there, so they would know if anyone approached from above.

By the time Mossy and the spiders had finished their work, the sun had set in a fiery glow behind the hill.

'I'm off to Jon's,' called Rollo. 'His parents said they'd give me a lift to the bonfire. I'll see you there.' The door slammed behind him, but it wasn't long before the others followed, heading off into the darkening night.

Mossy was glad his Dwellers would all be safely out of the way. Cautiously he emerged from the fireplace, checking carefully for any sign of strangers. He was just beginning to wonder if Tannor had left, when he caught sight of him hobbling slowly back across the yard.

'Plenty of space here,' snarled Tannor when Mossy met him by the front door. 'Though I have to say I prefer the open barn to the house. Too much soft stuff here. The barn is more my style, altogether a rougher place. Still, when I'm in control, I can sort that out. Once the fighting starts it'll soon become harsher.'

Mossy pointed a long finger at him. It was time to put him right.

'Not stay,' he croaked.

'Ah, but that's where you're wrong, my friend.' Mossy frowned at being called Tannor's friend. He'd never felt less friendly towards anyone. 'You see, you can't get rid of me. My Starting Stone is here. This has become my Holding as much as yours.'

Mossy felt as if the blood had been drained out of him; his legs felt weak, his head spun. He took a step back, reaching behind him for the strength of the wall, one of **his** walls, to support him.

How could Tannor have done that? No Holder had ever moved his Starting Stone. If somehow he possibly had managed to do it, then he might be right. Until it was moved away again, Tannor had the right to stay. But no Holding could have two Holders.

'That's right.' Tannor seemed to have read his mind. 'One of us has to go, and it won't be me. Prepare yourself. I only started with a flood because that seemed easy. I reckon that first little offering will take them plenty of time to sort out, but I have other tricks up my sleeve. Now, get lost, there's a good fellow.' He waved a dismissive hand at Mossy and limped away, quickly mingling with the darkness, his shadowy form a perfect disguise.

Never, thought Mossy, slumping down at the foot of the wall.

This is my Holding, these are my Dwellers, and I'm looking after them to the last breath in my body. He hurried after Tannor, but search as he might could find no sign of the monster. He's spent too much time in hiding, admitted Mossy. He's better at this than me.

With a sigh, he settled down on his hearth to keep guard, prepared for the first whisper of trouble. The soft darkness of a quiet night wrapped him gently in its safe stillness. A mouse ran across the sitting room floor, pausing by his feet to let out a flood of squeaks, before hurrying on its way. Mossy smiled. It was good to know that others were backing him too.

'… at quite a speed on those crutches,' finished Jack with a laugh when the family returned.

'And I can too,' added Rollo. 'He let me have a go.'

'Leave your wellies by the back door, JJ. I don't want mud traipsed through the house,' said Annie.

'I'm leaving mine there too,' added Cissy. 'I need them in school on Monday. We're doing outside stuff and they said to bring them.'

Patrolling through the dark hours, Mossy discovered a nightmare hovering over Cissy, already reaching out a tentacle towards her. He wrapped his long fingers around it and hurled the wraith from the window into the grasp of the Barn Owl's talons. He grinned as she wheeled away into the darkness. She was another valuable person to have on his side.

In JJ's room there was the usual chaos of clothes and possessions spread across the floor. In a heap in the corner lay the jumble of treasure brought back from the wood. Mossy inspected it carefully. Could this be where Tannor had hidden his Starting Stone? He checked each item one by one, but there was nothing among the levers, latches, broken shards of pottery and glass that could have been the first stone of any house. JJ turned over in his sleep, mumbling softly, and Mossy looked back just in time to catch a nightmare gathering its forces for an assault on him, too.

At the window he watched the Barn Owl fade into the darkness, the second nightmare struggling in her firm grip. I'm pretty sure I know how you got in here, he thought grimly. The only troubles to let you in were brought by Tannor, he thought grimly. Two down, he thought; how many more will I find? He checked that JJ's talisman was tucked under his pillow.

'Keep guard,' he projected, his fingers gently stroking the smooth surface. The hidden glow deep within vibrated softly in response.

He shivered as he entered Rollo's room. It was icy cold, far colder than it should be, he was sure. The duvet had more than half slipped from the bed, leaving Rollo at the tender mercies of a chill breeze that curled about him. Mossy hurried over to the open windows, closing one and pulling the curtains back over them before turning his attention to the bed.

The wafting breeze seemed to have formed a mist at its foot. Mossy scrunched his eyes. Was that a shadowy figure he saw? It slipped away, sliding over the covers before gathering again. Mossy reached out a hand. Where the mist hovered there was an icy coldness. It shuddered and split as Mossy's hand approached, spilling over the sleeping Rollo.

There was only one thing that could be that cold, shuddered Mossy. The chill of the grave. But where had it come from? There was no grave near Annanbourne, but if that mist lingered over Rollo he would become so cold that his whole being could freeze to stillness. Already his breathing was shallow and light, and there was a blue edge to his lips.

Mossy shook his head. He made a sweeping gesture through the chill mist with his arm, holding up one finger at the end.

'*There is no place for you here,*' he projected. The mist gathered, pulling together more densely. Mossy frowned. Was that a face he glimpsed? A young man with an expression of deepest sorrow. The thought had barely crossed his mind than any hint of an image disappeared, melting like ice in front of a warm flame. All that was left was the memory of its sadness. Mossy's heart tightened.

Again he swept his arm through the mist, stirring it softly, gathering it about his fingers and then pointing to the window.

'*Go home.*'

'*There is no home.*' The words echoed through Mossy's

mind as clearly as if they had been spoken. He looked around him. How could there be no home?

Maybe not all creatures had a home like his, a place where they belonged, that they came back to for rest and healing, a living space of warmth and love. Some of his Dwellers had lived their whole lives in Annanbourne, but even those who passed through knew that Annanbourne was their home while they were there. Mice had their nests, badgers their setts, spiders their webs. For some, home was the people who lived in it more than the place, but there was always somewhere. It might not be long-term, but he couldn't begin to understand the lostness that no home must mean.

Once again Mossy reached into the mist. The cold seeped into his fingers, turning them stiff and white. Closing his eyes, he breathed in the chill whiteness, pulling it deep into him as he tried to understand. The coldness crept up his arms.

Gradually an understanding grew. He felt the loss. Something missing, searched for but never found. Images flashed though his mind. A fire burning, huge flames. A damp place. The groan of a falling tree, and sudden darkness. And that cold still growing inside him.

Mossy's eyes sprang open as his teeth began to chatter.

'*You cannot bring your coldness here. This is no place for it, and leaving it here will not take away your loss or give you rest.*' He threw the projection into the constantly drifting white that rolled and roiled over Rollo. Somehow he had to protect his friend. Desperately he searched around the room. Was this Tannor at work again? There was no sign of him, and yet Mossy felt sure that in some way he was connected to this chill whiteness.

A huge yawn pulled itself through him. His shoulders slumped, dragged down by the cold. He was so tired. His eyes drooped. Again he shook his head to clear the fog that made him want to give in and sleep forever. He hunched his shoulders and stretched his fingers, pulling the last shred of warmth from his core. He had to speak, get his message across, before it was too late.

'If you need a home, I will help you.' He paused, panting. Splinters of glass tore at his throat. 'I'll find a way. But if this boy is hurt, it will no longer be possible. If you are lost, then we will find you, he and I. But take this chill away, or we can't do it.' His voice broke, finally shattered by the effort. Had he managed to say enough?

'*Promise?*' The icy voice echoed through his mind. The ever-shifting paleness gathered again, and Mossy wondered if he really was seeing dark eyes searching desperately into the depths of his being. He nodded his head, holding out his hand, palm upright. The mist swept through him. The deal was sealed.

'*Find me.*' And with that the haze melted through the wall and disappeared from sight.

It was only once it had gone that Mossy realised he had no idea where to look, or even start looking. And anyway, he thought, how do you look for something that was nothing more than a feeling?

As he gathered Rollo's duvet and tucked it round the sleeping boy, he tried to remember all the images he had caught. Somewhere in them there might be a clue. Rollo turned onto his side and pulled the duvet closer. Mossy blew a burst of warm air across his face, memories of sunny summer days and warm fireside evenings. Rollo's breathing steadied, became deeper and a soft flush of pink returned to his sleeping face.

If Mossy had had any doubts about Tannor's intentions before, they were gone now. The fact that he had started by attacking the children, the first of the family that he had encountered, made Mossy even more sure. This would be a long night. Throughout it Mossy patrolled, tired but ever vigilant, ensuring no more trouble showed its face.

The following morning the emergency plumber knocked on the door.

'Something to do with your header tank?' he asked cheerily, hauling his tools into the house. JJ sat on the landing and watched the work, his legs hanging down between the rails of the banisters. Mossy stood at his side, stifling a yawn.

'What's this for?' asked the boy, holding up a strange tool that Mossy had never seen before.

'Cutting pipes, mate,' the plumber replied. 'I'll be using it next,' he added, reaching out a hand. 'Want to watch?' As JJ scrambled up the ladder, Mossy heard raised voices in the kitchen. He tiptoed down the stairs.

'I just said I wanted the shower first.' Cissy had her hands on her hips.

'So that must be because you smell worst?' jeered Rollo.

'You're no bunch of roses,' Cissy threw at him, her chin jutting forward.

'Unnecessary, Cissy,' remarked Jack, passing through on his

way to his study. Mossy spotted a dark smudge lurking by the curtains.

'Yeah, well he started it,' grumbled Cissy.

'I never,' Rollo hurled back.

'I hate having brothers,' shouted Cissy, tears brimming in her eyes as she flounced into the sitting room. 'Just leave me alone,' she flung over her shoulder, slamming the door behind her.

'Willingly,' muttered Rollo, snapping his arms across his chest as he threw himself down on a chair, scowling. Mossy rested the lightest of fingers on Rollo's leg. Turbulent energy rumbled furiously through him. No wonder he was in such a bad temper, thought Mossy, keeping well out of sight.

'And don't think I don't know you're there,' muttered Rollo darkly, picking up a tea towel which he flicked at a serving plate on the corner of the table. Briefly the plate spun in place before lurching sideways, teetering on the edge and crashing to the floor.

Mossy heard a brief hiccup from the edge of the window, remembered the grey smudge and looked up. Tannor's pale face leered down at them, his charcoal eyes glinting as he lifted a knobbly finger to tick the air.

Mossy leapt towards him, but the door from the sitting room burst open and Tannor vanished from sight.

'What on earth?!' exclaimed Annie. 'Rollo, what's got into you? Cissy tells me you've been getting at her all morning, and now this?' She pointed at the broken plate.

'I... I...' Rollo stared at the floor. Then he put his head in his hands. He let out an exasperated breath. 'I dunno,' he mumbled.

'You don't know!' Annie stared at Rollo. 'Well you'd better think about it, and work it out pretty quickly. Breaking things for no good reason achieves nothing but trouble!'

Mossy stepped out of the way as Rollo started picking up the pieces, retreating to the other side of the kitchen. There was a tickle in his ear.

'Just a little argument that one, but see what I can do? Ready to go yet? You leave them to me and you never know, I **might** leave them alone.' Mossy spun round, his eyes burning red, but all he saw was a wisp of grey as Tannor slipped out of sight once again.

Follow him or stay? Mossy shook his head in frustration. He had work to do calming jangled nerves and frayed tempers. His Dwellers were more important than Tannor. He'd deal with him later.

CHAPTER 15

And On Another Front

Rollo had taken refuge in his room, and Cissy was storming around hers.

'I don't know what's got into them this morning,' Annie told Jack. 'It's not as if there won't soon be enough hot water for everyone.'

'They'll sort it out.' Jack put an arm round her shoulders. 'They always have in the past, and this'll soon blow over.'

I wouldn't count on it, thought Mossy, not if Tannor has his way. He wished he could ease the ache in his shoulders.

The plumber's cheery face popped round the door.

'Ah, there you are!' he grinned, coming to join them. 'All sorted. It'll take a little while for your water to be fully heated, but the system's up and running again.'

Mossy smiled. The chill that had wrapped him in its clutches was already beginning to ease. Sitting on his hearthstone, his back propped against the fireback, he watched his Dwellers come and go.

As darkness eased around them, Jack arrived with an armful of logs which he dumped beside Mossy.

'Who'd like roasted chestnuts?' he asked. JJ's face split into a wide grin.

'Can I make the holes?' he asked. Annie passed him a skewer. Carefully he pierced each chestnut before chucking them into a bowl by Mossy's feet. Mossy shuffled back once the fire took hold, wriggling himself into a comfortable position on the wood stack. He didn't want to be roasted along with the chestnuts. Footsteps clattered down the stairs.

'Mum, can you help me with my homework?' asked Cissy, waving some papers. Annie made space on the sofa.

'Let's have a look,' she suggested. JJ disappeared up the stairs and Jack picked up a book. Mossy wondered if he should go with him, but the warmth of the fire was making him lazy after his sleepless night. Surely Tannor had made enough trouble? he told himself.

Silence settled over the room, apart from the occasional murmur between Annie and Cissy. Mossy was just dozing off when the door to the stairs burst open again.

'Who's for a game of Racing Demon?' Rollo challenged them, holding up playing cards.

'Yup! That homework's done,' decided Cissy, her bad feelings towards Rollo forgotten.

'Are you sure?' asked Annie.

'It's done enough,' Cissy assured her.

By the time noisy games had been played and chestnuts had been eaten, the chill in Mossy's bones had been completely banished. He stretched his arms out. The ache between his shoulders had gone too. Looking around him he smiled. His

Dwellers seemed to be restored to their usual selves. Even so, he decided, he'd better do a thorough Nightwatch again.

He waited until Jack and Annie returned from saying goodnight to the children before abandoning the warm safety of the hearth. Cautiously he climbed the stairs, his eyes searching every dark corner for any sign of movement. Everything was still.

JJ was already asleep. Mossy checked the room for lurking nightmares, found an exciting dream and shunted it in his direction.

As soon as he peered round the door into Cissy's room though, he could see it had been abandoned. The duvet had gone. He listened carefully. Soft voices rose and fell in Rollo's room. Nevertheless he checked carefully for crouching nightmares lying in wait. He sniffed the air. The anger that had bounced off the walls earlier had disappeared. Despite being fairly sure that all was clear, he decided to recheck later.

He found Cissy wrapped in her duvet and perched on the end of Rollo's bed.

'I really mean it,' she was saying earnestly. 'It was as if something lit explosions inside me. All I could do was go banging on and bashing at things.'

'And I'm sorry, too. I was mean,' replied Rollo. 'There are lots of girls who are a complete pain, but you're not bad for a sister.' Cissy raised an eyebrow. 'Well,' he paused. 'Put it this way, you're almost as good as a boy.' He winked at her. Cissy grabbed his pillow, hauling it from behind his back and thumping it against his shoulder.

'I take it back,' he laughed, catching her arm, his voice

muffled by her smothering duvet. 'You're a whole lot better than most.' They don't need me, decided Mossy and left them to their banter.

Up on the roof the Barn Owl was waiting. Fixing her brown eyes on him, she hooted softly as he arrived. He raised his eyebrows in surprise, pointing at his throat with one hand and covering his mouth with the other, to explain his silence.

He had to agree, however, that she had a point. When Tannor made him feel afraid, he also felt weaker. Now was the time when he had to be strong, remember that he had friends who could help. He'd weathered worse in the past, he reminded himself.

The Barn Owl stretched her wings, beating them against the night, shaking the air. Feathers scattered around her, whirling into the dark, wafting slowly down to settle on the roof, snagging on the ancient timbers, one speckled wing feather curling down to rest in the crook of Mossy's arm. He smiled at her, his confidence restored.

The first part of his Nightwatch completed, Mossy installed himself on his hearthstone. He didn't wait long. Tannor materialised out of the gloom.

'How come they did it so quickly?' he demanded, getting as close to the hearth as he dared. Carefully emptying his mind of any thought that Tannor might pick up, Mossy shrugged his shoulders and then folded his arms across his chest.

'Back when I had Dwellers, something like that would have left them stranded for days, weeks, months, forever,' huffed Tannor. 'And who was that spare human that sprang out of nowhere? He didn't belong here and yet he did all the work.' His eyes smouldered like dark coals on a dying fire. Again Mossy shrugged his shoulders.

'Oh, for goodness' sake, stop blanking your mind,' snarled Tannor. 'You're shutting me out.' He sprang forward, reaching for Mossy. There was a brief fizz of warning before a sudden glow of pale blue light leapt from the stone towards Tannor's hand. He snatched it back. Mossy shook his head, pointed at him, then at his own throat before making a gesture as if passing his voice to the other Holder. Tannor chuckled.

'Too right, there!' His hiccupping laugh jolted through the dark room. 'I took your voice and I'll take your Holding yet. You ready to go now? Or do I have to show you more?' Mossy settled himself firmly on the stone and sent out a clear projection.

'I'm staying put.'

'Please yourself then,' jeered Tannor. 'I can think up plenty more to entertain your Dwellers and they'll soon realise who's in control here. And it's you they'll blame. They'll want you gone as much as I do.'

Mossy closed his mind to outside thoughts, concentrating instead on the sights and smells of a recent misty morning that had cleared to the brightest of autumn days.

'Ha! You think happy memories can help you. You'll forget them soon enough, and in the end all you'll remember is the fog,' Tannor taunted him. He faded from sight as he spoke, his words left hanging in the air.

Fog, thought Mossy. The mist in Rollo's room came back to mind. Now he was sure. It must have had something to do with Tannor. But where could he have found the chill of a grave?

The following morning Mossy was hugely relieved that his Dwellers were mostly out of the house again. It had been a lively night chasing round after Tannor, collecting nightmares, calming restless sleep and replacing bedclothes that kept being dragged to the floor.

As soon as the others had left for school, Annie went into her studio to work on a painting. Mossy joined her so that he could collect another dose of much-needed energy. He crept into the gap between the walls, found the studio's other residents and arranged for them to keep guard, warning him if any attacks attempts were attempted.

A van that arrived in the drive produced a man who followed Annie into the house.

'Not a problem, Mrs Breeze,' he told her enthusiastically. 'I can get that sorted. No worries. My Arthur goes to your husband's after-school class. He loves it, says it's not like any kind of school he's ever done before.' This time it was Mossy who grinned while the hole in the ceiling was repaired and fresh plaster spread smoothly over it. It was like swallowing a soothing spoonful of some delicious healing drink.

'I'll be back to do the finishing coat tomorrow,' the plasterer told Annie as he left.

Hoping to catch up on sleep lost during the night, Mossy curled up on his hearthstone for a quick kip before the others returned. He was just getting comfortable when Tannor's harsh voice sliced into his thoughts.

'Where do they find all these people?' Tannor's foot beat an angry rhythm on the wooden floor.

'Times have changed since you last got up to your tricks,' replied Mossy, glad to find that his voice worked again, maybe not quite as smoothly as before, but without the pain that he had endured from Tannor's mischief. 'These days it's not just the Dwellers who do work on a house. And this lot have friends.'

'I'll just have to think of something else then,' muttered Tannor. 'Remember, everything I do, all that they suffer, is your fault. You can stop it in a second. All you have to do… is leave.' He turned on his heel, spinning out of sight in a dark cloud of dust.

Mossy sighed. Forget sleep, he told himself. You've got to find Tannor's Starting Stone. That's the only way you're going to get rid of him. Find it, and find a way to get it out of the house.

He was halfway through a thorough, but fruitless, check of the kitchen when Cissy and Rollo arrived back from school. He ducked under the table.

'I tell you, I'll kill him,' thundered Cissy, banging her school bag down just above Mossy's head.

'You don't know it was him,' Rollo tried to reason with her.

'Who else could have stuffed mud down my wellies?' Cissy stamped around the kitchen, flinging open cupboards, collecting a plate and some bread. 'He knew I needed them today. Mr Caplan gave me all sorts of flack, and I missed out on the field work too. I got left in the class with extra work while everyone else was outside.' She fetched butter and jam from the larder. 'And now the butter's too hard to spread!' She flung the knife down on the table in a fury. 'I mean it, I'll throttle him!' She took a ferocious bite of the mangled bread.

'The butter's nothing to do with JJ,' Rollo pointed out. 'And why suddenly so cross with him? You weren't like this at school when it happened.' Ah, thought Mossy, that's because this temper wasn't Cissy's. His eyes darted round the room, and sure enough, there in a corner was a tell-tale smudge in the shadows.

'There you go again, Mr Oh-So-Reasonable.' Mossy could see Cissy's legs spin her in Rollo's direction. 'It's just that he does these things and he always gets away with it. I'm fed up with him.' Cissy stormed out of the room, heading towards Annie's studio.

Rollo sighed. Mossy was longing to talk to him, explain what was going on and get him to help, but he didn't dare risk Tannor working out that he was in contact with a Dweller. He might use it to all the worst ends. He would have to be even more careful than before.

Instead he went to the shadowy corner.

'*Go away,*' he projected. '*I'm pretty sure you know how that mud got in her boots. Just leave her alone.*'

'*You can't make me,*' shot back Tannor's rough response.

'*I'll find your Starting Stone and then we'll see,*' projected Mossy.

'*You can no more touch mine than I can yours. And anyway, you'll never find it. It's perfectly hidden.*'

Rollo's head jerked up, and he looked around the room at the strangled hiccup that punctured the quiet.

A reception committee was waiting in the kitchen when Jack and JJ arrived home half an hour later.

'Tell me what you know about wellies and mud,' asked Annie.

'Um...' JJ looked puzzled. 'Wellies keep your feet from getting muddy?'

'Oh yeah, very funny.' Cissy stood with her hands on her hips. 'You know perfectly well what Mum means.'

JJ looked from one face to the other.

'What does she mean?' he asked.

'Cissy's wellies?' suggested Annie.

'What about them?' JJ looked blank.

'Sweetheart, maybe he really doesn't know what you mean,' Annie suggested.

'It has to be him,' insisted Cissy. 'There isn't any mud at school, the playground is all tarmac and the mud was stuffed right down inside. It's just the sort of stupid thing little boys do. Go on, own up for once.'

'I didn't do it. Whatever it was, I didn't do it,' repeated JJ, his face looking flushed and hot, his fists clenched at his sides.

'Maybe he didn't do it,' Jack joined in.

'See!' Cissy was rigid with anger. 'See! Just like always, he's going to get away with it.' But he doesn't, thought Mossy. That's one of the things about JJ. He always owns up to everything. 'You always take his side. It's not fair.' She turned and ran from the room.

Mossy followed her. He had some comforting to do. She was right; it wasn't fair, but not in the way she meant. Tannor was attacking him through Cissy, dosing her with an anger that was totally unnatural, upsetting JJ with false accusations. A new shaft of pain shot down his legs, lodging in his knees, as he limped towards the stairs.

CHAPTER 16

Power Cut

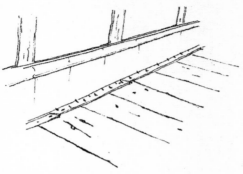

For the next seven days all was quiet. Mossy lived on tenterhooks. He kept glancing around, jumping at the smallest sound, but it was never more than a startled spider or sleepy ladybird sheltering from the winter winds. Tannor appeared to have vanished. Regardless, Mossy kept well away from Rollo, aware that the rogue holder could still be lurking unseen, and he wanted to avoid giving him any new ideas for ways to attack.

Although the repairs to the ceiling were finished, the landing remained bare of carpet.

'Make sure you keep your feet covered to protect them from splinters,' Annie reminded everybody. What about those sharp tacks? Mossy wanted to add, as he saw JJ's feet go skimming past them in socks.

Cissy quickly regained her normal sense of humour and the limp in Mossy's leg disappeared.

'You should have seen Frankie in school today,' she burst out when she erupted into the house on her return from school one evening.

'We were reading this book in English, and he had some BluTak, and he decorated his whole face with added eyebrows and moustache, a great fat nose, the works.' Her hands flew about her own face, describing grotesque additions. Mossy stroked his own nose. Always good to have a long one, he thought approvingly.

'He and Phil sit in front of me, and nobody had noticed, not Mrs Farthing, not Phil, not anyone. Anyway, just as we got to the bit where the ghost of Christmas Past turns up, he tapped Phil on the arm.' She nudged an imaginary neighbour.

'So Phil looked at him and got such a shock,' she pulled a horrified face, 'he tipped sideways off his chair.' She flung her arms in the air and staggered backwards, grinning.

'The whole class just fell about. It was so funny. Then Frankie stood up and bowed and somehow that was even funnier.' She bowed on his behalf. 'Of course The Old Bike got in a right tizz and sent him to stand outside the office.'

'The Old Bike?' interrupted Annie.

'Penny Farthing,' explained Rollo.

'I dread to think what nickname I might get in your school,' sighed Jack.

'You'd be OK,' grinned Cissy. 'People like your lessons. It's the rubbish teachers, that think they're fancy stuff, who get nicknames. Nobody gives people like Mr KP or Mrs Livvy nicknames – they're cool.'

'And they're good teachers too,' added Rollo. 'You learn stuff in their lessons.'

'And Frankie's always being sent to stand outside the

office,' said Cissy. 'It's not because he's bad. It's just that he's really funny, and teachers don't like it when you're funny.'

'Specially not if you make them laugh too,' added JJ, ruefully.

'So what happened to you today?' asked Jack, turning to him. JJ hung his head.

'Mrs Danby was talking about the way different particles link together in liquids and solids and gasses, and then he asked what I was doing, and I said I was just being a fart particle finding its way to Henry's nose.'

'Nice one, JJ' laughed Cissy. 'Sounds like the sort of thing I get into trouble for. Your problem is you own up too quickly.' At least she's remembered that, thought Mossy.

Jack disappeared into his study with a pile of books for marking.

'Rollo?' called Cissy. 'Can you give me some clues with this history homework?'

JJ stayed to help Annie make biscuits, and Mossy installed himself behind them on the dresser to enjoy the process.

'I don't like it getting dark so early,' JJ told his mother as he rolled out the biscuit mixture. 'It means we can't do half the things we do in the summer. It's dark almost as soon as we get home from school these days.'

'We have fires though now, which we don't have in summer,' Annie reminded him. 'And games together in the sitting room. Are you going to put icing on these?'

'Yeah, and hundreds and thousands.' Annie reached into the larder. Mmm, thought Mossy. Sounds like a tasty supper treat coming up. He craned his head forward to watch and then gasped in surprise.

His head spun: his vision spiralled. It felt as if someone had reached a hand through his chest, grasped his heart and was trying to pull it out through his stomach. He gripped the edge of the shelf, but his fingers were weak.

Then everything went black. He opened his eyes wide, realising that it wasn't just him. The whole room had been plunged into darkness.

'Mum? Why d'you turn the lights off?'

'Stay still,' Annie replied. 'Something must have blown.' Something more than that, thought Mossy as he slumped, exhausted, against a bowl. Feet clattered down the stairs.

'Rollo, that's my foot you're treading on,' complained Cissy.

'Sorry,' said Jack. 'It's me, not Rollo. You OK?'

'Yep,' admitted Cissy. 'I can cope with only half a foot, but why's it all gone dark? I can't do my homework.'

'It's OK, I'll just check the fuses and it'll all be fine again,' Jack reassured them. Mossy heard a soft crunch. His head had stopped spinning, but he still felt desperately weak. All his energy seemed to have disappeared with the lights.

'Oops, sorry. Was that your head?'

'Yeah, I'm not the fuse box, Dad,' said Rollo.

'It's OK. Got it now.' Mossy heard the click of the trip switch thumping down. The darkness seemed even blacker. Slowly he lowered himself to the floor. He could still get around, but it was a huge effort.

'Jack?' Annie sounded puzzled.

'I must have tried the wrong switch,' Jack apologised. 'It is the big one, isn't it?' he checked. 'I'll try it again.'

Again there was an audible click, but still nothing happened.

'Dad, why isn't it working?' Cissy's voice sounded a little tighter than before.

'Rollo, can you get the torch? It's on the windowsill of the washing room.' Mossy followed, and then listened as Rollo's hands patted the surfaces.

'Not here, Dad,' he called out. There was a scuffle as Annie joined them and bumped into the door. Mossy sheltered behind a broom.

'I saw it yesterday.' There was a dull dong as Annie's toe collided with the washing machine.

'Got it!' exclaimed Rollo. 'Oh no, this is something else.' Mossy heard a gloopy sound as Rollo shook what he held.

'Watch out, I lost the top off the detergent yesterday,' Annie warned him. There was a splot as liquid hit a firm surface.

'Yup, I've just worked that out; it's all over my hands.' Mossy could hear the grimace in Rollo's voice. Then his toe stubbed against something round on the floor. A dark cylinder by his feet turned out to be the torch wedged under the washing machine. He reached down, heaved hard, and pulled it free.

'*Down here,*' he projected. '*Look down.*' Rollo's feet shuffled closer, and a flower-scented hand groped along the floor. Mossy stepped neatly out of the way as he nudged the torch towards him.

'This time I really have got it,' said Rollo, standing up. 'We have li… Oh no, we don't. Dad, Mum, the torch isn't working.'

'But I put new batteries in on Bonfire Night!' exclaimed Annie. 'They can't have run out already. Pass it here, can you? I'll check.'

'OK. Matches,' said Jack. 'Cissy can you fetch them from the sitting room?'

'Eurgh!' Annie exclaimed. 'This torch is all sticky.' Mossy could hear Annie shaking the torch as he left the washing room and limped slowly to the kitchen. Skirting round JJ and Jack, he headed towards the sitting room, glad that he could see more clearly in the dark than his Dwellers. He flattened himself against the wall, panting softly as Cissy sidled past him with a guiding hand sliding along the wall.

'Here you are, Dad.' She held out the box, waving it in the darkness. 'But it feels weird.' Mossy could see Jack's hand reaching towards her, missing the box.

'Cissy?'

'Here, Dad.' Cissy thrust the box forward again, this time colliding with Jack's fingers, which grasped on air as the matches fell to the ground, landing between their feet. This was his chance. Mossy stumbled onto it. What had Cissy meant by 'weird'?

Ah, he thought, his fingers connecting with dampness. He rolled out of the way, heading for the safety of the space beneath the table. Cissy dropped to her knees, patting the floor around her as she and Jack both searched. Jack stood up first.

'These aren't just weird, my love. How come they're wet?' Mossy could see him trying to slide the box open. Jack heaved a sigh. 'Soggy matches aren't going to shed light on anything.'

'Why don't I go over to Jon's and ask them if we can borrow a torch?' suggested Rollo. 'Coming Cissy?'

'Whoops, sorry JJ,' said Cissy as she knocked against him

on her way to the door. 'Oh! It's easier to see out here. We've got the moon, nearly full too.'

'Back soon!' called Rollo. Mossy heard their footsteps disappearing at a run down the path.

'If it's a major power cut, the Raitatas will have no power either,' said Annie as she put an arm round JJ. 'They'll need their own torches.'

'I'm going to find the candles,' said Jack. 'I think I've got a lighter in my study.' Mossy heard a small scuffling noise by the door. He turned towards it, his eyes searching the darkness.

'What was that?' asked JJ.

'Don't say we've got mice in the house as well,' sighed Annie. I just hope that's what it is, thought Mossy. But he had a sinking feeling. He shook his head. There were too many coincidences.

'I only wanted the hundreds and thousands,' sighed JJ. 'Will I still be able to cook my biscuits?'

'Don't worry, we'll find a way somehow,' Annie reassured him.

Footsteps came running up the path, the door flung open and a shaft of light darted round the room.

'Matches and a torch!' announced Cissy with a flourish.

'It's just us, not them too,' Rollo informed them.

'And Mum says do you want to come for supper?' added Jon, hot on Rollo's heels.

The torch showed that no matter what switch was flicked, nothing was bringing the lights back on.

'Looks like we've no electricity until we can find someone to sort it out,' sighed Annie. 'Tell your Mum we'd love to come over for supper.'

'And can I bring my biscuits to cook?' added JJ.

'You won't believe it!' exclaimed Jack as he returned clutching some candles. 'You must be right about the mice. These candles have had the wicks eaten out of them. No way we can light them.' He dumped them on the table. 'And that lighter I mentioned? I sat down at my desk to get it out of the drawer, heard a crunch and found it had got under the foot of my chair somehow. I know I put it in there yesterday. Have any of you had it out?'

Cissy prowled around the kitchen, one hand holding the torch under her chin, shining upwards onto her face, the other held clawlike in front of her.

'I am the Ghost of Christmas Past,' she moaned. 'Trouble, trouble and more trouble,' she groaned.

'Well, I am the Spirit of Right Now,' interrupted Jack, 'and I say we get ourselves over to Sue and Rajesh's house pretty quickly, with homework and anything else we need.'

Jon was dispatched to warn his mother while the family gathered their essentials for the rest of the day.

'We'll be back,' called Cissy as they left. 'You watch out, you manky mice!'

Mossy eased himself out from under the table. It wasn't mice, he knew that. There were too many coincidences. The crushed lighter, the damaged candles, the soaked matches, the useless batteries in the torch, which someone had tried to hide anyway. It wasn't hard to work out.

'Tannor!' he shouted, his voice booming through the abandoned house. 'Too scared to show yourself?'

'Not at all,' hissed Tannor's scratchy voice from the

shadows. 'Right here beside you. Got rid of them fairly efficiently, didn't I?' His sinister hiccup rattled round the kitchen. 'Aren't you going with them? I can't imagine you feel up to much in the way of fighting your corner right now? OK, so I hadn't planned for this neighbour thing helping out. My Dwellers never had neighbours, or friends for that matter, I saw to that right from the beginning. But you're going to be useless for quite a while. Water they fixed, but this new energy thing should keep them foxed for a whole lot longer. And you're pretty much out of action, too.'

How do I fight this? thought Mossy. How do I protect Annanbourne and my Dwellers from this attack? Stand strong, the Barn Owl had warned him. But how do I do that when my energy has been sapped, drained away by Tannor's assault? Hiccupping laughter broke across his thoughts, hollow and twisted. So different he thought, remembering Cissy's laughter in describing the antics at school. He smiled as he remembered the warmth of it. Tannor fell abruptly silent.

'Don't!' he exclaimed, wincing as he felt Mossy's memory fill the room.

'Got it!' smiled Mossy. Now it was the memory of Annie's arm as it slipped round JJ's shoulder. Tannor's shoulders hunched, raising a barrier between him and any happiness. He took a step back.

'You may have taken my energy for now,' Mossy told him. 'But I warn you, it won't be for long, and meanwhile, I know what keeps us safe. Something you can't understand, you poor, broken Holder.'

'Don't!' screamed Tannor, his red eyes flaring in fury, his

hands lifted as if to attack Mossy again. 'Don't you dare! I will not have you feeling sorry for me! Go away!' he spat. 'Get out! Leave this Holding to me! Let me take my revenge!'

But Mossy noticed, even in the darkness, that Tannor's hands had dropped to his sides. Mossy couldn't fight, he was too weak. Instead he let Rollo's parting words fill his mind.

'Here, JJ. Take my hand. It's perfectly safe. We can see quite clearly now.'

Tannor turned and fled.

CHAPTER 17

Head To Head

'Well, I have to say, Mrs Breeze, it's the weirdest thing I've ever seen,' said the electrician when he called the next day. Mossy remembered him from the weeks he had spent rewiring the house soon after the Breezes first blew into his Holding. 'It's like someone jammed your mains cable. See here, where the plastic sheath's been broken? It's fine right up to that point; after it, nothing.'

'Not mice, then?' asked Annie, puzzled.

'No way!' chuckled the man. 'We'd have found some poor little fried mite if it had been mice chewing the cable.' Mossy winced at the thought. 'No.' The man carried on scratching his head. 'Your guess is as good as mine as to what happened exactly.'

'So not one of the children fiddling with it either?' checked Annie.

'Oh no!' The man's eyebrows shot up his forehead in alarm. 'They'd have been as fried as any mouse near that cable. There's enough power in there to blast most things from here to kingdom come.' Mossy wondered if by any chance it might have knocked some sense into Tannor. He hadn't managed to get a clear look at him in the darkness the evening before, but maybe the shock had even reached him.

'I'll have to get one or two extra bits and pieces, as well as my rubber boots,' the electrician said, 'but we should have you sorted out again by the end of the day,' He roared off in his van.

Leaving Annie to work in her studio, Mossy decided to borrow JJ's lucky talisman.

'I could do with a shot of your strength and calm,' he admitted. He curled one long finger through the hole, tucked his other hand under his head and settled for a much-needed rest on his hearthstone.

He woke to find Tannor pacing furiously in front of him, his broken leg making him lurch from side to side. In the light of day he could see now that his hair looked strangely frazzled, standing in spikes. His fingers had blackened tips.

'How come they've got a power man as well as a water man?' he demanded as soon as Mossy stirred. 'I thought if I cut off their water that would put them out of sorts, create the right atmosphere for me to cause some upset. But along came that fellow with his pipes and flames and in no time it was sorted out.' Tannor scowled at Mossy, who sat up and rubbed the sleep from his eyes but kept quiet. Carefully he extricated his finger from the talisman and rolled it softly into the ashes behind the fireback.

'It took hard work to create that little diversion,' continued Tannor, hobbling back and forth in front of the hearth, 'not to say risking my life in the process. Nasty stuff this new electricity, but I could see how dependent your precious Dwellers are on it, and stripping it out was supposed to leave you in the lurch for ages. Instead of which they spring this...' he spluttered to a stop. '...this... power man on me.' Mossy gazed at him. He waves his hands about almost as much as Cissy, he thought.

'And you can cut that out.' Tannor spun on his heel and pointed a finger at Mossy. The hearth fizzed a spurt of blue where the tip of his finger came too close, making him snatch his hand back. 'I'm nothing like that girl.'

'No,' agreed Mossy. 'More's the pity. She's a fine Dweller when you aren't tampering with her temper.'

'You wait 'til I get to the others,' taunted Tannor. Suddenly he stopped in his pacing and turned to glare at Mossy again. 'That older one, the Rollo. What's with him? I caught him sending out a projection the other day. He seemed to be trying to get hold of you. Are you up to something?' Mossy shut him out firmly. Deer, he thought. Blades of grass. Ash.

'You got something hidden in that ash?' hissed Tannor. Mossy could have kicked himself. Blue sky. Choose your thoughts, he reminded himself. Sunshine.

'Don't be pathetic,' sneered Tannor. Mossy racked his mind. Something active, busy. Got it.

'Bee,' he said.

'Bee sting,' Tannor flung back at him. Mossy looked up at the other Holder. His frustrated fury, combined with his damaged appearance, brought a bubble of sadness into Mossy's chest. It didn't have to be like this, a battle. If only he could show Tannor an easier way to settle his hurt.

Despite resting, Mossy was still drained of energy; the electrician had yet to complete his work. He needed a hand on the fire dogs to help pull himself to his feet. He searched deep to find the feeling he was looking for, the one he got when he listened to Annie reading a night time story to the children.

His eyes turned a soft, deep blue as he turned to face his tormentor. He held out a friendly hand and smiled.

'Don't do that,' screamed Tannor, lifting his arms to make a barrier between them. He grasped the leg of a nearby chair and turned his back on Mossy. 'I won't let you.' He hobbled from the room, leaving a grey smudge on the wood.

Mossy collapsed in a heap, all his remaining energy used up in that one gesture. JJ's lucky talisman rolled into his rejected hand, the warm glow at its core comforting him with its steady strength.

'I hope that electrician gets here quickly,' he sighed.

By the time Annie went to pick JJ up from school, Mossy was back on his feet.

The rush of energy when the power came back on had carried him round the house, but there was no sign of Tannor anywhere. On his way to return JJ's talisman to its place under his pillow, he hunted in dusty corners, under beds and in cupboards. There was no sign of him. He didn't for one moment believe the other Holder had gone, but there was no harm in hoping.

Rollo and Cissy arrived soon after, bubbling with noisy chatter. Silently Mossy trailed after them, keeping well back and making sure that no thoughts escaped to give away his presence to the Place Reader.

'I've got to finish that science thing,' Rollo sighed eventually. 'Gimme a shout if you need me,' he added hopefully, swinging his bag over his shoulder as he set off for his room. Mossy trailed in his wake, still searching around for any sign of Tannor. On the landing he paused, wrinkling his nose at the sharp smell that accosted him. The farmers must be spreading manure, he thought. Funny time of year for it.

Rollo's door stood ajar, and he wriggled round it into the room, slipping silently towards the bookshelf before climbing upwards. Rollo paused in arranging his books. He looked around the room, a pencil held in one hand.

'Mossy?' he said softly. Sitting on the pile of books, Mossy shimmered into visibility. Rollo's face broke into a broad smile that disappeared quickly when Mossy lifted a finger to his lips.

'*Say nothing,*' he projected. '*Look out of the window and find something interesting to watch, but listen carefully. I've got to be quick. There is trouble in the house. Don't worry, I'm working on it, but most importantly you must avoid any contact with me until I tell you it's safe.*' Rollo's eyes slipped round to catch a glimpse of Mossy.

'*No. Contact,*' repeated Mossy, holding up a forbidding finger. '*Clear out all thoughts of me. It's to keep you safe,*' he finished, slipping back out of sight.

Rollo sat back on his chair, his elbows on the table, his face a forlorn mask. Mossy longed to comfort him, tell him more fully what was happening, but he didn't dare risk

Tannor finding out that he could talk to the boy. The more he said, the riskier it would be. With Tannor in such an angry and embittered state it could only mean worse trouble for Rollo.

Suddenly Rollo straightened his shoulders, looked at where Mossy had been sitting and then grabbed a pencil, scribbling quickly on the paper in front of him. What was he up to? Silently Mossy leaned a little closer to read the words.

Are you OK?

The words made him smile. Yes, he was much better, and a plan was forming to find a resolution. Now Rollo had hit upon a method that they could use to communicate in an emergency. Mossy was pretty sure that none of Tannor's Dwellers had ever been able to read or write. If that was the case, then there was no way Tannor could have learned to read either.

'*Fine*,' he projected. It was stretching the truth a bit, but he had to stop Rollo thinking about him. '*Writing for emergencies only*,' he added. '*Now blank me out of your mind*,' he finished, climbing back down the bookcase and leaving as quickly as he could, before anyone else could latch on.

The acrid smell on the landing caught at Mossy's nose again. It was as if he had walked straight past a sheep! He skirted round one of Cissy's slippers, which seemed to have crept out of her room, and headed downstairs to the sitting room. He still didn't trust Tannor not to attack the hearthstone.

Outside, darkness settled around them. Jack and Annie

clattered about in the kitchen. JJ bounced in and out with questions, rattling up and down the stairs as he came and went.

'Is it true that if we lived on Mars we'd be twice the height we are now?'

'Why has Shiva got so many arms?'

'Where does the Gulf stream come from?'

Mossy was tapping his toes on one of the firedogs and humming a tune quietly under his breath when he saw Tannor sauntering across the room towards him.

'I wanted to see you when it happened,' he hissed. Mossy looked up in alarm. What did he mean? Tannor steepled his fingers together and then sprang them apart with a snap. 'Any minute now,' he purred. Mossy looked up into the chimney. The spider webs were intact, a little sootier than when they had first been spun, but none had been broken by any unwanted passer-by. A horrid thought crossed his mind. He hadn't checked the top of the chimney. Had Tannor come at it from above? A hiccupping chuckle broke across the turmoil of his thoughts.

'No idea, have you?' Mossy raced to the front of the hearth. Tannor met him, the fingers of both hands poised and pointing.

'One step off there and I'll belt you for six,' he threatened. 'I'm not letting you stop this one.' Mossy took no notice. He had to protect his Dwellers. He stepped off the hearthstone and Tannor pounced, flicking his fingers out at him. Shooting pain fired through Mossy. He reeled back, grasping for the familiar stone to break his fall.

'Stay where you are,' ordered Tannor. 'I've got plenty

more where that came from.'

JJ burst out of the kitchen again, running across the sitting room towards the stairs.

'And tell the others while you're up there,' Annie called after him.

JJ swung round the door and pounded up.

Mossy sunk down, focused his thoughts.

'Be careful!' he projected. *'Careful…'* But then he caught Tannor's simultaneous projection.

'Go for it! Run like crazy! Run, little boy, run!'

'Cissy! Rollo! Supper's…'

There was a terrible crashing bang; a sound of breaking wood followed by silence, then a wail of shocked pain. Mossy felt a sharp, slicing twist in his little finger. Doors crashed open.

Annie and Jack raced through the sitting room, abandoning a rattle of crockery in the kitchen.

'JJ?' called Annie.

'Mum! There's blood everywhere!' Cissy's voice came from the stairs as Tannor stepped back, courteously ushering Mossy off the hearth.

'You may go and inspect my handiwork,' he said with one of his stretched leers.

Mossy raced across the sitting room and up the steps. Annie was cradling JJ in her arms. Cissy was proffering towels. Jack and Rollo were collecting broken struts from the banister.

'That's a shame,' admitted Tannor, hobbling behind him. 'I was hoping he might fall all the way through. Could have broken his…'

'Shut up! Mossy turned on him, his eyes a fiery orange. And then he saw Tannor's look of triumph. This was what he wanted. He wanted to goad Mossy into anger; anger was what he fed off. Concentrating hard, he pushed it back, forced himself to calm his breathing. He had work to do.

'Antiseptic,' he projected, as clearly as he dared. Then he caught the sound of Jack's voice raised.

'How many times, Cissy, have I told you that slippers are supposed to be in your room or on your feet?' He held up the one Mossy had seen earlier in his hand. 'I take it this is what JJ tripped on?' Cissy clapped a hand over her mouth in horror.

'I... Oh my... Oh JJ, I'm so sorry.' Cissy sank down beside her brother, tears welling up in her eyes. 'Oh JJ... Mum, it's not that bad is it?'

Annie lifted the towel from JJ's arm. They looked at the damage. There was a deep gash on his hand and fresh blood welled up along his arm. JJ grimaced. Rollo handed Annie a bottle and some cotton wool he had brought from the bathroom.

'I'm sorry Mum,' JJ said through clenched teeth. Annie shook her head, mopping up some of the blood, before pouring liquid from the bottle onto his arm.

'Don't you worry, my love, it's just another visit to A&E,' she said as she re-wrapped the wound. 'It's not as if we don't know the way already. I think your hand is going to need stitches, though the rest isn't too bad.' She looked up at Jack. 'We should have taken those old tacks out. Cissy, you aren't the only one who made a mistake.' Mossy moved among them, placing a comforting finger to ease an anxious mind or to strengthen a sore heart.

Jack put an arm round Cissy.

'Mum's right, it's my fault as much as yours. I should have made the landing safe after we took the carpet away. We'll do it now, while Mum takes him to the hospital.'

As soon as Annie and JJ had left, the others busied themselves with tools, levering out all the old tacks. Cissy scrubbed at the wood with a sponge.

'The blood has stained the wood,' she sighed. 'I can't get it out.'

'Something to remember him by,' murmured Tannor under his breath.

Mossy had had enough of his dark mutterings. He took Tannor firmly by the arm and dragged him away.

'How dare you touch me?' fizzed Tannor, his eyes a deep, burning red.

'This is still my Holding,' Mossy reminded him. 'You may be on the attack, but you haven't won yet.'

'Ah ha!' Tannor pounced on Mossy's words. 'But you accept that I might. That was just the first step. She's taken him to a hospital, and we all know that hospitals are places where people die.'

'No,' Mossy shook his head. 'These days people get better in hospital.'

'Not with what I've done. That wound will be infected in no time. I rubbed sheep droppings all along those tacks. Old, mouldy droppings,' Tannor chortled, rubbing his hands together in glee. 'I wasn't leaving anything to chance.'

'Remember that stuff she poured on his arm?' Mossy said quietly. 'It kills germs. It stings a bit, but JJ's used to it.

They'll give him more stuff to fight any badness at the hospital. People don't die of infections like they used to. You got it wrong. You're out of date. He'll be fine.'

Tannor stopped in his tracks. His eyes faded to a dull grey.

'He'll be fine?' he echoed. His fists clenched and then he lifted one hand, pointing a scraggy finger towards the woods, back to where his damaged Holding was crumbling through the final stages of decay.

'They made me suffer,' he said. 'For all those years, every time they came or went, that pivot ground further into us. I had to survive against the odds, and I found my strength through anger. Then I took my revenge, stopped the constant suffering, but I was trapped. You broke my silence, bringing your noisy batch of happy Dwellers traipsing through my Holding, unearthing our last remnants. Then, when he found my Starting Stone and brought it here, I swore one last revenge, not just on them, but on you too, for allowing them to do it. I won't let you steal my revenge from me. I won't. There has to be some payback for all that pain.'

CHAPTER 18

What And Where?

Mossy sat on the roof and watched the scudding clouds race across the night sky. He had checked the chimney and found all the webs intact. As he peered down into the sooty blackness, one of the spiders had hauled himself over the rim of the pot, waving three legs energetically.

'Thanks,' smiled Mossy. 'That'll help a lot. I can keep a better eye on things if you're going to let me know what goes on here. But with only the two of you...' The spider displayed another pair of legs.

'Oh right!' grinned Mossy. 'I'd forgotten about all the cousins, uncles and aunts. In that case, there's nothing to hold me back!'

Now he sat racking his brains, going over and over what Tannor had said. Sureley there was a clue in there somewhere.

Careless Dwellers could do things which damaged a house and its Holder. If they neglected their home, the Holder suffered and in time would become unable to look after his Dwellers.

But Tannor seemed to think his Dwellers had deliberately set out to hurt him. What had he said? 'Every time they came or went': that was it! What was it Dwellers did every time they arrived or left? Was it something they wore? Something they knocked against? Mossy tried to conjure up memories of past Dwellers. They came in, they went out. They hung up hats, they knocked on knockers, they scraped boots clean. Could that be it? Could Tannor's Starting Stone be something to do with scraping boots clean? All that muck dumped on them all the time would have been pretty unpleasant.

Mossy shook his head. Tannor had said he'd suffered, he wanted to pay back the pain. Having muck dumped on you wasn't much fun, but it didn't hurt. No, it had to be something else.

Once again he went back to the idea of the doorstep. Tannor had laughed when he'd suggested it, but maybe he'd been covering up. Again Mossy shook his head. He'd seen the broken threshold stone after the children had left. And anyway, if it had been broken, then Tannor would have disappeared. No Holder could survive a broken Starting Stone.

And Tannor had seemed to imply that one of the boys had moved it. At least that would be an explanation. It must have been either Rollo or JJ, not Tannor.

He pulled a face, and then grasped an idea slipping by. The gargoyle. Could that be it? JJ had persuaded Jack to prop it beside the front door. He frowned. Strange sort of Starting Stone. Gargoyles were usually added later. Still worth investigating, and the sooner the better.

Mossy lowered himself over the lip of the roof and then

climbed nimbly down the drainpipe. At the front door two mice scurried across the lawn towards him.

'I've got to check the gargoyle,' he told them. They skipped over the doorstep and jumped onto the lip of the hideous face. One climbed onto its ear and sat washing her paws.

'It's all very well for you,' he said. 'You won't get the shock from it that I will if I'm right. But that's the only way I can be sure.' Mossy looked at the face. It grimaced back at him, tongue stuck out, lips stretched wide, eyes bulging.

'It would be hard to feel good about myself if that was my Starting Stone,' he admitted. 'But would it be enough to drive me to the sort of things that Tannor's doing?' A rabbit loped by, paused and rubbed its nose.

'You're right,' he sighed. 'I'll only find out by doing it.' He took a deep breath. Every muscle in his body was tense. If he was right, this was going to hurt; more than hurt. He hoped it wouldn't damage his house. He stretched out a finger, then paused. Everything around him seemed to hold its breath. The mice jumped down to the ground. They looked up at him. Mossy leaned forward. His finger touched the stone.

His breath burst out in a rush of disappointment. This was no Starting Stone. The face still grimaced, but nothing moved, no light flashed. Mossy sank to the ground, propping himself against the elbow of the gargoyle, relieved and frustrated in equal measure.

In his mind he saw again the remaining stones of Tannery Cottage. There was the paved floor, the threshold stone and the tanning pits. Rollo had dug about in one of them. Had he picked something up? Again he shook his head. Starting Stones were always part of the main Dwelling, and those pits would have been dug later. Or were they? Which came first, the house or the tanning? If it were the pits, then maybe one of them had contained Tannor's Starting Stone. That might account for it, the stinking smell – the burning acid of the tanning process that made the leather so soft. He had seen the damage it could do to the skin of a Dweller, so what might that do to a Holder who started there? If that were the case, he felt sorry for poor Tannor.

Or was it one of those paving stones on the floor? Mossy slapped his hand against his head. Oh come on, think, he berated himself. No one starts a building with the floor.

The stars were beginning to fade. Mossy got to his feet, stretched his arms wide to embrace the last remaining starlight and took a few paces down the path. He turned to look back at his beloved Annanbourne. The moon emerged from behind a cloud, shooting out a shaft of light that glinted off the smooth stone by the front door.

Not that, he thought. No. He stopped, closed his eyes, remembering the entrance stone he had seen in the wood. It was cracked, shattered and beside it…

All of a sudden Mossy's eyes sprang open. He'd seen it. He'd seen the hole. The place where something was missing. Suddenly he understood! Beside the threshold stone something had been moved. That was what he had to find. The stone which had held the door post. That must have been Tannor's Starting Stone! Now at last he knew what he was looking for. He looked back at his own door. There, at the base of his doorpost, was a block of stone on which it rested, holding the wood free of the ground, keeping it safe from the wet.

What was it that Tannor's Dwellers had done to make it hurt so much? Had they kicked the doorpost stone? Scraped their feet against it as they came in and out? It was hefty though. He cast his mind back. He couldn't remember either of the boys carrying something that big. But then he hadn't been looking for it at the time.

The early sun was still trapped in the bare branches of the wood behind the house, but Mossy's spirit shone brightly. A stone as big as that should be easy to find. Tannor had said that he'd never find it, but that was because he'd been looking in the house. If it were that big, it would have been left outside.

He searched through the barn, examining stacks of roof tiles leaning against a tower of breeze block, beside which a heap of broken stones tumbled across the floor. Mossy checked them carefully. All were chipped or damaged in some way, none was big enough to be a post stone and from the way the dust and dirt had settled on them they had all been there for far too long. A beetle ambled out of a pile of flints.

'Seen any new stone arrive recently?' asked Mossy. The beetle waved his antennae and marched on by. Undaunted, Mossy inspected a couple of slabs by the entrance. Could one of those…? No, he remembered Jack using them to prop the door open when he was getting the mowing machine out.

By the entrance to Annie's studio he found the smooth round rock that Cissy had hauled back from the beach during the summer. The stone he was looking for would be square, wouldn't it? Carved? He paused in his search. Were they all the same shape as his? He went back and started again. Any stone, he told himself, any unfamiliar stone.

By the time Rollo returned from his paper round Mossy had to admit he had found nothing usual in the yard or in any of the outbuildings.

'Surely it's still too bad for me to go to school?' insisted JJ, waving his bandaged hand at his mother over breakfast.

'I didn't notice it holding you back from eating your food,' laughed Annie.

'And fortunately you use the other hand for writing,' smiled Jack. 'What a lucky lad you are!'

'Remember I've got After-School Club today,' JJ called out to Jack as they headed towards the car. Cissy chased after him.

'You forgot your lunchbox,' she called, waving it at him.

Carefully Mossy trawled through every room of the house after they had left. The children dumped stuff in the washing room when they came home, but he only found some bits of wood, JJ's sports kit and a bag of conkers beside the muddy boots on the floor. Cissy's school bag was slung across a pile of damp towels on top of the washing machine. It looked like JJ wasn't the only one leaving things behind that day.

In the sitting room he found one of JJ's shoes under the sofa. Several coins, three paper clips, a rather hairy sweet and the pen that Rollo had been hunting for the previous night emerged from under its cushions.

Most of JJ's possessions lay scattered across the floor of his room. Mossy worked his way through the piles of treasure: shells, dried leaves, drawings, pebbles, twisted bits of metal and strangely shaped twigs competed with t-shirts, socks and jeans for space on the floor. There were no stones of any size to be seen anywhere. The chest of drawers was nearly empty, bar a few old outgrown clothes that had yet to find a new home. Tucked away at the back of the bottom drawer was a shallow cardboard box labelled DO NOT TOUCH THIS, SPECIALLY NOT YOU DAD.

Mossy smiled. He knew what it held – JJ's collection of paintings, including the one he was keeping for his Dad's Christmas present. He had come into the room a few nights before, just as the little boy was tucking the box away, flinging a pair of old trousers on top of it. No need to check that, and anyway it wasn't big enough to hold a post stone.

In Cissy's room he found the bits and pieces that he had last seen in JJ's room, the window latch, several pieces of wood, broken shards of pottery and a couple of slates. A pot she had made at school the previous term contained a bunch of dried leaves and some paper sunflowers she and Annie had made. Holding his breath he carefully he ran his hands over everything, but not a single spark could he raise.

Cissy's clothes lay in a heap on her chair, but there was nothing hard hidden amongst them, and her bed was made, so anything big and blocky would have shown up instantly.

Books were stacked in towers beside the bookshelf in Rollo's room, another pile leaning against the leg of the desk where he sat to do homework. Positive that this was where he would finally find something, Mossy went over the whole place. The dust under the bed tickled his nose, and he sneezed loudly as he emerged dragging yet another book.

Rollo's clothes were all in the chest of drawers, but it did look as if someone had exploded a bomb in there with them. Would Rollo hide a stone in there? wondered Mossy, lightly patting the surface. His hand jagged against something hard. Cautiously he lifted the hem of a t-shirt and then let his breath out again as he spotted yet another book tumbled in amongst the socks and jumpers.

Forlornly Mossy climbed onto Rollo's desk. A scrap of crumpled paper lay on the workpad. Idly he ran his eyes over it. All sorts of people had written messages.

You would!!!!

A drawing of a pig running.

Have you done the French homework?

Did you see Matty's?

Ha Ha Ha!

A pencil lay, as if underlining a final couple of comments which were in Rollo's handwriting.

M – Are you OK? Let me know if I can help.

He smiled. Rollo had found a way to leave him a message that no one but he would recognise.

But could Rollo help? Mossy glanced out of the window and saw Annie coming over from her studio. His searches had taken him all morning and still he hadn't found anything. He felt despondent and scratched his head, racking his brains. He had said only to write in an emergency, but just maybe Rollo could help, and this way Tannor wouldn't know.

Carefully he picked up a pencil. Learning to read had been fun, but writing was another matter altogether. He very seldom did it and was out of practice. Pencils were such long, awkward things, and he had very little need to write. After all who was going to read it?

He wrapped himself around the great shaft and knelt down on the paper to hold it in place, his knees as wide as possible to give him space to make the letters. After a few test squiggles to check that he could still manage at all, he drew a slightly wonky bee. Shifting his position and frowning slightly he adjusted his grip and set to work. Finally he managed it.

Anything stone from woods?

Hearing footsteps approaching up the stairs, he dropped the pencil and slipped behind the curtain just in time, as Annie came into the room with a pile of folded clothes which she dumped on the bed.

Waiting until she was heading back downstairs, Mossy slowly dared to emerge from his hiding place. Tannor was standing in the middle of the room.

'What're you up to?' he hissed. Mossy shook his head.

'What could I be up to?' he asked in return.

'You were doing something up there with that pencil and paper. What were you doing?' Mossy's heart sank. He had been so engrossed in his search for the stone that he hadn't felt Tannor hidden in the room.

How much had he seen? Desperately he hoped Tannor hadn't been there all the time. Could he get away with this? He took a big breath.

'I wanted to have a go,' he said.

'You can write?' asked Tannor, climbing towards him.

'Why would any Holder need to write?' asked Mossy. 'I drew a bee,' he finished lamely, as Tannor arrived beside him and stared down at the paper.

'That's supposed to be a bee? It's got no sting,' he sneered. 'And what are all those worms? What's that all about?' Tannor's smouldering eyes burned into Mossy, who shut his mind tightly.

'You tell me,' Mossy replied, shrugging his shoulders. Tannor glared at the writing, then back at him. Suddenly his fist flashed out, landing a hefty punch on Mossy's shoulder, spinning him off balance, his arms windmilling wildly as he tipped further and further backwards. As he fell towards the ground his leg caught against the unevenly stacked books, knocking them to scatter noisily across the floor around him.

Annie was back in a flash.

'Oh Rollo,' she sighed. 'How many times have I told you?' As soon as Annie picked the book off his finger, Mossy rolled silently under the bed. The last thing he needed was to be trodden on.

Only once she had disappeared again, leaving the books heaped on Rollo's bed, did Mossy dare to emerge. Tannor was nowhere to be seen, but Mossy could still see the crumpled curl of the paper on the desk. Reluctant to check further in case Tannor was still spying on him, he quickly drew himself straight and set off to continue his abandoned hunt.

CHAPTER 19

Blockage

'It's so unfair!' Cissy kicked her shoes across the washing room floor. 'It's not as if I'd left it behind on purpose, and she made me do it all over again in lunch.'

'It can't have taken long. I saw you out with your friends before lunch break was over.' Rollo dropped his school bag on the kitchen table and fished out a book.

'You've got some sorting out to do in your rooms,' Annie told them. 'Clean clothes, and Rollo, will you please organise those books properly? A whole stack fell all over the floor giving me the fright of my life. I thought a fight had broken out.' Mossy raised an eyebrow. It had certainly felt like a fight as far as he was concerned.

'There's always someone on my case,' complained Cissy as she stomped up the stairs.

Mossy decided to leave them to their own devices. He sat on the hearth and flicked his toes in the ash bed. He couldn't think of anywhere else to look. How on earth he was going to get rid of Tannor if he couldn't find his stone? He'd been counting on Rollo disposing of it and bringing their troubles to an end. He gave a big sigh, hands hanging limply between his knees.

Above him there was a bellow of rage from Cissy's room. Mossy ran to the stairs, flattening himself against the wall as Annie hurried past him.

'I really will kill him this time! Why does JJ keep picking on me?' Cissy's voice was at least as upset as it was angry. 'I didn't leave my slipper out on the landing on purpose, and he knows it.'

By the time Mossy peered round the door into her room, Annie had her arm round her daughter.

'...couldn't be him, now could it?' she was saying.

'Frogs don't get into beds by themselves,' wailed Cissy. 'It must've been him.'

'Cissy, think about it sensibly.' Annie brushed the hair from Cissy's damp face.

'No one else would put **that** in my bed, though,' she sobbed, pointing at a frog who rolled yellow eyes at Mossy and croaked.

'*Don't worry, we'll find you a nice muddy patch for you to get back to sleep soon,*' he projected.

'I hate him,' Cissy ranted on. 'Not the frog: JJ. I almost wish I had done it on purpose. Made him hurt his hand. He deserves it.'

'Cissy, he's had no chance,' Rollo reminded her, leaning against the door. 'He left for school before us this morning and he isn't back yet.'

'Then he must have done it before he went.' Cissy blew her nose loudly and wiped her eyes with the back of her sleeve. 'And I gave him his lunch. That's why I forgot my homework. Next time he can starve. It's all his fault I got into such trouble, and Mrs Farthing says if I miss another homework I'll get extra work at school and she'll have to call you in too.' Mossy looked around the room. Tannor has to be here somewhere, he thought.

He found him crouched in the shadows by the foot of her bed, dark eyes fixed on Cissy, oblivious to anyone else, his hands reaching out towards her. Mossy strode over, grabbed his ears and pulled him backwards. There was no way Tannor would dare to make any serious protest for fear of being discovered by Dwellers.

'Ooh,' sighed Cissy, as soon as Tannor's attention was pulled away from her. She sunk into her mother's arms as Mossy dragged him out of the room. 'I'm so tired.'

Mossy didn't care that Tannor bumped down the stairs. The troublesome Holder wriggled and struggled, trying to get to his feet, but Mossy hauled him through the sitting room, determined to put him out of the house.

'Attacking Cissy isn't fair,' he said. 'She never did anything to hurt you. Nothing!' He pointed a long finger at his own chest. 'If you want to pick a fight, pick it with me, not them.'

'Who cares about fair?' sneered Tannor, baring his teeth in a fake smile that made Mossy's stomach clench uncomfortably. 'She laughs, she's happy. I told you, you shouldn't have brought them. If you care about them as much as you say, why don't protect them the way I suggest? Leave. Leave, and let me do the looking after.' He pointed at his chest with a gnarled hand.

'But why do you keep picking on her?' insisted Mossy. He

had to understand.

'She has imagination, she's easy to work on. She sees the pictures I plant. But don't worry, I'm about to start on the others.'

He looked sideways at Mossy, his nose twitching. 'That Rollo,' his eyes narrowed as if a thought had just occurred to him. 'I've a feeling I could work with him too. That should be interesting. Go on; do me a favour and get lost.'

'Never!' Mossy exclaimed. 'You don't know how to look after Dwellers properly any longer.' With an extra twist Tannor broke free of his grip.

'Then remember that what happens next is **your** doing,' he chortled as he turned his back. 'I gave you the opportunity to stop it.' He twirled the three remaining fingers of his injured hand as he left the room.

Mossy stared after him. Why could he not stop him? The Barn Owl had said he just had to be strong, stay out of Tannor's games, keep calm. He let out a heavy sigh and decided the best way to keep calm was to take himself down to the pond and check out a hibernation spot for the frog when she was finally released.

Whatever it was that Annie and Rollo discussed with her, by the time JJ returned home, Cissy had decided to refrain from killing him. She thumped the cutlery down on the table as they prepared for supper and then sat, frowning and grim-faced, between Rollo and Jack.

'Guess what I found in my bed,' she said finally, glowering across the table at JJ, whose face lit up in delight.

'My shoe?' he suggested. 'The one I lost?'

'A frog,' Cissy declared, folding her arms across her chest.

'A frog! In your bed? How did it get there? You didn't try kissing it, I hope.' He grinned at her, so clearly surprised that no one could doubt this was the first he had heard of it. 'Only princesses can turn frogs into princes. Mum?' he turned to Annie. 'Did you ever wonder if Dad was a frog?' Cissy's face began to melt. 'I've seen you kissing him, but, you know, he's never going to turn into a prince.'

'I wouldn't want Dad to turn into a prince,' laughed Annie. 'I'd be no good at being polite to all the dull people princesses have to pretend to find interesting.'

'Yes, but then we could live in a palace,' Cissy pointed out.

'And what if it was a girl frog?' Rollo butted in, passing Cissy the bowl of mashed potato.

'No way do princesses ever get turned into frogs. That's for princes.' There was a sparkle in Cissy's eyes now. 'Princesses get turned into swans and plants, things like that.' She squeezed a dollop of tomato ketchup onto her peas.

'So if you're getting turned into something by the wicked magician, what d'you think you'd like to be?' asked JJ. 'I'd be a boa constrictor so I could wrap up the magician and squeeze him until he turned me back into a JJ.'

'I'd be a Siberian Tiger,' decided Cissy. 'Very rare and highly sought after. And very beautiful.' She smiled. 'Oh, by the way, I saw your shoe by the sofa.'

Mossy sat back on his dresser shelf and swung his legs gently. Cissy, helped by her brothers' cheerful chatter, was recovering from Tannor's ministrations more quickly than the previous time. Maybe his Dwellers could fight back on their own.

It wasn't until Mossy had done a second Nightwatch,

patrolled the garden and been reassured by the mice in Annie's studio that all was well, that he decided he could finally allow himself a rest.

'Maybe he just said he'd got something up his sleeve to give me a sleepless night,' he told one of the spider's cousins who had come to report on the state of the webs in the chimney. He yawned, stretching his arms before holding his hands out to the last glowing embers of the fire. He rubbed his tummy. It felt slightly odd, as if he'd pulled a muscle. Maybe he'd twisted something in all that hunting about, he decided, as he curled up beside the chestnut roasting pan.

Mossy was woken by a sharp stab of pain as Rollo hurried past on the way to collect his bike. He clutched his stomach, drawing his knees in tight. He cast a quick glance upwards. Was this it? Was this Tannor finally attacking the chimney stonework so a section would drop down and kill him? He pushed himself into a sitting position.

Two spiders swung down on silken threads.

'Is he there?' Mossy whispered, pointing into the darkness. One scrambled back up his thread. The other swung gently on a current of air, reaching out for the fireback. 'Thanks,' said Mossy, rocking himself slowly.

Somewhere in Annanbourne there was trouble brewing. He sat still, racking his brains. Had he missed something in his checks last night? Tannor had mentioned trying to get at Rollo. What if he had tampered with his bike?

He should never have gone to sleep.

A terrible ache welled up in Mossy's throat. This didn't

feel like the chimney under attack. He clapped a hand over his mouth and staggered from the room. A cold sweat broke over him. He leaned against the garden door and hoped he wasn't going to be sick. There was no cat or dog to blame it on, and he hadn't the strength to climb out of the house.

Upstairs he heard the rest of the family preparing to start the day. Jack filled the kettle in the kitchen. The clatter of cutlery was followed by the chink of breakfast plates and bowls before Jack disappeared towards his study.

'Where'd she say the other one was?' muttered JJ as he hopped across the kitchen in one shoe. Noisy feet thundered down the stairs and Cissy burst into the kitchen, grabbed JJ by the back of his jumper and spun him round to face her.

'And last night I let you con me into thinking you had nothing to do with that frog. But this is the proof!' She thrust a stiff sprig of holly in JJ's face. He backed against the dresser. I ought to be doing something to help, thought Mossy, shuffling slowly towards the door. Another wave of nausea leapt up his throat, stopping him in his tracks.

'What are you on about?' JJ asked, putting both hands on her chest and pushing back. 'Get off me.'

'Holly in my socks now. Just grow up, can't you?' Cissy was a tower of fury.

'I didn't,' protested JJ, pushing at her again.

'Well you can have it back yourself,' growled Cissy, shoving the holly down his shirt.

'That hurts,' protested JJ.

'First the mud in my wellies, then that stupid frog in my bed, and now this!' Cissy's voice ricocheted round the kitchen. 'Everyone keeps saying 'Oh, JJ wouldn't do that'.

Well, it can't have been anyone else. I'm sick of you. I think your pathetic little tricks are just that; pathetic. It's time you had a taste of your own medicine!' She pulled her hand back, opening her palm, her fingers stiff with anger and then hit him hard with the flat of her hand across his face.

For one brief second JJ stood still, and then he bunched his fists and launched himself at her.

'I never did it, whatever you say,' he shouted, hitting her shoulder. 'I didn't do the mud thing.' He hit her chest. Cissy grabbed his shoulder.

'You liar!' she bellowed, shaking him. 'Liar!' A plate was jolted from the dresser, shattering on the floor. Mossy ducked to avoid a sharp splinter that shot in his direction.

'And I don't know what you're on about, with frogs and holly.' Now JJ was crying. 'Cissy stop it!' Cissy landed a clenched fist of her own on JJ's cheek, smearing it with blood. Two more plates crashed onto the floor.

And then Annie and Jack came racing through from the sitting room.

'Cissy!' Jack put his arms round her, pulling her away from her brother.

'JJ! What on earth is going on here?'

'She stuffed holly down my shirt!' JJ wailed, one hand searching for it. 'I'm all scratched.'

'Only because he put it in my socks.' Cissy wriggled free of Jack.

Mossy slipped to the side of the washing machine as Rollo came in through the door. A smell of sewage wafted in with him. Mossy turned a pale shade of green.

'It stinks out there,' Rollo told them. 'And there's sludgy

stuff all over the lawn, by the path.' Mossy made the most of the open door to step outside.

'Have you touched any of Cissy's things?' Jack turned to JJ.

'I never,' JJ insisted.

'He's lying.' Cissy was equally determined. 'And those other times.'

'I'm not lying.' JJ launched himself at her again, but she ducked out of the way.

'See? He's just horrid.'

'It's as if someone's dumped a load of mud and muck on the lawn,' Annie remarked from the window.

'You don't care,' thundered Cissy. 'None of you care.' She stormed towards the sitting room.

Mossy skirted around the edge of the mess outside. Now he understood why he felt so sick. Foul water, bits of used loo paper, revolting stuff that he didn't want to look at too closely, had erupted around the edges of a manhole cover and were slithering across the front garden. No wonder his tummy felt so strange. There must be a major blockage in the drain. So this was what Tannor had been meaning. He was hoping to spread every kind of infection and disease.

'See, Mum,' Rollo was pointing at the manhole. 'I think it's coming from there.' Jack and JJ arrived, JJ still defending his honour.

'Oh, yuk.'

'What's happening to us?' Annie turned to Jack. 'Everything's going wrong. First the water pipe, then the electricity cable, fighting children and now this. We can't afford to get a new carpet for the stairs and landing as it is.

How can we possibly afford to sort this out?' Jack slipped an arm round her shoulders.

'It's a good thing it's term time. We can let the warring factions calm down in school, and I'll ask some of the others at work for suggestions.'

Tannor didn't wait for Mossy to find him this time.

'Got you now, haven't I?!' he chortled, coming up behind Mossy as he examined the sludge. He rubbed his hands together. 'It won't be long before the first of your precious Dwellers sickens.'

'Don't count on it,' Mossy reminded him. 'Just as they're making JJ's hand better, so they'll tackle this. Cholera's not the killer it used to be.'

Annie covered herself in rubber gloves and overalls.

'Hmm,' grunted Tannor. 'I hadn't planned on them protecting themselves like that.'

She levered up the manhole covers and peered into the drains.

'Ha!' grinned Tannor. 'I made sure it was well beyond arm's length.'

Mid-morning, Jack came home briefly.

'I can't stay,' he said, 'but the caretaker has lent us some rods for clearing the drains. I'll have a go when I get home.'

'I'll have a go right now,' said Annie. Tannor frowned.

He frowned even more when she thrust the first of the rods into the drain and attached another to the end that still stuck out.

'That's cheating,' he muttered darkly. Mossy sat quietly to

one side. Annie added another length to the growing rod, and it was his turn to smile. 'Women aren't supposed to do this sort of thing,' grumbled Tannor as Annie got to grips with the drain.

By the time Rollo and Cissy arrived home, everything was working properly again. The pain in Mossy's tummy had gone, though he still felt a little queasy. Tannor had departed in a fit of temper.

'There was a great wodge of paper, and other stuff. Newspaper?' she told them. Do either of you know anything about newspaper getting into the drains?'

'Ask JJ, I expect it was another of his cunning plans,' Cissy suggested. 'Filling things with stuff that shouldn't be there seems to be his idea of fun these days.'

'I thought you agreed to give him a break,' Rollo reminded her.

'I know, it just makes me cross that you all take his side. I don't mean to be harsh, Mum, but it's still pretty stinky.'

'Dad's bringing home a pressure hose,' Annie told her.

'Can we all have a go?' asked Cissy, brightening.

'All help welcome,' her mother smiled.

Sludge was briskly hosed back into the drain when Jack returned. Mossy felt much better. The children slopped about the sodden garden pointing out bits that had been missed.

'It was almost as if someone had blocked the drain on purpose,' Annie told Jack. 'Stuffed with shredded newspaper, dead leaves and things. It was real effort to free it, but once that first bit was cleared it all went easily. There was no sign of roots or anything like that. Cissy seems to think that JJ might have done it.'

Jack shook his head.

'Cissy keeps blaming others for things, telling tales on them. It's not like her at all. And JJ swears blind that he's done nothing. You know, these are just not the sort of things he does. He falls over, he crashes into stuff. He hurts himself. Can you think of any time when he's ever set out to hurt someone else?'

'That's why I was so surprised to see him hitting Cissy this morning. She's not the only one who's behaving oddly,' Annie reminded him. Mossy nodded his head. That was a sign of how far Tannor was changing things in Annanbourne.

'Your turn, Cissy!' called JJ, passing the spray to his sister. 'There's just that last bit to do.'

Cissy fired the jet of water at the path, drumming the last debris of the overflowing sewage back into the drain. The path gleamed wetly in the light of the setting sun that was already painting the sky crimson.

'Well done, troops,' smiled Jack. 'That was quicker than I thought it would be. Thank goodness for friends who can lend us the stuff we need to clear up. I thought it would take us weeks.' That's what Tannor was hoping, grinned Mossy, lifting his face to let a light shower of refreshing droplets wash over it. Time was when something like this would have brought deadly disease in its wake.

Cissy glanced over her shoulder. Jack and Annie were heading into the house. She turned towards her brothers.

'Watch out, Rollo,' JJ warned. 'She's all over the place with th…'

'I know just what I'm doing.' Cissy was grim faced. Mossy didn't like the glint in her eyes.

JJ caught the blast of water directly on his chest. His arms flailed as he tried to get his balance, but Cissy wasn't letting up. She moved the jet of water upwards. JJ tried to cover his face, but water spurted in all directions. Rollo dived round to the back of her, grabbing her arms and bringing them down to her sides, taking the nozzle, but not before JJ landed in a heap on the muddy grass.

'That's horrid,' Rollo told her. 'He hasn't done anything to you.'

'Maybe at least it'll make him think twice, before he tries to do anything else.' Cissy flung the jet wash on the ground, where it writhed like a furious snake as she ran laughing indoors.

Annie stuck her head out of the kitchen door.

'What on earth are you boys doing?! Get yourselves in here right now, and I've a good mind to make you wash your own clothes by hand to get that mud out.'

JJ opened his mouth, shut it again and struggled to his feet in silence. That's right, agreed Mossy. No telling tales. Maybe that will help Cissy to see things more clearly.

CHAPTER 20

Time To Give In?

As soon as Rollo left on his paper round, Mossy slipped into his bedroom. Climbing onto the desk, he soon found the paper on which he had written before. There was another message under the one he had left.

Cissy – stones from beach

JJ – candlestick

Me – nothing

'You're at it again,' Tannor's voice grated by Mossy's shoulder, making him jump. How come he could never tell when Tannor was sneaking up? He looked at him and once again, despite all the damage that Tannor was trying to do to him and his Dwellers, he felt sorry for the other Holder. He looked at the broken leg that could never mend, the fragile body covered in sores and bruises, the damaged hands with missing fingers, the charred skin, the shadowed eyes, and his heart felt Tannor's hurt.

'Don't you dare,' Tannor snarled, distracted from quizzing Mossy's reading by the sympathy.

Seeing him prepare to attack, his fingers bunched together, Mossy stepped backwards. His heel slipped over the edge of the desk, and he looked down at the floor below. Not again, he sighed, sympathy evaporating as he teetered briefly on the edge of the desk, reaching his hands towards Tannor, asking for help.

He landed with a crunch in the wastepaper basket and was glad that Rollo hadn't emptied it for a while. Above him Tannor peered over the edge of the desk, his teeth showing in a lopsided smile of delight. Mossy shifted an old apple core that was tickling his ear and had swung a leg over the side when Cissy came into the room. Both Holders froze.

'Rollo?' She glanced about the room, a puzzled expression settling on her face. 'JJ?' she called out. 'D'you know where Rollo is? I thought I heard him, but he's not here.

'What d'you want him for?' asked JJ, ambling in in pyjamas.

'Mum's birthday, remember? Tomorrow?' whispered Cissy, her voice dropping low. 'I need some last stuff for making her present, and Rollo said he wanted to get something too.'

'I've got mine all sorted,' grinned JJ, jerking a thumb over his shoulder. 'It's hidden in my bedroom.'

'Aren't you just Mr Goody Two Shoes?' Mossy looked sharply up at Tannor, who had twisted round and was staring fixedly over his shoulder at Cissy, one finger pointing stiffly in her direction. Regardless of what might happen, Mossy started to climb the desk, determined to break

Tannor's grip on her.

'What's with you Cissy?' JJ was standing up for himself. Mossy stopped in his tracks. 'What's got into you? It's like someone else speaking, not you, not my proper sister, who makes me laugh and tells me funny stories and knows I don't do horrid things to her.'

'Who cares about 'making you laugh'?' Cissy imitated him.

'You do. Well, you did,' JJ reminded her.

'Not anymore; not since you became such a pain with all your stupid little tricks.' Cissy flounced past him, buffeting him with her elbow. JJ watched her go to the top of the stairs, his head on one side as he rubbed his arm where she had jolted him.

'But I never did those things,' he murmured, more to himself than her. Mossy felt his ache, and his shoulder ached with him.

By the time Mossy looked back to where Tannor had been standing, the other Holder had gone.

'Huh,' he sighed. Gone to make more trouble. He sat down on the bed. Had Rollo really understood what he'd asked? This was always the problem when you couldn't speak clearly to someone. He'd seen his Dwellers have just this sort of muddle before. Misunderstandings could lead to all sorts of disasters.

The message seemed to imply that the only stones Cissy had brought home were the big ones from the beach during the summer. They were nothing to worry about. Mossy had enjoyed their smooth surface, feeling the tumbling of the oceans, the strength of ages past.

JJ had clearly got the wrong end of the stick. Mossy laughed quietly to himself. Candlesticks weren't made of stone! Not that he'd seen any candlesticks in his hunt through JJ's room, neither metal, wood nor pottery, which was what they were usually made of.

And Rollo had brought nothing. That he could understand. His hands had been full of his friend, making sure he got home safely. He heaved another sigh, one that carried all his frustration and feeling of looming disaster.

What could he do? Might he even be driven to taking up Tannor's suggestion? Abandon his Holding in the hope that Tannor might somehow learn to care for his Dwellers? And what would happen to him if he did? Would he become a wandering Holder, homeless and lost? The words he had caught in the night – no home – came back to him. What would he be with no home? How did anyone cope with that?

He thought then of his friend, the Travelling Holder. **He** didn't seem to be fixed to any proper Holding. Appearing out of the blue with no warning, but so often just as he was needed. Mind you, he smiled ruefully, rubbing the tip of his nose, I could do with you right now. Where are you? he wondered. And who are you, exactly? He rubbed his hand the full length of his nose. Or should I know the answer to that?

'If you want a hand, just give me a shout,' called Rollo's voice from outside. Mossy clambered onto the windowsill and looked down into the yard. Cissy emerged from the barn, pushing her bike and waving a pump.

'I think I've got a bit of a flat tyre,' she told him. Rollo propped his bicycle against the barn wall and squatted down by her back wheel. There was no sign of JJ.

A flicker by the door caught his attention. A large black spider was hurrying across the room, waving two front legs at him.

'Coming,' replied Mossy, jumping lightly to the floor and racing for the sitting room.

He saw the crumble of mortar on the hearth as soon as he entered. Two more spiders were hanging off the top of the fireback. One pointed a back leg up the chimney.

'You actually saw him?' asked Mossy as he leapt from the firedogs onto the soot-coated fireback. He peered upwards at the spiders, who swung down towards him, their eyes glinting in the shadows.

'How many?' asked Mossy, hardly believing his ears. He laughed. He didn't envy Tannor. These spiders were friends of his, but even he'd have felt daunted at the sight of an army of them, arriving, wave after wave, all throwing out their webs to ensnare him.

Just under the chimney pot he saw the place where Tannor had started to chip away at the mortar. He had chosen his spot carefully, right at the highest point where a falling brick would gather plenty of speed. It would have made quite a crack on the hearthstone from that height. He shuddered. Had it not been for his friends...

'Thank you,' said Mossy. 'I wish there was a way that I could tell you how much I mean that. Catching him at it so quickly has stopped him doing more than the slightest damage. This won't even let water in. And I wouldn't be surprised if you've put him off now. You didn't happen to see what direction he headed in afterwards?'

Half a dozen spiders spilled over the top of the chimney, waving their legs in all directions at once. Others were already busy respinning their webs, knitting strands across the spaces to make sure they would be alerted of any further incursions.

Mossy followed them out onto the top of the chimney stack. He dusted soot off himself as he looked about him. The spiders seemed to have as many opinions about Tannor's whereabouts as they had legs. He examined the garden. Where might Tannor have taken himself off to, and what kind of trouble would he be thinking up next?

He saw Jack and Annie buried in conversation, heading into her studio. He had heard Annie asking Jack to look at her latest painting. They would be busy there for a while.

He followed the curved line of the stream as it flowed along the edge of the garden, dividing it from the farmer's fields beyond. A silver flash sparkled up at him as a trout swam upstream. A blackbird flew across the sky, battling the wind. He wasn't the only one who sometimes had to work to get where he wanted.

'You're right,' he told the spiders. 'I mustn't give up. There has to be a way through. After all, I've survived worse than this in the past.' Suddenly his eye was caught by a distant movement. He leaned forward, squinting to get a clearer view. Beyond the meadow, where the path crossed the next field as it headed towards Widow Knight's Wood… Was that a person he had spotted? Was it someone coming towards them or…? His heart clenched and a shiver ran through him. Rollo and Cissy had gone to town on their bikes. Annie and Jack were busy in the studio. JJ...?

High above him he heard the falling cry of a buzzard spiralling upwards on a thermal. He waved his hands frantically to catch the attention of her needle-sharp eyes, then dropped lightly from the chimney stack onto the roof ridge. There was a sharp rush of wind as the bird plummeted towards them.

'Over there,' called Mossy, waving towards the woods. 'Can you check for me? Who's that in the field? One of my dwellers may be missing,' he called as the buzzard flicked a wing tip, curving over the meadow and sailing towards the trees.

Mossy had already scrambled down the roof and was preparing to lower himself over the guttering when she returned. He paused, hooking his toes around the drainpipe, and looked upwards. Again the falling cry rang through the crisp air. Mossy's spirits fell with it. The buzzard's sharp eyes confirmed his worst suspicion. The description was spot on.

'It must be him,' he agreed. 'And you say he's nearly at the far wood already?' The buzzard gripped the edge of the tile by Mossy's hand. She dipped her head, her dark eye shooting a fierce look at him. Mossy nearly lost his grip on the gutter.

'What?' he exclaimed. 'Are you sure?' The buzzard straightened her neck and shook her wings. 'How close behind him?' She launched herself into the air, her last call confirming his worst fears as she soared once more into the sky, swinging out over the trees of the copse and the high hills of the downs.

CHAPTER 21

Where Has He Got To?

Mossy tore across the grass, catching his toe on a loose stone and tumbling head over heels down to the rough track, where he rolled to a stop at the grass ridge on the far side. He leapt back onto his feet, turned towards the woods and set off at a run.

JJ would have already reached Widow Knight's Copse by now, he told himself, and he had a ghastly feeling that he was aiming for Tannery Cottage. Tannor had threatened dire consequences if any of the children returned, that what had happened to Jon would seem mild in comparison.

Lots of people threaten all sorts of things that they never do, Mossy reassured himself as his feet beat a tattoo along the track. On the other hand, the trouble with Tannor was that he seemed to carry out his threats, he chided himself. He ducked under a bramble that lunged from the hedge. Another loose stone jolted his heel, sending a sharp pain up his lower leg, but there was no time to worry.

He was panting heavily by the time he reached the gate

into the big field. His chest ached, but he couldn't afford to rest or draw breath. He climbed through the bars, dodging the clods of mud churned up by the cows.

Drops of water clung to the grass, bending it over, making it harder to get through. He pushed the blades apart, but they clung to his limbs, quickly soaking him so that his feet squelched at every step.

'Find his footprints,' Mossy told himself, brushing droplets off his face with the back of his sleeve. Sure enough the trail left by JJ's feet was clear, even though the grass was already springing back. It would have been easier for Tannor, tracking his prey, following just close behind.

Mossy struggled on.

'I've got to get there before it's too late,' he panted.

By the time he turned off the track in the wood Mossy thought his chest would burst. His legs were shaking, and sweat trickled down his back as he bent over to examine the ground, one hand supporting himself on the tree. He was right. There were fresh marks in the mud; two sets — JJ's, and on top of them the narrow Holder footprints.

Pushing a bramble out of the way, Mossy forced himself on towards Tannery Cottage.

'Help! Someone, please help!' JJ's voice was shaky. Mossy looked around him. The rope the children had used as a swing lay curled across the ground. Beyond it he spotted the boy. His head was propped on the lip of one of the old tanning pits, his tear-streaked face resting against the stones that Rollo had scraped clean. He was curled up, groaning.

'Please… someone help.' His voice faded at he slid into unconsciousness. Above him Mossy saw Tannor sitting on a branch, his broken leg hooked casually over his stronger one, arms folded across his chest.

'What have you done?' shouted Mossy, rushing to JJ's side. He gasped, horrified at the sight of the rusty blade that jutted from his thigh. Dark blood had soaked into his jeans, and Mossy could see streaks of it on his hands as well. What if...?

'It was a piece of cake.' Tannor swung his legs in the air. 'I told you not to let them come back here. You only have yourself to blame, you know. I used that rope you so conveniently let them bring.' His hiccup of laughter jarred in Mossy's ears. 'That'll teach you to stop them making fun and games in my Holding.'

Mossy laid a finger against JJ's wrist. There was a gentle pulse. It wasn't too late, yet. But any kind of delay and it might well be. He had to find help, but he needed to keep Tannor from doing any more damage in the meantime. There was no one to call on here. Everybody was too frightened to come into this wretched place.

Scooping up a handful of earth, he pressed it into the palm of JJ's outstretched hand, folding his fingers over to hold it in place.

'You still think the Old Things work?' jeered Tannor. 'How long will it be before I wipe that off?'

'The Old Things do more than you care to admit,' Mossy replied calmly as he rubbed a smear of blood from JJ's cheek. He turned to face Tannor. 'As far as I can tell, you have continually tried to bring harm here, but see how the trees have grown through it?' He swept a hand in a wide arc that embraced the last remnants of Tannery Cottage. 'You may have scared away the animals, but nature heals the scars that humans make. See how they have covered the acid of the pits? That was scorched earth, but now it's lush with flowering plants in spring. Even you can't stop that. The Old Things take their time, but they always get there in the end.'

'Huh!' coughed Tannor, spitting into the air. 'That boy can't wait the time you're talking about.'

'Once people didn't dare come here, for fear of the terrible feel of the place,' Mossy reminded him. He spoke gently, knowing that Tannor would find it hard to have to hear what he said. 'But my Dwellers didn't notice that. What they saw was the beauty of the trees, the light of the stream, a place to play. Your grip here is fading.'

Tannor looked over his shoulder to the bank at the back of the clearing. It was overgrown with brambles and other vegetation. Mossy wondered what he was looking at. He racked his brains. What was it that Tannor had said a few weeks back? Something about 'trapped'? He had trapped someone. Was that it? Or was it he that was trapped?

JJ groaned, eyes flickering open, then closing again. Save the boy, Mossy reminded himself. He stood up and held his arms wide to the sky.

'Help!' he called, his voice clear and strong. 'Anyone who can hear me. Help! We have a life to look after!'

'Too late,' sneered Tannor. 'He's still losing blood, your precious Dweller, and there's no one here to help you.' Far away a faint, falling cry drifted down on the breeze. Mossy looked up, his mind focused on the dark eyes, the sleek head, the soft feathers still out of sight.

'Here!' he called, looking up into the grey sky, waving a hand above his head. A speck of brown plummeted down towards them. Mossy smiled as he spread his arms wide. 'See!' he exclaimed. 'They are no longer as frightened as you wish.'

'Thank you!' he called upwards.

Tannor looked up in time to see the sharp talons spread wide before they clamped on his shoulder. He gave a howl of frustration as the buzzard's claws gripped tightly, ripping him from his perch, as she swept between the branches and then glided out over the stream and into the valley beyond, Tannor kicking uselessly at the empty air below them.

'Don't hurt him,' Mossy called after her. 'He's not edible. But I'll give you something that is.'

With Tannor safely out of the way it was time to concentrate on finding help. He turned and set off at a run, his mind focused. Now he had no doubts. He knew who he was fetching.

'Rollo,' he shouted at maximum volume, sending it as a projection too. This time he had to try to get his attention any way he could. 'Rollo, we need you. By the swing.' He ducked under the brambles, dodged the branches that stretched out towards him, slipped through the gate into the field. His heart thudded in his chest. His lungs burned. He slammed the grass out of his way.

'JJ needs you! Bring help, the best help you can find!' Never before had he wanted a Dweller to hear him so clearly.

He was three-quarters of the way across the field when he spotted Rollo climbing the stile beside the gate and running towards him. He stopped, chest heaving, legs wobbly from the exertion. His Place Reader had heard him. Thank goodness. His friend had responded.

'Rollo!' called Cissy's voice. 'Why the panic? If you run like that I can't keep up.'

Mossy grinned. He had indeed brought help. And maybe of all the people who could help, this was the one that could make an important difference, comfort JJ's spirit as well as his body.

As Rollo reached him, and with his sister blocked from view, Mossy briefly let himself be visible.

'Oh, wait, can't you?' called Cissy, as Rollo stopped abruptly.

'Catch up quickly,' he shouted back.

He sank onto one knee, fiddling with the strap of his trainer.

'What is it, Mossy?' he whispered, waving an encouraging hand at his sister. 'Something about JJ? I can't find him anywhere at home. You sounded really worried.'

'He's badly hurt and needs your help.' Mossy replied, slipping out of visibility again. He had got his message across.

'D'you want a lift?' Rollo asked, reaching out a hand into the grass. 'You could ride on my shoulder.'

Mossy's eyes widened in alarm. He'd ridden horses, dogs, carts and in cars, but never a Dweller. But with the trouble so urgent he hesitated only a moment. Oh well, in for a penny, in for a pound, he decided. After all, you've been in his pocket before now.

'OK,' he muttered, taking Rollo's hand and climbing onto his arm.

Rollo stood up swiftly, and casually dropped Mossy onto his shoulder as Cissy arrived, panting. She bent over to catch her breath, hands on her knees.

'What's spooked you?' she gasped. Mossy adjusted his position, one leg either side of Rollo's neck.

'You know we couldn't see JJ when we got back?' Rollo held himself still. 'Well, I've got this horrid feeling he's gone back to the swing we made. And somehow I just don't think it's safe. Jon got hurt, and I know you think it was all my fault, but something odd went on and I don't trust that place. You ready?' he asked.

Mossy wasn't sure who the question was directed at. He patted the top of Rollo's head.

'OK, come on then,' said Rollo, breaking into a run again. 'You've got to keep up.'

Mossy clamped his hands onto his young friend's ears and clasped his toes together under his chin. Galloping horses have nothing on this, he thought, wondering if he was going to be shaken to pieces as he desperately held his nose out of the way to avoid bashing it on Rollo's head.

'*By the further tanning pit,*' Mossy urged him, glad they were well ahead of Cissy again as they turned off the track.

'JJ!' called Rollo as he entered the clearing. Silence muffled everything.

'Over there.' Mossy pointed to where he saw the tousled top of JJ's head, forgetting entirely that Rollo couldn't see an invisible finger. It felt like the times when he had the Travelling Holder with him.

Rollo crashed to his knees by the edge of the shallow dip in the ground.

'Oh my ...! It's OK, JJ. It's going to be OK.' Mossy slipped to the ground.

'*He's passed out. He needs water,*' he added, stepping to one side as Cissy arrived, shoved aside a branch and flung herself to the ground beside them.

'Oh JJ! Rollo, what's all that mess on his leg? And what on earth's that... that thing sticking out of it?' She reached out a hand to him.

'You stay here,' Rollo told her. 'I'm getting some water.' In no time he was back with some scooped in his hands, which he splashed onto JJ's face.

'He isn't dead, is he?' Cissy looked ashen.

'Not yet,' grinned JJ, opening his eyes. 'Though I think Rollo's trying to drown me.'

Cissy laughed, pulling the sleeve of her jumper over her hand to rub the muddy water from his face.

'Don't move,' she said. 'You look ghastly. Trust you to mangle yourself, but why do it here? What happened?'

'I wanted to see if I could work out what made you so cross.' Mossy saw Cissy blush.

'It all started here,' he went on, 'when we made the swing and then when Jon got hurt, and I wondered if there was something here that I could find.' Cissy sunk her head in her hands.

'Oh JJ, I'm so sorry. I don't know what's got into me. It's like a great ball of anger fills me up sometimes, and it rumbles about in me and I say horrid things and I keep on saying them until I make everybody miserable. Including me. And then afterwards I don't understand why, not any more than you do. I was telling Rollo when we were in town

197

shopping. I was horrid to you this morning, and I don't mean it, really I don't.'

'I know…' JJ's eyelids fluttered down again and he went a shade paler. 'That's why I wanted to see if I could find something that made it bad here.' His voice faded.

'JJ?' Cissy leaned forward. 'JJ, keep looking at us. Tell us what happened.' Mossy was surprised. This was Cissy, the drama queen, calm. Rollo stood up and stripped off his jumper. He bent down by his brother's leg.

'Don't take that out,' Mossy projected. *'That's when it'll be really dangerous. You've got to get him home with that still there.'*

'I'm going to tie this round your leg above the injury,' Rollo warned JJ.

'Don't move it.' JJ winced. 'It really hurts if I move it at all.'

'It might move a bit, I'm afraid, but keep telling Cissy about what happened,' Rollo replied. He turned to his sister. 'Hold his hand now.'

Cissy did so.

'You can squeeze as hard as you like, if that helps. See if you can squash my fingers into jam.'

Mossy stepped between her and JJ, a strengthening finger placed softly on both their ankles.

'I wandered about,' JJ continued, 'but I couldn't see anything. And then I spotted something moving in the undergrowth.' He gasped sharply, his eyes closing, and gripped his sister with both hands as Rollo slid his jumper under his leg.

'Squeeze harder; I can hardly feel you,' Cissy encouraged

him. 'And then?'

'And I went to look, but I tripped on the rope. Rollo! Rollo!' JJ's voice rose higher. 'That really hurts. Ow! Ooow!' he yelped, sitting up sharply as Rollo brought the ends of the jumper together to tie them. Brighter red blood oozed around the spike.

'How come you tripped on the rope?' Cissy interrupted.

'What?' JJ stared blankly at her.

'Just look at me,' Cissy reminded him. 'Not your leg. How come you tripped?' she repeated, carefully looking away from the blood.

'Erm,' JJ frowned.

Still gripping Cissy with one hand, he wiped sweat from his forehead with the back of the other. 'It sort of looped around my leg. One minute it was lying on the ground, half buried in leaves, and the next it seemed to come alive.' Tears rose in his eyes. 'Rollo, just take that jabby thing out of my leg and stop making it hurt so much. Please.'

'I can't,' Rollo told him. Mossy nodded approval. 'I think they've got to do that in the hospital, but I want it to stop bleeding so much while we take you home. Go on telling Cissy.'

'I just want it to stop…' murmured JJ, his head slipping back as he slumped onto the ground. Cissy caught an arm round him in time to stop his head hitting the stone rim of the dip.

'Rollo, he's passed out again, and he's a horrid yellow colour,' she said, her eyes large and hollow as she looked up at her older brother intently. 'You're not to let him die, d'you understand? If you do, I'll kill you.'

'Right. Well, I'm going to have to carry him. You run ahead and get Mum and Dad.'

Mossy stepped neatly out of the way as Cissy helped Rollo cradle JJ in his arms.

'OK?' she checked.

'I'm coming as fast as I can, but I don't want to jolt him. You just go for it.'

Cissy leapt over a fallen branch and disappeared in the direction of the track. As Rollo set off in her wake, Mossy shimmered into visibility.

'He's going to be OK,' he reassured Rollo, with a confidence that came from somewhere deep inside him. 'You're doing all the right things.'

'But that's only because you called me in time,' Rollo muttered through gritted teeth. 'Gosh, I hadn't realised how heavy he is.'

'Don't worry,' said Mossy, an unnoticed finger on Rollo's ankle streaming in his supporting strength. Raising an encouraging hand towards JJ's limp form, he smiled up at his friend. 'You're doing fine.'

Mossy kept pace, pushing shut the gate that Cissy had left open for them as soon as they were through. Halfway across the field they heard the sound of a car by the far hedge. Jack leapt the stile and came running towards them, Annie on his heels.

'Cissy told us,' Jack called out. 'Thank goodness you found him. Oh, that looks horrible. Here, let me take him. That swing has been nothing but trouble.' It's not the swing, thought Mossy, wondering where the buzzard had dropped Tannor off, hoping it would be a long while before the other

Holder found his way back. We all need a break from his attentions, he admitted grimly.

'I left the engine running,' Annie told them as she stroked the damp hair from JJ's forehead. 'Come on. Let's get him sorted out.'

'You go with them,' Mossy whispered to Rollo. 'I'll look after things here.'

CHAPTER 22

Out And About

'So what on earth made you think of going to look in the woods?' Jack asked when they returned a few hours after Mossy had made his way home.

'Just a feeling I had,' Rollo shrugged.

'I was my fault,' Cissy told them both. 'I'd been really crabby with him before we went into town, and I'd made him miserable.'

'Have you sorted it out now?' asked Jack, putting food on the table.

'Sort of,' admitted Cissy. 'Though he may not realise it much.'

'He looked OK in the hospital by the time we left,' Rollo reminded her. 'And he was laughing so much at your impression of that woman in the shop this morning; even the nurse who was doing the stitches was laughing.'

'D'you ever get that, Dad?' Cissy turned to her father. 'Times when you feel so cross and mean inside yourself that you just want to hit out at everyone and everything? And then once it starts you just can't seem to stop.'

'I think we all do, Cissy. It's a matter of recognising it, and remembering to stop it taking over. Sometimes we do need to be cross to make sure bad things aren't allowed to happen, but if it's bad temper without reason, then you have to be on top of it. It's not easy, but knowing it can happen is half the battle, my love.' Jack put an arm round her and gave her a hug. 'Learning from our mistakes is how we get it right the next time.'

'He said he wanted his proper sister back,' Cissy told them. 'I do too. I don't like me like that.'

He's already found his proper sister, thought Mossy. You helped save his life today, something you'll both remember for the rest of your lives. And I'm here too. Whatever tricks Tannor may get up to, you're not on your own.

Mossy was delighted when Annie brought JJ home with her that evening.

'Just for tonight you can put your feet up on the sofa and we'll bring things to you,' she told him.

'Promise me you won't go stabbing yourself in the leg each time you want me to bring you a cup of hot chocolate,' said Cissy when she came to join him.

'Mum says I may not even get days off school. Can you believe it?' asked JJ.

'You'll have to cut your leg right off next time,' suggested Rollo.

'I wouldn't count on that making much difference with Mum,' Cissy warned them. 'She's the kind of mother who'd send us down a mine given half a chance.'

'No point in having children if you can't make them work to keep you comfortable in your middle age,' joked Annie, handing out biscuits.

'No baths either, until the stitches come out,' JJ warned them.

'Don't worry, we'll find clothes pegs for our noses if you get really stinky,' said Rollo, already holding his.

Mossy toasted his toes by the fire and lapped up the gentle teasing. This was what he remembered from before Tannor's arrival. How long ago was it? It seemed like ages, and yet it was less than a month. He heaved a big sigh. How much longer? He looked around him. There was no sign of Tannor's return, and there was no point in looking for trouble before it arrived. Maybe the buzzard had dropped him so far away that he'd never make it back, he told himself cheerfully.

He waited until the family were all tucked into their beds, before he went up. There were questions he needed to ask Rollo.

'You awake?' he asked in a low voice.

'Mossy?' Rollo sprang up in his bed, flicking on his bedside light. 'I was right, wasn't I, when I said there was something unfinished, a sadness in that place? JJ felt it too, didn't he? Isn't that why he wanted to go back there, because he could feel that it had messed Cissy up?'

Mossy crossed his ankles and leaned his back against the base of the lamp.

'You're right, there is a sadness there, and I think I'm going to need your help to sort it out, but that's not what turned Cissy's feelings upside down.'

'You mean this other Holder has been deliberately making her like that?' exclaimed Rollo when Mossy finished explaining.

'He's been damaged,' Mossy said. 'I think since way back at the beginning of his Holding. If only I could find his Starting Stone, then maybe we could put it right and keep him away from here. But that's harder than I thought.'

'Perhaps if we could put right whatever went wrong at his house, then that would make him feel differently,' suggested Rollo.

'You can't change the past,' Mossy reminded him.

'It's not the past I want to change. I just want to understand what makes it feel the way it does. It feels heavy and sad there, but I don't know why. Dad says if you understand why someone feels the way they do, then it's easier to sort out whatever has gone wrong. It guess it might be the same way with places, don't you?'

'You're the Place Reader,' Mossy reminded him. 'You tell me.'

'Cissy said she'd come with me tomorrow, and we're going to have a good look. Who knows what we might find?'

'If you go, then I'm coming too,' Mossy insisted. 'Tannor will be bound to be back soon, and he'll still be trying to hurt you.'

Determined to protect his Holding, Mossy said goodnight to Rollo and departed to make his Nightwatch.

Moonlight shone across the garden, and the first hint of

frost was crisping the tips of the grass as he returned to the house after checking the barns and studio. There was no sign of Tannor anywhere. All was calm, as if the stream had washed away all the troubles that had entangled them for the past few weeks.

By the time he returned to Rollo's room the Place Reader was fast asleep, the duvet pulled up over his shoulder and tucked under his chin. Mossy smiled. Sleep puts everything right, he thought, and tonight even I might get some.

In the corner he spotted a tangle of movement, a flash of light and a whisper of shadow. Was that a nightmare sneaking up on them? Mossy lingered by the corner of Rollo's bed, ready to jump and grab something unpleasant, but equally reluctant to stop an exciting dream.

Softly the night vision wafted towards Rollo. Was that a flicker of flame? Mossy wondered. Gently he curled his long fingers around the sleeping head as the dream slipped over his friend. He nodded. It may not be a bed of rose petals, but then that was hardly what he'd expect a teenage boy to dream about, and maybe this would be more useful.

Mossy was ready when Rollo shambled past his hearthstone on the way to collect his bike the next morning.

'Fancy some company?' he asked. Rollo stopped in his tracks and looked down at him.

'I never thought I'd hear you suggest that!' he exclaimed.

'I always like a bike ride,' laughed Mossy, 'if you don't mind the extra weight.'

Mossy hung on tightly as they bumped down the rough

track to the lane. On the smoother roads, he wound his legs round the light fixing and lifted his hands to let the wind whistle through his fingers.

'I had a weird dream last night,' Rollo told him as they set off from the village shop with the double load of papers he carried while covering Jon's job since his injury.

'Oh yes?' Mossy had wondered if he might mention it.

'About that place where we made the swing. Do you know if there was ever a fire there?' Mossy hung on tight as they swung round the corner towards Rollo's first delivery.

'The whole house was burnt down,' he replied.

'That must have been pretty scary,' muttered Rollo, as he picked out the first of the papers, folded it and pushed it through the letter box. 'What happened to the people who lived there?'

'It was only one man. He had no family, and he lived there alone. He was a strange fellow, bad-tempered and unfriendly.' Mossy remembered him well from visits his Dwellers had made to buy leather for their needs. He suspected that Tannor had helped to keep the bad temper hot, needling him and reminding him of any small difficulty. It wasn't helped by the acid tanning pits that burned the skin of the Dwellers who worked there, and by the terrible smells. It wouldn't have been easy to be kind and loving in a place like that, and Dwellers would have needed the help of a very skilled Holder to guide them through it all. Instead of which they'd had Tannor.

'In my dream there were lots of people, and shouting and flames.' Rollo folded another paper and slipped it into a box on the wall of the next house. A dog came bounding round the corner, leaping up at the gate, barking loudly. Mossy shook his head, then gave it a nod of greeting. The barking stopped, and the tail wagging increased.

'So how did the fire start?' asked Rollo when he returned.

'It was a bad business,' Mossy answered, remembering the discussions at Annanbourne at the time. 'A young lad from the town had gone missing, and rumours flew about as to what had happened. He'd been seen heading this way, but Denny, up at Prior's Farm, told me he'd seen him heading through in the direction of Winchester with some travelling players. Local people never knew that though, and there were some that decided the disappearance had something to do with Tannery Cottage.'

'Hang on, I've got to do another paper,' said Rollo, leaping off again. Mossy waved at the house's Holder, a fresh-faced young fellow who popped his head through the straggly hedge. They were in an estate of new houses that had been finished only a few years before. The grass was barely green in the gardens, and the Holder looked a bit wild and chaotic.

'Does he know you're on his bike?' The young Holder pointed in all directions, indicating Mossy, the bike and Rollo all at once.

'Long story,' Mossy told him. 'First time in nearly six hundred years. Don't try it until you're my age at least, or it'll give you no end of trouble to sort out.' He looked at the house, which already had peeling paint and a tatty garden. 'And time you did a bit more looking after yourself, if you want to get through the next hundred years or so.' On Rollo's return they cruised past the next two houses, leaving the poor young Holder staring after them wide-eyed.

'So what happened?' checked Rollo.

'It reached a stage where the only person who would come to Tannery Cottage was the man's cousin. He was young, and I think there may have been talk of him helping in the business. Anyway, the local squire had checked into all the rumours about the missing boy, and with no evidence it was decided that nothing could be done. Well, there were those for whom that wasn't good enough, and they took the law into their own hands. It happened in the night.' Rollo propped his bike by a low wall.

'Was that what my dream was about?' he asked, as he rolled a paper and two magazines into a cylinder and slid them into another box, before swinging his leg back over the saddle. 'Did they set fire to the house deliberately? Is that what I'm feeling? If they did, wouldn't that be enough to make it feel horrible there?'

'I think it may be worse than that.' Mossy wasn't sure quite what it might be, but he remembered that feeling, the chill of the grave, and the promise he had made. 'You see, Albi over at Aller Farm said he'd seen the tanner walk by in the night. He got away, never came back. But Tannor said something about someone or something being trapped. I'm not sure if he was talking about himself, or maybe someone else.'

Mossy remembered the images that had flashed through his mind when that strange cold mist had wafted through Rollo's room. Fire, a falling tree, and sudden darkness. No home, and a home that was needed. Something lost that needed to be found.

'Maybe there was something else that went missing that

night. Something connected to the fire. And somehow that has kept Tannor there, waiting all these years.'

Suddenly Rollo slammed on the brakes so hard that Mossy was catapulted over the handlebars to land, facing backwards, astride the mudguard over the front wheel.

'Oh, sorry!' Rollo bent over to look at Mossy struggling to sort himself out. 'You OK? It's just I was so caught up in listening to you, and I missed that house. You mean someone got caught in the cottage? While it was burning? Hang on there, back in a tick.'

Rollo grabbed a couple of papers and ran back to the house they had just passed, while Mossy rearranged himself. A cat examined him disdainfully from the top of a wall, pausing from washing the back of a back leg to purr softly.

'Not exactly,' Mossy admitted. 'I'm not quite the acrobat you cats are.'

'You mean someone was stuck inside while it burned down?' repeated Rollo on his return. 'That's awful. No wonder it feels so terrible.'

'No, no one was in the house,' Mossy said. 'We'd have seen something at the time. But maybe there's something we haven't found, that I don't know about. A place where something, or maybe even someone, could have been lost, or hurt, or trapped. I'm not sure where or how, but I had this feeling …' He paused.

'So maybe that's what I can sort out,' interrupted Rollo. 'I can't change what happened, but if we can find what was lost and give it back to the original family it belonged to, then maybe that can put it right somehow. What if someone did die that night and no one knew?'

'Well, you're right. Sorting that out might free Tannor,' agreed Mossy, gripping the handlebars tightly as they swung round at the end of the cul-de-sac. 'Mind you, if you do go, you're to take someone with you, and I'm coming too. I don't trust Tannor one bit, and he'll make no end of trouble. It's bound to be dangerous.'

As they sailed back up the road they went past the house where Mossy had spoken to the young Holder. Loud voices and wails were coming out of an upstairs window.

'I will not have you telling lies like that,' shouted a woman's voice. There was the crack of a harsh slap. 'Little men, indeed. A fairy story's all very well, but you are not to try telling me it's real.'

'But Mummy, I did,' sobbed a child's voice. Mossy shook his head. He'd tried to warn him, but obviously his advice had gone unheeded.

He did so hope that Rollo had been paying more attention.

CHAPTER 23

Hidden

'But it only hurts a bit,' complained JJ when Annie refused to let him join the expedition.

'I'm not keen on the others going, but you need another day of rest before you go traipsing about the woods,' she insisted. 'Why not join me in the studio? I need someone to help me sort out my paints. Dad'll be back from his mystery trip into town soon, and then we can get ready for birthday lunch.'

'We'll be quick,' promised Cissy, 'and then you can help me ice Mum's birthday cake. OK?'

Mossy kept close on Rollo and Cissy's heels as they headed off across the fields. A good night's rest, an invigorating morning bike ride and happy Dwellers had filled him with energy, and he had no problem keeping up, unseen, behind them.

'So not just tidying up?' said Cissy. 'Whatever you told Mum. What exactly are we looking for?' she asked as they turned off the track in the wood.

'I'm not sure, maybe I'll know better when we get there,' Rollo told her. He and Mossy had decided that this time it would just be a general hunt to find any places where something could have been lost or damaged.

The clearing was still and quiet. Ah, thought Mossy, spotting a woodlouse scuttle past his toes. Not completely still; that's a change for the better.

'Look, see here, this end of the rope is all knotted into that bush!' exclaimed Cissy as she tugged it free. 'Maybe that's why JJ tripped on it.'

'Yes, but we left it over there,' Rollo reminded her, pointing at the big oak. 'Where Jon fell off.'

'Maybe some animal shifted it?' suggested Cissy.

'And tied it into the bush?'

'Are you saying someone did this deliberately? To trip JJ? No one else knew it was here, apart from Jon. And he'd never do that kind of thing. He likes JJ. And he still couldn't make it back here without us anyway.' Cissy tied the rope into a coil and hung it on a low branch.

Well done to put that out of the way, thought Mossy, glancing around nervously.

A shaft of sunlight shone down through the bare branches, lighting a mound in the bank that rose behind the clearing.

'Wow!' breathed Cissy. 'Wouldn't JJ love that? It's perfect for jumping from, and with all those dead leaves at the bottom, even he would have a soft landing.' She set off towards it.

'Cissy! Wait!' called Rollo. 'Hang on 'til I'm with you.'

'You and your 'feelings'!' laughed Cissy. 'I'm fine.' She

grabbed a branch that jutted out and pulled herself upwards. There was a loud crack.

Rollo jumped towards her as she rolled back down the bank. Mossy jumped with him.

'Cissy!'

'I'm fine,' she laughed, sitting up, her hair spiked with leaves and twigs. 'I just slipped.'

Rollo stood still in the centre of the clearing, gazing around him.

'What is it?' Cissy asked, dusting earth off her hands as she sat on the ground. That's it, thought Mossy, knowing he had no need to project his ideas for Rollo to catch them.

'Read the place. Even if I can't find it, I'm sure you can.'

'You know I said there must have been a house here once? Well I reckon it ended badly. Someone got hurt, badly hurt, here. Come on.' Rollo stretched out a hand and pulled her to her feet. 'Maybe we should head home.'

'Not yet,' thought Mossy. *'I'm sure you can find it if you keep looking.'*

'Just one jump,' insisted Cissy, setting off again. 'On JJ's behalf.' She scrabbled up the slope, reaching up to grab at a sapling that sprouted near the top. She hauled herself upwards.

'Watch out,' warned Rollo. 'It's not holding...' Cissy let out a shout of exasperation as the sapling pulled free of the earth, tumbling her back down the bank again.

'Right!' she exclaimed, getting to her feet once more. 'I'm not going to let it beat me!'

Rollo wasn't paying attention. He was staring at the wall that had been exposed by the collapse of the tree and its surrounding earth. A dark hole could be seen where a stone had pulled free.

'Cissy watch out. There's a hidden wall there. It's probably weak from being covered by earth for so long.'

Cissy stopped in her tracks. Her eyes sparkled with excitement.

'Maybe there's treasure!' she suggested. Mossy shook his head. The Dwellers of Tannery Cottage never had treasure. 'Buried for years,' she went on. 'We'll be millionaires.'

'Nothing like that here,' said Rollo, joining her. He gave her a leg up as she reached towards the wall, setting off another cascade of earth and vegetation. Rollo pulled at it too, dragging ivy and other plants away. Another stone tumbled free, doubling the size of the hole.

'Mind my foot,' called Cissy.

Mossy recognised the tingle on the back of his neck. He spun round, hunting for the tell-tale sign that would show him where Tannor was hiding. Over by the oak tree, under a thicket of bramble, he spotted two dark, glowing spots of light.

'Got you,' he muttered under his breath, ducking hurriedly through the undergrowth towards him.

'I told you not to bring them here, but you keep ignoring me,' hissed Tannor. 'You're making it worse. Didn't what happened to that boy make you understand? And yet this time you've brought the girl. She'll help me make another 'accident'. She can't help herself.' Tannor turned away from Mossy to focus on Cissy. Glancing over, Mossy saw her frown in pain as she rubbed the side of her head.

Mossy reached out and gripped Tannor's ear, tugging hard.

'I won't let you hurt my Dwellers,' he insisted. Cissy's hand fell back to her side as Tannor's concentration was broken.

'Help me pull this away,' Rollo said to her, pointing at a thick mat of ivy. He looked at her. 'You OK?'

'Sudden headache,' she replied.

'You forget where you are,' growled Tannor, jerking his head to one side.

'Oh no, I don't,' grinned Mossy. 'We're out in Widow Knight's Wood, but, according to you, neither of us has any tie to this place any longer. Neither of us is the stronger here, with no Starting Stone you are no longer its proper Holder.'

He grabbed Tannor's shoulder, shaking him firmly.

'Look at me when I talk to you.' Mossy's determination forced Tannor to flick a glance in his direction.

'I'm busy,' he muttered. Cissy shook her head, shoving her hand through her hair.

Mossy bent down and grabbed Tannor's feet in both hands, jerking them backwards so he fell flat on his face in the muddy earth.

'Ah, that's better,' said Cissy. 'Headache's gone.' She launched herself up to where Rollo had cleared a section of curved wall.

Tannor scrabbled onto his hands and knees, kicking backwards at Mossy who stepped neatly to one side.

'If you want to get rid of me, you'll have to pay more attention,' Mossy reminded him, looping an ivy tendril round Tannor's shoulder and pulling back sharply.

'Get off me,' grunted Tannor. 'I have to stop them. They'll ruin everything.'

'No,' Mossy said, gently now. 'This may be the only way

that it can all begin to finally get better. For you, too. I won't let you hurt them. This has to stop.'

Tannor lashed out, swinging his hand round, his fingers bunched in attack. Mossy ducked, but he needn't have worried. Thorns from the bramble hooked into Tannor's sleeve and brought his arm up short, his fist inches from Mossy's nose.

Then Rollo was calling. 'Watch out Cissy, I'm going to pull some more of these stones away. I think there's some kind of chamber. I think it may have been a cold store. I can't see an entrance, but maybe it got blocked up at some time in the past. I want to see what's inside.'

'I told you!' Cissy's eyes sparkled in anticipation as she slithered back down the bank. 'Treasure! Gold and jewels. I know you said you thought it was a tannery, but I reckon it was a gold mine. Bags I first pick.'

Tannor battled with the bramble. Another spiral of thorns wrapped itself around his leg. A twist of wild clematis slipped round his wrist. He glared down at them, then at Mossy.

'What are you doing? You brought in those vile children, then that hideous buzzard that dragged me away.'

'She isn't hideous,' protested Mossy. 'She's actually rather beautiful.'

'No bird or animal has dared come here in centuries,' continued Tannor furiously, 'and now even the plants are turning against me.'

'You disregarded the Old Things,' Mossy said quietly, sitting still and watching as Tannor's struggles sank him further into the mud. 'But they have been working to heal this place, and ultimately to heal you, if you let them. That shaft of light just now made Cissy want to climb the place that needed to be found. Her fall when the sapling pulled free helped to show them. It is harder when there are no animals, but sun, rain and roots can work their magic too. They have been breaking down the last remnants of this Holding, returning it to fresh growth. You can let them heal you too.'

'If you heap up those stones at the bottom, we can stand on them to look into the hole you've made,' Cissy was suggesting.

Tannor put his head in his hands. His struggles slowed.

'They're going to find him, when no one else could. They're going to find him, and then there will be no one left to tie me here. Don't you see? It gives me no option.' He lifted his coal black eyes to smoulder at Mossy again. 'I have to take your Holding now.'

'Find him?' Mossy's brow furrowed. Maybe that chill he'd felt wasn't the chill of the grave. He so hoped that was the case. There was a good chance that this was Tannery Cottage's old cold store, built away from the house and hidden over the years by the growth of plants.

'Give us a hand and I'll pull you up,' Rollo told Cissy, one hand resting on the lip of the hole as he turned to look back at her.

'My Holding is mine, until the day that it and I are gone for good,' Mossy said softly, looking back at Tannor pinned by the brambles. 'I cannot leave it. It is not mine to hand over. In your heart of hearts, you know that.' Tannor groaned.

'No looking 'til I can see too,' insisted Cissy, reaching up to her brother.

'Ready?' he checked.

Both children pressed their heads to the hole. There was silence.

'Oh…' Cissy gasped. 'Rollo?' Her voice sounded pale. 'Rollo, is that what I think it is?

'It's OK.' Rollo slipped an arm round her shoulder, as she leaned against him. 'I think it's been there a very long time.' Mossy felt the shiver of fear shoot through them both.

'I'm going to have to look after them now,' Mossy told Tannor, standing up and stepping out of the briars.

'You were right.' Cissy gripped Rollo's hand. Mossy arrived to see her eyes shining with unshed tears. He laid the lightest of fingers on her ankle. 'It isn't treasure.' Her head hung down.

'No.' Rollo kept his arm around her shoulder. 'And now we need to go home and tell Mum and Dad that we've found a skeleton.'

CHAPTER 24

Corrections

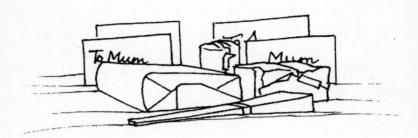

Mossy was impressed by the speed at which the police arrived.

'I'm afraid we're going to have to shut off this area of the wood,' announced the inspector. 'Investigations will have to be undertaken, and until proper procedures have been followed this whole area is off limits.'

Mossy was delighted. At last he wasn't the only one telling the children they had to keep away. Plastic streamers were tied around the trees, and people in dark blue, followed by others in white overalls, stomped about the place, digging things up and putting them in plastic bags.

Birthday lunch turned into sandwiches, while police people in jeans and jumpers sat with Rollo, Cissy and their parents, and asked a whole multitude of questions. JJ listened in.

'I found the house to begin with,' he volunteered.

'Hmm,' said the detective. 'Who might you be? And what happened to that leg?'

'I missed out on the best bit,' he grumbled later as they sat roasting chestnuts by the sitting room fire. Outside the day had faded into darkness, but Mossy felt cosy in the chatter of the family.

'It wasn't that great,' admitted Cissy. 'In fact I felt all weird when I realised what it was. You know, a real person?'

'But if it hadn't have been for you, we'd never have gone back to have a look at all,' Rollo told him.

'So, in a way, it's thanks to you that we had the fright of our lives,' grinned Cissy. 'And at least the poor old skeleton gets to be properly buried now.'

'Imagine being lost for all those years and nobody knowing that you're there all that time.'

'In fact we still don't know who he was,' mused Rollo.

'It might've been a 'she', for that matter,' Cissy reminded them.

'Never mind all that,' Jack interrupted them. 'I think we all need something to cheer us up, and Mum and I have decided that even though it's late in the day we still need to remember it's her birthday.'

'Great!' grinned JJ, hobbling off to the stairs ahead of the others. Mossy toasted his toes and leaned back against the warm stones of the hearth.

'Ta da!' sang Cissy moments later, launching herself through the door. 'Presents!'

'Dad, are you doing yours first or last?' asked Rollo.

'I'm giving mine last,' JJ butted in.

'Then mine's first,' decided Cissy, holding out a shiny parcel.

Exclamations of delight and hugs of thanks followed the ripping of paper.

'Cissy it's beautiful, and made entirely by you. I love it!' said Annie, holding up the book that had emerged. 'I shall keep records of all my painting sales in it.'

Mossy saw a shadowy movement in a far corner of the room and crept over to investigate. Tannor looked different, as if someone had shaken all the fight out of him. He looked more stooped than Mossy had ever seen before.

'They've taken him away,' Tannor told him in a hollow voice.

'It was bound to happen,' Mossy reminded him. 'It should have happened years ago. And with him gone, you aren't trapped any longer. You're free.'

'But I don't want freedom,' Tannor sighed. 'I've lived with my anger, and off its energy, all these empty years. By taking him away, they've taken another part of me. What else can I do?' His lower lip trembled, and he bit down on it with his broken teeth, but Mossy noticed that he seemed less there, as if he had faded somehow.

'You'll be free to go, find the rest you need, let everything heal,' Mossy replied, knowing that it was a hard prospect to face.

'I can't seem to get through to that girl any longer,' lamented Tannor. Mossy looked at his dejected face and almost felt sorry for him. Without his anger, all that was left was an empty, shattered shell of a Holder. His broken leg sagged, and his twisted hands hung loosely at his sides.

'It's as if the whole family have wrapped her up, keeping me out. I don't know what to do any longer,' he moaned.

'Watch what's happening here,' Mossy suggested, gently taking Tannor's hand and tugging him towards the light around the family. 'This is something that can work wonders for us Holders. It's one of their celebrations. If you haven't seen one of these before, you'll be surprised how good it can feel. I thrive on this energy, and it's a feast we can share.'

'How did you know this was precisely what I needed?' Annie asked Rollo, waving a wide fan of a brush as if painting the air.

'I heard you saying that you wanted to soften the edge of something, so I asked Ursula in the art shop,' Rollo explained. 'She says if it's not right you can change it.'

'It's perfect. I couldn't have chosen better for myself.'

'And my present comes in two parts,' announced JJ.

'I don't do this kind of thing,' muttered the visiting Holder. 'I don't know how to cope with it.'

'First this part,' continued the boy, holding out a crumpled parcel. 'Watch out, it's heavy.'

'My goodness, it is!' said Annie, holding it carefully.

'What's happening?' murmured Tannor, his pale skin blanching even whiter, his eyes looking even darker. 'He had it hidden. What's he doing with it?'

'Had it hidden?' Mossy was confused. 'They always keep presents hidden until they give them; it's part of the surprise. Didn't any of your Dwellers ever give a present?'

'But that's not a present,' confessed Tannor with a groan. 'It's my Starting Stone,'

'Your **what**?!' Mossy couldn't believe his ears. He stared at the square flat stone that emerged from the wrapping. 'It's barely big enough to start anything, let alone a house! And what's that hole in the centre?'

'Like I told you, it's where they used to grind me down. It

stood at the bottom of the door post, and the iron rod of the door pivot drilled into it, just a little, every single time they opened or closed the door.'

Mossy stared at him aghast.

'Every time?' he echoed Tannor. 'You poor, poor Holder. It must have been agony.'

'And then there's this to go with it,' added JJ, handing his mother another smaller, but equally crumpled, parcel.

For the first time Mossy's sadness for him no longer fired Tannor's anger. Instead he turned his aching eyes on Mossy.

'How come you can feel sorry for me when I've done nothing but cause you trouble? I've tried my best to drive you out of here, and yet you still find kindness for me. I don't understand.'

'If you lived with that all that time I'm not surprised you're filled with pain.'

'What if they put my stone under another door pivot?' Tannor's face crumpled at the thought. 'One day they will grind right through it and then... Then what?'

'Look,' said Mossy, pointing towards Annie as she placed the candle she had just unwrapped into the hole in the centre of the stone.

'It's a perfect fit, my JJ. A candlestick. Oh Jack, can you turn out the lights so that we can see it work properly?' A candlestick, remembered Mossy. JJ had said he'd brought one from the cottage, but he had ignored it because all he could think of was a big, square, post stone. He had never thought JJ could make one from another of the stones with holes in them that he loved so much.

'Here, Mum; matches,' said Rollo, passing them to her.

There was a flare in the darkness and then a glowing light, that grew to shine on the surrounding faces. Mossy could feel Tannor trembling beside him.

'Darling, it's beautiful. It's as if the stone shines too,' said Annie.

'She's right,' breathed Tannor in a voice that Mossy hardly recognised, a voice that had lost its harsh edge and found a new softness. 'I've never seen it like that before – but it does shine.' Mossy stood silently, seeing the warmth gradually fill the stone and then spread beyond.

'Feel that,' he said at last. 'That's what Dwellers can give you if you let them.' Looking at Tannor, he saw his cracked cheeks wet with tears.

'What have I done all this time? I've lived off anger and pain, created fights, fury and hurt. What is this amazing thing, this warmth, this feast of energy? What makes it?'

'See the light in these Dwellers,' Mossy whispered softly. 'See the way they look at each other? Give to each other? It's love. Your Starting Stone has been given in love by a son to his mother. That candle simply makes it visible.'

'Ace one, JJ,' said Rollo, giving his younger brother a hug. 'You always find such brilliant stones.'

'It was in the wood,' he told them. 'By the paving where we made the swing. As soon as I saw it I just knew it was special.'

'And now who wants cake?' Cissy leapt to her feet. 'I made stacks of icing!'

Mossy tucked Tannor into a corner of the woodpile by the fire as his Dwellers headed into the kitchen. The candle was left glowing quietly, shedding a golden light.

'Mind the hearthstone,' he reminded him.

'It's still good, even though they've gone,' said Tannor, his eyes riveted to the candle. 'He said he knew as soon as he saw it that it was special.' His eyes lit with a soft glow. 'My Starting Stone, special. Me,' he breathed.

'We all can be,' Mossy added. 'It's only in your stone if it's in you.'

'I don't know about that.' Tannor hung his head in shame.

'The light is always there. Even if it's hidden for a while, it's still there. All you have to do is let it out,' Mossy reassured him.

Singing floated through from the kitchen.

'And when you cut the knife down to the bottom of the cake, we'll all scream to scare away the evil spirits!' announced Cissy.

'Does she mean me?' asked Tannor, looking up anxiously.

'No,' chuckled Mossy. 'They don't even know we're here.'

Shrieks, screams and laughter rang through the house. Tannor lifted his hands to his ears, as if to protect them. Then he paused, his hands wavering as the corners of his mouth curled upwards.

'It tickles,' he whispered. Mossy nodded. The outside corner of Tannor's eyes wrinkled as a smile reached them for the first time, and then Mossy caught the soft gurgle of a first laugh breaking out, with not a single hiccup to be heard.

'You wait 'til they really get cracking,' he chuckled.

The evening slid into a dark, moonless night, starlight sparkling in the clearness of frost to come. There was no need for a Nightwatch. The trouble was put to rest. Instead Mossy invited Tannor onto the roof. It was a difficult climb, and Mossy had to give him a hand at several points, waiting patiently as Tannor hauled himself slowly upwards.

'That's Orion, and those two are the heavenly twins, see, launching themselves off his shoulders.' Mossy pointed to the stars from their seat by the chimney stack, the scent of wood smoke drifting about their shoulders.

'It's so clear; no twigs or chaos to get in the way,' sighed Tannor. He turned, his dark eyes full of sorrow. 'You know, I've done terrible things; things I am ashamed to remember now. I made people's lives a misery because I couldn't see past my own pain, and now it's too late to put it right, isn't it?'

Low on the sky, just above the trees of Widow Knight's Wood, a huge star shone brighter than those around it.

'That's Vega,' explained Mossy, pointing at it. Tannor squinted upwards.

'I don't see things as well as you,' he reminded him. Mossy put an arm around his shoulders.

'Let me describe it for you, and that way we can share it.'

CHAPTER 25

A Change Of Heart

Mossy spent the next day taking Tannor round Annanbourne, showing it to him so he could enjoy it for once, now that he felt so different. He pointed out things that had changed, where places had been made better, the lost mill.

'I thought you were a bit in the skinny side,' remarked Tannor.

'And I'm still tripping over my extensions,' laughed Mossy, as he reached a hand out to help him up the steps to Annie's studio.

'Wow,' Tannor gasped, when the blast of creative energy hit him. Two mice peered cautiously round the leg of the table, their whiskers twitching. He shook his head.

'Promise I won't,' he assured them. 'Even I can have a change of heart.'

By the time the children came home from school, Tannor was exhausted. His thin chest heaved with each shallow effort to breathe. Mossy could see that he was fading fast now. His skin was paler, the light in his eyes dimmer, each step was a struggle.

'Mossy, I'm going to have to go. This isn't my Holding. Whatever I may have said before, I know now that it's yours, through and through. My time is up. My Starting Stone has been moved from my Holding. In fact it isn't really my Starting Stone any more, if it's not in my Holding, is it?' he sighed. Mossy shook his head, reluctant to tell Tannor the things he had clearly worked out for himself.

'I can see now that what I did was wrong. All I could feel before was pain, so I made it my task to give trouble to others. If I had tried to do my best for them, who knows? Maybe I wouldn't have suffered so much. There might have been other things that could have taken the pain away. I never knew I could do something that was good until I saw the light shine out of my stone. I didn't know it was there.' He stopped, and Mossy let the silence rest easily between them.

'We can all make mistakes.'

'And that's just it!' Tannor exclaimed. 'Before I go I need to put right some of what I've done wrong. Your Dwellers found my lost Dweller, but there is something else they need. Before he hid in the cold store he dropped something which I found and hid, so that if anyone came searching he would remain lost.' Tannor fell silent, his breath coming in short pants. Mossy waited.

'You know I didn't kill him, don't you? It was the falling stones that killed him when the tree crushed the cold store. Even at my worst I couldn't have killed a Dweller, but it was my fault he was never found. I wanted him trapped so that I had to stay. I'm so ashamed now of what I did. It's still hidden, but if I bring it here, can you give it back?'

'Who would I give it to after all this time?' asked Mossy.

'To the family of the young man who died. So they know he's been found.'

'How on earth would I find him?' asked Mossy. 'Do you know his name?'

Tannor shook his head.

'My Dweller was called Josiah Tanner, and the lost one was his cousin.'

'I don't know.' Mossy stared down at the ground. Then a small smile crept across his face. 'But maybe I know someone who might be able to find a way. Do you need me to come with you?'

'No.' Tannor shook his head. 'This is something I must do by myself, even if it's hard. I have to be the one who starts the process of putting it right, even if I can't do it all myself.'

That night Mossy waited until the children were in bed before he shimmered into visibility next to Rollo's bedside lamp.

'Something's changed, hasn't it?' said Rollo immediately, closing his book and dumping it on the duvet.

'Yes, but I need to ask for your help again.'

'Brilliant!' Rollo looked excited once Mossy had explained the problem. 'Finding out who he was will give me an excuse to look into the archives, and I've been longing to do that, find real, living history. What exactly is it you've got?'

'I won't know until I see it tomorrow,' grinned Mossy, anxious to keep Tannor out of sight.

It was one thing for him to let himself be seen by Rollo, but he wasn't going to force any other Holder into having to cope with it. After all, it had taken him quite a while to get used to it. Tannor was too fragile now, and neither of them wanted to frighten the children, Tannor's reluctance showing yet more clearly how much he had changed.

Rollo was excited the following day, when he saw the stained, folded pages that Mossy and Tannor had smuggled into his room.

'Wow! Even the paper feels different to ours,' he said, his hands smoothing the document flat. 'And just think, it's been hidden all this time. We're the first people to see this in hundreds of years. If only I could read this kind of writing.' He turned bright eyes on Mossy. 'I'm sure Doc Mallon at school will be able to show me. He runs the history club. If this gives us some clues as to who the skeleton was, we could find out if there are any of his family still living round here.'

'You can't read it?' Mossy was amazed. 'You've always got your head buried in a book. I thought you could read everything! Even I can read that. It's the way everybody used to write when I first learned to read.' He craned his head over Rollo's arm. 'See there?' His fingers traced the spidery sprawl. 'That's a name – Samuel Goodyear – and there's a date, April 27th 1723. I can't remember exactly, but that's close to when Tannery Cottage burned down.'

'And what about this bit here?' asked Rollo, pointing to another section.

'It's a list of house goods. See?' Mossy pointed to a

column of writing, picking out several items. 'Two stools, four knives, one ewer.'

'Ewer?'

'What you'd call a jug.'

'Ah.' Rollo nodded his head. 'And this word here; is that belle house? What does that mean?' he asked. 'Is it French?'

'No!' laughed Mossy. 'They just didn't spell like you. See, it's in the kitchen section. Read it out loud.'

'I already did,' protested Rollo. 'Belle House.'

'Faster!' chuckled Mossy. 'And think about what you'd find in a kitchen.'

'Belle House. Bel hous. Bel'ous. Ah, got it!' exclaimed Rollo. 'Bellows! But why in the kitchen? Surely they'd have that sort of thing in the sitting room?' Mossy shook his head.

'No, you'd keep a slow burn in the sitting room. It's the kitchen that needs a roaring fire for cooking,' he grinned. 'Or a blacksmith may be.'

'And that one – rotherbeastes? What are they?'

'Young cattle. We used to have lots of them here, in the barn where you lot keep your cars and bikes.'

It took a while to decipher the whole document, and there were places where even Mossy got stuck.

'It looks to me like this is some sort of will, saying who gets what, and then this list of stuff. In which case,' Rollo smiled broadly, 'we ought to be able to find out who this was quite quickly. If it's a missing will, someone will have wondered what happened to it.'

Tannor was pleased when Mossy reported back to him.

'So you think it might make a difference to someone? I don't want to cause any more trouble, just to help a bit in the end. And Mossy, when I've gone, will you look after my stone? Remind them to keep a candle that shines in it, so that you can remember me now, not as I was.'

'See how things have worked out?' said Mossy, his arms wrapped round his folded legs as he sat beside Tannor. 'I know you weren't pleased by the children coming, but it turned out alright in the end, didn't it? I wouldn't be surprised if the roots of the trees had pushed your Starting Stone up again to make sure that it could be found, to make it possible for everything to be healed and restored. But now it is you who's putting things right.'

Tannor nodded, smiling weakly.

'I couldn't have done it without you and your friend. But I'm finished, and it's time for me to rest at last.' He paused, looking up at Mossy with wan eyes. 'Do you want to break it? If you ask that Dweller boy to help, you could do it between you, couldn't you?'

'Break what?' Mossy frowned in confusion.

'My Starting Stone It's what I deserve.'

'No, you don't,' said Mossy, smiling gently as he rested a hand on Tannor's lopsided shoulder. 'And we'd all miss it. I'd have nothing to remember you by, and think how sad Annie would be, after the pleasure when she was given it? Do you want to take that from her?' Tannor shook his head.

'Then I have one last request,' he said. 'Can we leave the candle alight as I go?'

'You stay here, and I'll bring a flame,' Mossy told him. He returned with a long slender twig which he had lit from the last cinders of the fire. He watched as Tannor curled himself round the base of the candle, and then touched the taper to the wick at the top. The flame transferred and grew, pale at first, then golden, the soft light flickering over the broken Holder as he closed his eyes.

'There you are, lit from the fire on my hearth, so that I always remember you at your best,' Mossy told him.

'Thank you,' Tannor murmured. 'You've been a better friend than I deserved.'

'You're welcome,' said Mossy. 'I'm glad we got it sorted out in time.' He rested his long thin hand gently over Tannor's, and settled beside him in the quiet darkness of the night sitting room.

Mossy was startled awake by Rollo hurrying through the next morning. He looked at the candle. It had burned down to a small stump, the flame no longer flickering, but still alight, and steady.

He looked around the room. There was no sign of the other Holder. Mossy reached out a long finger. He held his breath, unsure what to expect, and then briefly touched the stone. There was no blue flame, no flash, no burning pain. The stone felt smooth and warm. He let his hand rest on it and sighed heavily.

Tannor was gone.

CHAPTER 26

Another Day

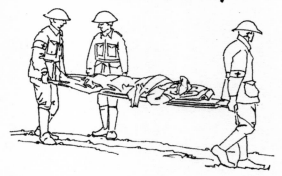

Annie frowned at the burned-down stump.

'I don't remember lighting this after supper. And who left it burning all night long?' Cissy and JJ shook their heads as they prepared their breakfasts.

Oh dear, thought Mossy, I should have thought of that. Maybe Tannor couldn't help leaving a small problem in his wake still.

'Rollo?' Annie pointed at the candle when Rollo returned from his deliveries.

'*I lit it last night,*' projected Mossy. '*I'll explain later.*'

'I lit it last night,' said Rollo. 'And then forgot,' he added.

'I'm really sorry about that,' Mossy apologised that evening. 'I hadn't realised she'd be so cross.'

'At least replacing the burned candle won't cost too much,' mused Rollo. 'And by the sound of things it was in a good cause.'

'The trouble is over, and everything is settled again,' Mossy assured him. 'And if you ever go back to the woods, it'll be quite safe. No more dropping swings, or dangerous spikes.'

'It's all been pretty bad for you, hasn't it?' said Rollo. 'It's not been much fun for us either, actually. I guess this whole business must have been one of the worst things you've ever had to deal with,' he suggested, snuggling under his duvet.

Mossy looked over at him. Strangely, over the past few days he had come to think of Rollo much as he did the person that he reminded him of, a person he could count on in any difficult situation, someone he would trust with his life. A friend, he admitted to himself.

'No, actually,' he said after a pause. 'There was another time, back in the last century, when things were, in fact, much worse.' He shivered at the memory. 'That makes dealing with a Holder gone bad look like a piece of cake. But I had help.' He looked over at Rollo. 'I was rescued by a friend.'

'A friend?' Rollo stretched his arms out, then rubbed his face. 'Someone like me, another boy?'

'No…,' Mossy shook his head, unsure. How much could he tell him? 'He's a Holder like me really. But not here all the time, he just visits. We call him the Travelling Holder.'

'Was he trying to steal your house too?' asked Rollo. He yawned. 'Oh, sorry, I'm really tired,' he admitted.

'It was about as far from stealing anything as you could get. No, he sort of comes and goes, sometimes when I need help, and at others just to join in. But there was one time when I was in a desperate state. ...You see, there'd been a war.' Mossy shuddered, his eyes clouding. It still frightened him to remember it.

'What? Here?' checked Rollo, perking up and rolling onto his side.

'No, that was another time.' Mossy looked over at Rollo. 'You may have read about this one in your books; they called it The Great War?'

'The First World War? We did a project on it at school,' Rollo nodded. 'I never thought I'd meet someone who'd been there when it happened.'

'I wasn't there,' Mossy shook his head. 'And the fighting never happened here, but when people are caught up in bad events the hurt can go through everyone and everything. At that time it was terrible. Everything suffered. There was hardly a family that wasn't affected. We Holders found it tough looking after our Dwellers.'

Rollo curled up his legs and Mossy relaxed back onto the warm softness of the duvet. Maybe it would do him good to tell this boy, this Place Reader who seemed to understand him so well. He'd never really told anyone, and the trapped pain of the memory still made him fearful. He'd seen, often enough, how one of his Dwellers could drain away the bad feelings out of something by describing it to an outsider. After all, hadn't that been what had finally helped Tannor, that at last someone had understood all he had suffered? Maybe Rollo was the one human he could trust.

'You see, when the people who live in our Holdings suffer, we do too, and we have to try to help them cope with it, whatever it is. During that war so many young men died. All around us there were families where someone was missing; a father, a son, a cousin, brothers, friends. Some of them hardly more than boys your age.'

Mossy's voice shook, his eyes glistening at the memory. 'Up at Mount Pleasant Farm, it was two of their sons. Poor Petis, endlessly having to look after death in that Holding. Over at Hangar Farm the daughter of the family lost her young man a month before the wedding. She never did marry and the farm had to be sold. It was like that everywhere.' He paused, a huge sigh washing through him. A tear trickled down his cheek.

'And here... Here it was Joe Samson. Killed over in France, in some battle which achieved nothing but the destruction of lives. And his death destroyed his wife. She lost the will to live and sickened. Nothing I could do could bring her out of it. I tried everything. I called in all the help I could, the stream, the trees, everything that grew, to show her that there was still life to be found and enjoyed. But she just saw the blankness of her missing man. Even her children couldn't bring her round. They were little ones and needed her. Madge and Phyl...'

Mossy looked over at Rollo. Although he was still focused on Mossy, his eyes were drooping, his pale face looking drained in the darkness.

'You're tired. I'll tell you another time,' he suggested.

'No, no,' protested Rollo, 'Go on. Madge and Phil, a sister and brother ...'

'Not a brother and sister – two girls: Margaret and Phyllis,' Mossy continued, his eyes lifting to softest blue at the memory. 'Dear little girls they were too, but eventually the three of them were in such a state that Dorrie's parents came from Norfolk and took them all away. And the house was left, abandoned.' Mossy sat still, as if frozen, as the colour drained from him, his eyes now washing out to a pale grey.

'Mossy, you look terrible!' said Rollo, stifling a yawn as he reached out a hand towards him.

'There was no one here to tend the land, to make repairs.' Mossy's voice cracked as he continued. It was almost as if he no longer saw Rollo, just memories that filled his vision like a film in a cinema.

'The fields grew nothing but weeds. The mill, which hadn't been used for ages, finally collapsed. Years passed, but they never came back. Will Earp's grandfather took over the fields beyond the stream, and the rest of the fields and the wood at the back went to Lower Farm. Neighbours took stone from the mill for repairs to their own houses, and I got thinner and thinner. Windows broke, which made it hard for me to see clearly. I could barely look after the place. But worst of all there were no Dwellers, not just for a day or so, a week or a month, but for years. Year after year. With no one at all.' Mossy shook his head at the memory. 'With no laughter here, no happiness, kindness or love, we starved. The walls began to crack, timbers rotted, the roof had holes, pipes leaked...'

Mossy paused and looked over at Rollo. But Rollo had fallen asleep.

'Never mind,' Mossy spoke quietly, more to himself than to Rollo. 'Maybe it's not really something you need to know about, and in the end we pulled through, but that was down to someone you've never met.'

He closed his eyes, his breathing stilling, and in the silence of the dark room the words of the old tortoise came back to him. He opened his eyes again and looked over at Rollo. How would he know if it worked?

CHAPTER 27

Home Alone

When Rollo woke up he was instantly aware of a change. He was cold, shivering. The duvet had gone. He reached out, searching in the dark. His hand hit hard wood. Suddenly wide awake he sat bolt upright, puzzled to find himself on hard, bare floorboards. A faint dawn light slipped through the window. Where were the curtains? As he leapt to his feet, his eyes searched the room.

It wasn't just the duvet that was missing. His bed, his books, the chest of drawers, everything in fact, had gone.

'Some joke, Cissy!' he called. 'How d'you do it?' His voice echoed in the empty room. Then he realised that his missing things were not the only change. The soft green of the walls was now a dingy white. The window seemed higher than he expected. It was definitely his window, he assured himself, but different. It wasn't just the dirt on it, the cobwebs that hung across the corner and the peeling paint. Just what had changed? It didn't make sense. This couldn't be Cissy's work. He rubbed his eyes. Was this some weird kind of dream?

Roughness on the soles of his feet made him look down. Not only had the carpet gone, but the floorboards seemed bigger. He racked his mind, remembering when the room had been decorated. It hadn't had huge, wide boards then. They'd been about as wide as his foot was long. Now he'd have to stride out to cross them in one step.

'Don't panic,' he told himself, trying to calm his racing heart. 'It's just a dream. I'll wake up and I'll be in bed.' He looked up at the ceiling, far above him, to where a cracked glass lampshade tipped at an angle. He shut his eyes and then opened them again. Nothing had changed; everything was still wrong.

'Cissy!' he called. 'JJ?' Silence swallowed the sound. No voice called back.

OK, so it was a strange dream, he decided, but so long as he was in it, he might as well make the most of it. As he headed for the door, his footsteps echoed around him. He paused. It was a good thing it was open, he realised; he couldn't reach the handle.

Out on the landing, it was no better. Although in one way he recognised everything, the place looked utterly different. The ceiling soared overhead. The landing window had a broken pane. At Cissy's door he paused, glancing into her room. Hoping.

No sign of her. Or her things. His eyes darting about him, heart hammering in his chest, Rollo edged across the room to a damp stain on the floor. A careful touch confirmed what his eyes had told him. The wood was beginning to rot. Looking up, he could see where water had damaged the ceiling. It bulged and sagged, as the landing ceiling had not long before it collapsed from the flood of the burst header tank. A crack showed where small pieces of plaster had broken away and now lay in powdery spatterings across the floor.

What kind of dream was this that made the house look as if it were falling down? What had he been doing when he fell asleep to make him dream like this? He remembered Mossy's voice. They'd been talking, hadn't they?

Carefully Rollo backed out of the room. Skirting past JJ's door, he looked beyond it to his parents' bedroom at the far end of the corridor. Gone was the soft blue green of the walls, the white curtains. The door hung ajar, paint peeling around the handle. Beyond it he caught a glimpse of green, the colour JJ had turned just before he was sick after eating all his birthday cake in one go. A draught snaked round him, making him shiver, catching at a leaf and sending it skittering across the floor, trailing tracks through the dust. If only JJ were here now. Suddenly Rollo wanted to get out of there, be away from it. It felt too desolate.

This must be his home, but not as he'd ever seen it. Everything that made it a home was gone. All the warmth, the clattering sounds of busy people. He couldn't imagine anyone wanting to live in a place like this.

Turning, he began to run, but at the top of the stairs he grabbed at the wall to stop himself from crashing over a precipice. This was no dream. It was a nightmare. How on earth could he get down the steps?

'Come on,' he told himself. 'Think it through.' With a hand resting on one of the banister struts he looked down at the stairs. He could jump down to the next step, he decided.

It was nothing he couldn't manage if he took it one drop at a time. The clatter of his feet landing on the bare wood shouted back at him, bouncing off the walls.

Far away, downstairs, something rustled in the sitting room. He froze.

'How much worse can this get?' he asked himself. A dream is a dream, even when it's a nightmare. He'd heard his Dad tell JJ that. Suddenly it was as if his father were standing beside him, his strong voice calming his fears.

'If it's a dream, you can change it, make it go the way you want it to go. If you want to head on through a wall, just go for it. Walk straight through. That's the whole thing about dreams. In a dream you can do the impossible. You can face your worst fear and win.'

So if I want to go down these stairs quickly, he decided, it should be a piece of cake. Just think myself there.

Standing on the third step from the top, Rollo braced himself, looked at the bottom and decided to 'go for it'. His toes curled over the lip of the tread.

'This is a dream,' he announced loudly. 'I can reach the bottom in one go.' He paused at the edge, took a breath and stepped boldly out.

Always before, when he'd fallen in a dream, he'd woken with a jolt, but long before he hit the ground. This time it was as if every sharp edge was trying to find a new place to thump him as he fell.

Hands over head! he remembered. Wasn't that what had saved JJ when he fell down the stairs? So much for Dad's famous 'make your dreams do what you want', he grimaced.

Now the steps were taking it out on his arms and legs, as

well as his back and sides. How long does it take to fall down a staircase? he wondered as he somersaulted past the last step and fell spread-eagled onto the cold stone of the floor.

Lying quite still, Rollo wondered if he had any bones that weren't broken. Slowly he shifted first his arms and then his legs. There were no sharp pains, though breathing wasn't easy. All the air had been knocked out of him.

And suddenly he felt desperately alone. If only there were someone else in this dream. Someone there to help him. Anyone. But nothing stirred. No one conveniently stuck their head round the door with a cheery greeting. Or any greeting at all.

Rolling onto his side, he felt a dull ache across his left shoulder. As he pushed a hand through his hair, he felt a lump already growing above his right ear. But it seemed he'd been lucky; he hadn't hurt himself seriously.

As he struggled to his feet he looked at the front door. Water was seeping under it, and leaves had gathered in corners by the walls. An enormous spider swung gracefully towards him. Rollo stared, wide-eyed. He'd never seen one that big before. It waved its legs cheerily in his direction, then disappeared into a crack by the hinge. It was strange, he'd never thought of spiders as cheerful creatures before. Turning round, he had another shock.

The walls of the entrance hall had gone!

Instead it was as if the front door opened straight into the main room of the house. He was standing in a much larger room along one wall of which he could see the big beam of the sitting room fireplace. Underneath was a cavernous darkness instead of the familiar hearth round which they sat in winter evenings. But that wasn't the most surprising difference; opposite the fireplace half the sitting room had gone!

Where he should have been able to see the pillar, the one that held up the big ceiling beam, there was now a wall, with two doors in it. The nearer one creaked as it swung briefly in a draught. The other one stood open, the darkness beyond oozing into the room, creeping across the floor. On the far side a tattered curtain was snagged against the window frame, light from the risen sun struggling to push through the grimy glass, falling in soft puddles on the bare stone. Rollo put his hands to his face. He didn't want to see this, dream or no dream.

Keeping well away from whatever lay beyond those strange, dark doors, he stepped tentatively into the room, turning towards the kitchen.

He crossed his fingers. Maybe that would be the same. He'd go through, and everything would be fine again. His family would be there, and the house would be back to normal. The door stood ajar. Beyond it light washed across the familiar red of the old brick floor.

Just as he reached out to push the door further open, he heard a sound. He spun round, a flash of pure fear shooting down his spine, the hair on his neck bristling, his legs weak. There **was** something moving in the room.

One hand held defensively in front of him, prepared to fight off any assault, he scanned the darkness beyond the two doors. Nothing.

But his ears hadn't deceived him. He knew he'd heard something. He took a step towards the centre of the abandoned room. Were there more giant spiders? Less friendly ones this time? Slowly he turned towards the fireplace, the only place he hadn't inspected before. Was something lurking in the shadows of the huge open space, waiting to leap out at him when his back was turned?

An old poker stood propped in the far corner beside a couple of worm-eaten logs. A brick that had fallen down the chimney lay, surrounded by soot, on the hearthstone, a heaped bundle of rubbish beside it. I know, thought Rollo, I'll take that poker and then, if I do need to defend myself, at least I've got something. As he crept stealthily past the fireplace, his eyes constantly scanned the room, looking for any hint of attack.

And that's when he saw it. The rubbish moved.

CHAPTER 28

Time To Go

Rollo froze to the spot, his eyes fixed on the heap. It had only been the smallest movement, but there it was again. This time he caught a glint of light, something faintly shining out at him. Two things. Eyes.

Hardly daring to breathe, Rollo stared back. The eyes blinked, and then there was another movement. Was it some kind of animal?

'Is that you, Tollo?' The voice was hoarse, barely more than a whisper, but there was something about it that he recognised. Rollo took a step closer. Again the eyes blinked, pale grey eyes in an even paler face, smudged with soot, creased and lined, ancient and worn out. But, with a start, he recognised the long nose, the peaked tips of the ears.

'Mossy?' The eyes blinked again. 'What on earth's happened to you?' Rushing over and climbing onto the worn hearthstone, he fell to his knees at Mossy's side, reaching towards him with both hands. As he did so, he realised something extraordinary.

'Hey, Mossy! You're as big as me!' He paused, looking up at the huge wooden beam that arched over them. 'Or is it… that I am now as small as you?' A frown of confusion crossed his face. Mossy's pale lips curled into the hint of a smile.

'Weak I may be right now, and a touch too skinny these days, but I've been the same height as you ever since my extensions. You do talk rubbish sometimes, Tollo.' Mossy's brow creased. Tollo could say the strangest things, but he had never been gladder to see him. If he had to go, it was better done with his friend at his side.

Rollo frowned too. Tollo? Why was Mossy calling him by this weird name? Things must be seriously wrong if he couldn't even get his name right. He waved a hand as if to brush the idea away.

'Who cares? What matters is that you look dreadful. And what's happened to Annanbourne?'

'We're done for,' Mossy's voiced croaked. 'We've been empty, abandoned, for goodness knows how long. I've lost count of the years, but it must be decades now. After Joe died and Dorrie took the girls away, there's been no one here. No laughter, no love, no happiness or kindness; nothing to keep us going. We're dying. Soon we'll be gone and there's nothing you can do this time.'

Mossy watched as his friend drew closer and gazed down at him. Now that he was close up he would be able to see the flaking skin, places where it had rubbed raw. He looked steadily back from eyes that were sunk deep into dark hollows in his pale face. The bones showed sharply under skin that was almost translucent, and he hoped that he wasn't too frightening to look at.

Mossy was thin at the best of times, thought Rollo, but this was different.

'Mossy, you're starving. But you can't die, you can't.' Now it was Rollo's voice that cracked with anxiety as he hung onto Mossy's fragile hand, the long fingers lying limp, almost lifeless, in his.

His mind raced. Dorrie, Joe – weren't they the people that Mossy had been telling him about as he fell asleep? Joe who died in the First World War, and Dorrie who couldn't cope? And the girls, what were they called? But they'd left in 1916. That wasn't decades ago, that was more like a century. He shook his head. He'd think about it later. What mattered now was looking after Mossy.

'You can't die,' he repeated, more to himself than to his Holder friend. 'You told me; you and the house go together. If you die the house will fall down.'

'It's started already.' Mossy knew he had to prepare Tollo, though speaking was almost more than he could manage. 'I've tried my best, but there's no point any longer. There are cracks all over the place, the roof is spotted with holes, the mill has been destroyed, the barns are losing their walls where the wood has rotted away, and water leaks in each time it rains. I give up.'

Slowly Mossy's eyes drooped, the pale light dimming out of the grey, his breathing becoming shallower. Somewhere a beam shifted in the walls above them as a shower of soot and brick dust skittered down the chimney.

'No! Mossy! No.' Rollo's voice was sharp in the stillness of the room. 'You've got to hang on. I won't let you die. It isn't time for you to go yet. You can't. We need you,' he pleaded. Tenderly he slipped an arm behind Mossy's back, the other under his knees, cradling him in his arms, just as he had JJ when he'd carried him back from the woods. He rose to his feet.

'Mossy,' he begged. 'Look at me. I'm here, and I'll show you. It'll get better, it has to.'

Mossy allowed his head to rest against his friend's shoulder, the light barely flickering in his eyes any longer as he struggled to look into his face. Rollo carried him through to the kitchen, heading for the door to the back garden.

'I'm taking you outside,' he explained. 'See, the sun has risen now, and it's going to be a beautiful day. You can't die when the sun is shining.'

'Thank you for trying, Tollo. And thank you for coming this last time,' Mossy added, his voice the faintest of whispers. He no longer had the breath to spare for speaking. 'But it really is too late; I've run out of...' His voiced faded away, leaving the words hanging in the air.

But Rollo was no longer paying attention. Barely glancing at the rusting black range that filled the chimney breast, he crossed the worn brick floor to the back door. Mossy's legs hung limply down; he could feel his toes trailing on the ground, as Rollo skirted a broken chair that lolled drunkenly in front of an absent table.

'You just stay there,' he said, lying Mossy down. Mossy almost smiled. As if he could go anywhere!

Rollo shoved at the corner of the door in the vain hope that it would swing open. The wood was spongy and soft, but nothing moved. His frustration building, he kicked at it in fury. A mouldy section fell away. Mossy's hand gained another bruise.

'I'm sorry, but this is the only thing I can think of.'

Using all his energy, Rollo kicked and kicked, again and again, scrabbling with his hands until he had made a hole big enough to crawl through.

'Come on,' he said, turning to Mossy. 'I've thought of something.' Gently he hooked his hands under Mossy's shoulders, lifting the top half of his body and shifting him into position. 'It's going to be a bit bumpy, but it's the only way we can get out.'

Crawling through the hole, he reached back to pull Mossy towards him. The aching Holder groaned, and lath and plaster from the wall above them fell to the ground beside Rollo's legs.

'Hang on,' Rollo encouraged him. 'Look, see that sun, and the clear blue sky? That's what you'd call a good sign.'

Mossy opened his eyes wider, their paleness briefly mirroring the blue of the sky, before the lids drooped down again. A soft sigh escaped his lips as the early sun caressed his worn face.

'So good...' The corners of his mouth flickered upwards.

As soon as Rollo had pulled Mossy clear of the door, he scooped him back into his arms.

'Come on then, old fellow. We're going down to the stream.' Mossy felt the tall grasses part as Rollo pushed a way through, following the corner of the house, passing under the apple tree laden with the blossom that promised a fruitful autumn to come.

'Apple blossom in winter?' asked Rollo.

'Spring,' Mossy corrected him, waving a limp hand at the last of the daffodils that arched their heads above the bent grasses. His friend staggered down the bank, to where the stream struggled through the silt-filled pond. Dried hogweed heads that had long since scattered their seeds, matted grasses, stinging nettles and docks made it hard for the water to find its way. Mossy glanced over to the broken and damaged barns. You could still see the shape of the old farmyard, even overgrown and neglected as it was. A wagtail danced on the rotting thatch of the granary roof.

'What's happened to it all?' asked Rollo.

The track from the lane to the house was rough and unkempt, speckled with weeds, but still a point of connection. Did anyone even know it was there still?

'Listen, can you hear?' Mossy's attention was caught by the question. The familiar, laughing rush of water had faded to a quiet gurgle, but the stream was still there, struggling to find a way through the overgrown watercress and rushes that competed to block its course. Gently Rollo laid him by the damp edge.

'Fresh water,' he explained, cupping some in his hands to wash the dirt from Mossy's face. 'And feel this.' He grinned as he trickled some of the soft earth into the palm of Mossy's hand. 'Didn't you say you took some to London that time you went to sort out Mum's boss?' Mossy felt a tingle tickle through his bones.

'Never been to London,' he whispered, a frown creasing his forehead, but his voice was a little stronger.

'But you told me all about it, how worried you'd been at the idea of travelling on the train, the Holders you met who helped you?'

'What do you mean 'travelled on a train', and 'Mum', who's 'Mum'?' Mossy interrupted him.

'Never mind,' Rollo shook his head. 'You know me – talking rubbish, like you said before.' Mossy's eyes drifted shut again.

'So tired, so…' But even as he said it, Mossy felt a long-forgotten tingle of energy, an unfamiliar surge, somewhere deep in the core of him.

There was a soft rustling beside them as a small, sharp beak appeared, followed by a dark head with a flash of red on it. Bright eyes peered at them, and then Mossy caught a voice.

'Who was that?' Rollo looked up. He couldn't see anyone. Leaping to his feet he looked all around, craning his head over the tallest grasses, but there was no sign of anybody at all.

'Who was it who asked how we got here?'

'He brought me out.' Mossy replied. The moorhen dipped her head, quietly dropping a small piece of watercress by Mossy's hand. Rollo stared at her. Am I going mad in this dream? he asked himself.

'Full of iron, you say?' he heard his voice reply weakly to the advice he could have sworn she'd just given him. 'Erm…, thank you.'

Lifting Mossy's head a little, he held the watercress so that his friend could nibble a tiny piece.

'I know it's not your real food, but maybe it'll help a bit.' One small mouthful and Mossy sank back in Rollo's arms again, exhausted by the effort. Rollo looked down at him.

'That's it,' he encouraged him quietly. 'We'll get you better again.'

Somewhere beyond the clogged stream a bird was singing. A lark, rising into the spring morning, scattered his song down on them, a song that sang of life renewed, of dark days passing, of love that brings healing.

'See, we're not the only ones,' murmured Rollo, searching the arching blue for the tiny brown bird whose message of hope lifted his heart.

Mossy drank it in too, stretching out his hand, his long fingers reaching out to touch Rollo's arm.

'So what brought you this time, Tollo?' he croaked, his voice a fraction stronger. Rollo looked down at him. There was a long pause. Mossy wondered if he hadn't heard him and took another breath to repeat his question.

'Oh, you know… been busy… I just woke up and…' Rollo muttered.

'I should know better than to ask by now,' Mossy's hand patted his arm, a touch as light as a leaf drifting by. 'You never say anyway, and at least you aren't trying to tell me it's just a dream.' Rollo looked relieved, and this time Mossy's smile crept up to his eyes.

'Listen carefully,' Rollo spoke slowly, weighing his words. Mossy turned to look at him. 'Things are going to get better. Don't ask me how I know: I just do. You're going to get new Dwellers, families who will bring back everything you need. Laughter and fun, people who need you. You have to hang on for them, because without you here, without Annanbourne… it can't happen. Honestly Mossy, I promise you, it's going to be fine.' Mossy summoned all his energy, looking intently into his friend's face.

'What can't happen?' he asked.

'It's too complicated to explain right now, and I'm not sure I know anyway, but you have to believe me. You're going to find new Dwellers.'

There was a long pause.

'You've been right before…' Although Mossy spoke quietly, his voice sounded a little stronger. Rollo looked at him, but said nothing. How could he when he had no idea what Mossy was talking about? When had he been right before? 'Times when I found it hard to believe what you were saying. Times when I needed help, or was struggling to understand. And I've never needed you so much as I do now.'

A new sound broke across the stillness of the morning, the rumble of an old vehicle. Rollo stood up, turning to pull Mossy into a sitting position.

'Look,' he said, pointing down the track towards the lane. 'There are people passing, and one day they'll be coming here.'

The sound of the engine grew closer, and then it changed. A car was slowing.

CHAPTER 29

A Helping Hand

There was a crunch as the green Ford turned onto the track, weaving its way cautiously past potholes. Slowly it ground its way round the corner, stopping in front of the barn. A young man in a smart suit emerged and stood looking at the house.

Rollo crouched behind the grass.

'I don't think we ought to let ourselves be seen, do you?' There was a quiet chuckle from behind him.

'Still not sure that you're invisible?' Mossy whispered. 'How come you're never really sure? They can't see you. You faded fine. Look at your hands…'

Glancing down, Rollo was alarmed to find that the grass was clearly visible, not just through them, but through his feet and legs too.

'At least you sound a little stronger, even if I am fading,' he replied in a perplexed tone.

Standing up, he looked at the young man wandering up the path towards the front door. He was checking his watch.

'What can you see?' asked Mossy.

'He's got a briefcase, slicked down hair and a great fat tie with flowers all over it. Like something out of the sixties, a kind of fancy dress.'

Another car turned off the lane and bumped down the drive, interrupting him. Ducking out of sight, he watched through the parted grasses.

'Someone else coming too,' he explained.

'Help me up?' asked Mossy, reaching out a hand. 'I need to see.'

Mossy was glad of the support as Rollo pulled him to his feet. He was still seriously shaky and had to lean heavily on him, but, as they watched, the second car stopped beside the first. The sight of the young couple – who climbed out and hurried to join the first visitor – brought a sparkle to his eyes.

'We need to get closer,' he urged Rollo.

'Put your arm round my shoulders,' Rollo responded, wrapping one of his round Mossy's waist. Allowing himself to be half carried, Mossy struggled slowly towards the group on the path.

'Not so fast,' he whispered, as they crossed the pebbles. They paused, out of sight, but not out of earshot, behind a heap of rubble.

'As I said in the office,' the young man was advising, 'it needs a lot of attention. It's been empty for a long time. There's been talk of demolition.' Mossy felt a blank shiver of horror go through him, one that shook him to the core.

'Not demolition,' he groaned. 'That's the worst possible way to go.'

'I know Lower Farm would be quite happy to add the garden into part of their fields,' the young man rattled on.

'Surely not!' exclaimed a young woman. 'A house this old... It's in need of looking after, but pulling it down would be so sad!' Rollo looked at her carefully. There was something about her that seemed vaguely familiar, but he wasn't sure what.

'But Nicky, darling, it would be a huge job,' the young woman's husband reasoned with her. 'Are you sure we could manage it? With the baby coming? And I won't be able to help you, I'll be working.'

Rollo felt a tug on his arm and turned to face Mossy.

'Applicants!' Now Mossy's eyes were shining. 'These are Applicants! We have to make them want to stay. Keep close.'

Mossy and Rollo shadowed the group as they walked up the path. Rollo, still half carrying Mossy as they struggled in their wake, turned to his friend.

'What do you mean, Applicants?'

'People who are applying to be Dwellers. This is our chance; we have to help them see that they can be happy in Annanbourne. Thank goodness you're here too. I'm too weak to do it on my own.'

Mossy couldn't climb the steps when the group went upstairs and, having crashed down them such a short while ago, Rollo was glad that Mossy held him back.

'We need to send a projection, Tollo,' he explained.

'Projection?' For a moment Rollo was puzzled, and then he remembered how he and Mossy seemed able to send each other ideas. 'What, me too?'

'I don't think I've got the strength to do it alone, but with both of us together we should manage. You can be quite good at it sometimes,' Mossy assured him. Rollo was still puzzled; Mossy kept using that strange version of his name, but it seemed he genuinely thought that was it. And he appeared to think Rollo knew what he was doing, could perform all sorts of feats that Mossy had only hinted at before. Dreams, he sighed silently.

'Forget dreams.' Mossy was business-like now, if still a little pale. The presence of his friend and the hope of future Dwellers was helping him find the determination to carry on. 'What we need to send them is 'home'. I think just that on its own will do. You take Nicky; I'll tackle her husband. Catch them as they come down.'

They waited at the foot of the stairs, trying to track progress from the sound of footsteps above them. The voices were muffled, with only the occasional word wriggling down through the floorboards.

'They're in Cissy's room,' said Rollo.

'Cissy's room?' Mossy frowned at him. 'You're full of it today – Mum, Cissy – who are these people?' Fortunately Rollo was saved from having to explain by the sight of feet arriving at the top of the landing.

'Now!' Mossy gripped Rollo's shoulder, his long fingers shaking with the effort.

Rollo closed his eyes. Holding Nicky's face clearly in his mind he silently repeated the word 'home', over and over again, as he listened to the footsteps coming down the stairs. He hoped this was what Mossy meant by projecting. It was all he could think of. A feeling of warmth seemed to fill the space around him, and suddenly it was as if his mind was filled with light. A smile spread across his face. He'd felt Mossy do this before.

Opening his eyes as the group passed, he caught a glimpse of the husband taking his wife's hand and giving it a squeeze.

'I always say you can tell whether a place is right by the way it feels.'

'Can you sense it too?' Nicky asked, looping her arm through his, as they walked across the old brick floor of the kitchen.

'I know it's in a terrible state, but there's something about this house...' he paused. 'Mice?' he asked, looking at the hole Rollo had made in the back door.

'If they are, they're giant ones!' Nicky laughed. 'And that looks recent!'

'This takes us out into the back garden.' The estate agent pulled another bunch of keys out of his pocket and sifted through them. 'I just need to find the right one.'

Bill and Nicky looked at the old range.

'That will have to be replaced,' Nicky remarked. Bill looked at her, then grinned as she rubbed some of the grime off one of the panes of glass in the window, while he tested the taps by the sink. There was a loud screech of complaint, but no water came out. Mossy winced in silent pain, and Rollo put an arm round him to stop him collapsing.

'Um... I can't seem to find the right key,' sighed the young man. 'We'll have to go out through the front door, but we can walk round to the back, if you don't mind wading through the grass.'

'Quick, Tollo, through the hole,' said Mossy, as soon as

they had gone. 'We need you in position before they get there.' Rollo helped pull him through again.

'In position?' Rollo asked. Exhausted, Mossy sank to the ground and then pointed at the old apple tree.

'You'll have to climb up,' he explained. 'When they come round, they'll walk under it. Shake the branch and it'll free the blossom.'

'Climb the tree?' Rollo felt daunted. He'd never thought it particularly big before, but now it towered over them.

'Come on, no time to waste,' Mossy urged him on. 'The hollow trunk. You've never found it difficult before.'

'Oh right. Fine.' Rollo knew he had never climbed it before. In his normal size he'd never have fitted inside. Nevertheless he decided to keep quiet. 'Just remind me how to get in.' Mossy stared at him wide-eyed.

'You're the one who worked it out last time you were here! By the crack on the far side, remember?'

'Of course!' said Rollo, slapping his head and instantly regretting it. The bruise from falling down the stairs was still very tender.

'You go. I'll catch up,' Mossy added, preparing to crawl after him.

Heading off in what he hoped looked a confident manner, Rollo luckily found the crack and squeezed through. A shaft of light poured down the hollow trunk, from where the branches spread up into the blue. Briefly amazed at the space, Rollo spotted the ivy growing up the smooth walls. Grasping it firmly, he started climbing and soon poked his head out of the top. He immediately spotted Mossy by the base of the tree, and from the other direction he caught the sound of voices.

'...I don't think there should be any problem with that. The two sisters who still own it are simply looking to get it settled. They live in Suffolk, and none of their children has any interest in the place. They sold the land off long ago.' The young estate agent strode on energetically towards the far side of the garden.

Balancing carefully, Rollo edged himself along the bough, aiming for the blossom-covered twigs. Nicky and Bill walked underneath him and then paused. He looked down. Mossy, now propped against the base of the trunk, and panting slightly from the effort, waved his hands at him with a thumbs-up. Rollo gently shook the branch. Nothing happened.

'What do you think, my love?' asked Bill. Rollo eased himself a bit further out, the branch bending under his weight.

'It's lovely,' sighed Nicky. 'Or it will be. Not too far from the town, but wonderfully quiet. Space for this little one,' she patted her tummy, 'and any brothers or sisters that might come.' Rollo grasped a slender twig that was covered in blossom.

'You think this could really be our home?' checked Bill.

'Oh yes, for years and years,' Nicky smiled up at him. Suddenly Rollo remembered where he'd seen that face before. Not looking like this, but much older, creased and with a halo of white hair. But how did that work? Looking down at Bill, he tried to remember a photograph that he'd seen in the house when he'd first come to visit it with his parents, before they had come to live there. Could this possibly be a younger version of the man in the picture?

He leaned forward for a better look. The small twig under his foot bent, and then sprang sideways, flinging him off balance. He grabbed at the branch beside him, giving it a major jolt as his feet danced on empty space. A shower of petals fluttered through the air, decorating Nicky like confetti at a wedding. At the base of the tree Mossy clapped his hands together silently.

'It's almost as if the house wants us to be here,' Nicky laughed, and Bill brushed a speck of pink blossom off her nose.

'And we think this might once have been a vegetable garden,' called the agent.

By the time Rollo had clambered back down to the ground, Mossy was sitting with his back against the warm wood.

'That was brilliant!' he beamed. 'Though I thought you were going to fall off at one point!'

'So did I!' agreed Rollo. 'I'm glad I didn't. I think I've bashed myself enough for one day! Still, these people are going to come to be your new Dwellers.'

'We don't know for sure, yet,' mused Mossy. But Rollo was convinced.

'I told you it'd be fine. I told you new Dwellers would come. And children arriving soon. See, you're going to be fine. You've just got to hang on a bit longer.' Mossy looked at him.

'How come you're so positive?'

'Well,' Rollo started, and then stopped. How could he explain that the young woman examining the weed-infested vegetable garden was the old woman he'd met a few years ago? 'Trust me.'

To stop Mossy fretting, and to prevent him asking any more questions he couldn't answer anyway, Rollo spent the rest of the day carefully helping Mossy around, reminding the Holder of all the places he loved and cared for. Nicky and Bill walked to and fro, inspecting every nook and cranny, peering up chimneys, revisiting places two, or even three times. Sometimes they asked questions the estate agent couldn't answer.

'It's not an oven, it's where the washing copper stood!' Mossy exclaimed under his breath. They were standing in one of the little rooms whose doors Rollo had spotted when he'd first entered the downstairs room. Rollo nodded his head sagely, although he wasn't quite sure what a washing copper was.

'No, no, no!' Mossy muttered when the agent told Nicky and Bill that the other small space they were exploring was a store. 'That's beyond; this is the dairy.' Oh, so that's what Dad's study used to be! thought Rollo. And as far as I'm concerned, both this dairy and the washing copper room are part of the sitting room. But he kept that to himself.

Each time the couple smiled or laughed Rollo saw Mossy change. It wasn't that he suddenly looked better, but his breathing was deeper and he looked about him with interest. There were still dark rings under his eyes, and he needed help to walk anywhere. He was very weak and struggled to see things that Rollo pointed out to him, completely missing the kingfisher darting up the stream, or the deer that peered timidly through the hedge.

After every little thing had been inspected, sometimes twice, the visitors finally returned to their cars and left.

'You really think they'll really come back as my Dwellers?' Mossy checked yet again.

'Absolutely,' said Rollo, nodding his head. 'And meanwhile, let's go into the garden and enjoy the day.' They lazed by the stream, watching trout swim by, and spotting dragonflies skimming over clear patches of water.

'I should have found a Forget-Me-Not,' muttered Mossy, 'but they're not in flower yet. Or one of the Moon Pennies to slip in their car. Something to make them remember us.'

'They won't forget Annanbourne,' Rollo reassured him.

Eventually the sun sank, glowing and red behind the hill. The pair ambled back to the house, creeping in through the hole in the back door.

'I can still feel that there have been people here,' Mossy said, smiling, as they crossed the kitchen and headed for the sitting room. He eased himself down onto the edge of the hearthstone.

'You staying long?' he asked.

'Dunno,' replied Rollo, wondering how long a dream could last.

'You're welcome as long as you like, you know.' Mossy swung his legs up and then lay back on the stone, his fingers laced under his head. 'I'm still really tired, but somehow I think I'm going to sleep well for once. I haven't in ages. But, like you said, there's something to look forward to, and I can hope again.'

Rollo sat with his back against the worn wall of the old chimney and looked up into the blackness. He was tired too.

His eyelids drooped, sleep making them heavy. Somewhere far above in the dark night sky an owl hooted as she flew by on silent wings. The last thing he heard was Mossy's voice.

'I couldn't have managed today without you. I'd given up. The state I was in, those Applicants could have come and gone and I'd never have known, never have been able to make the effort to persuade them to become real Dwellers. Now I think we might stand a chance. You've saved my life, Tollo. And not just mine, Annanbourne's too. We can never thank you enough.'

CHAPTER 30

Understanding

Waking just before the alarm went off, Rollo lay snuggled and warm for a while, puzzling, pondering his dream. Some night! But he'd been right all along. That was all it had been, a dream.

Funny how they can feel so real at times, he told himself, pushing the duvet off and getting out of bed. As he wriggled his toes in the soft carpet, he became aware of an ache on his left side and looked down to see a ruddy bruise that stretched from his hip to the top of his leg. He poked it with a finger and winced at the pain.

'Hmm, not surprised, the way you fling yourself about on that bike,' thought Mossy, lurking in the corner of the room.

Down in the kitchen, Annie was busy watching the kettle boil.

'Hot chocolate for you, my love?' she asked as she reached for a couple of mugs.

'Mmm, please,' replied Rollo, hunting out cereal. His mother brought the steaming mugs over and sat down beside him.

'What on earth have you done to your head? There's a great purple bruise above your ear.' Rollo reached up to touch it and flinched. It was worse than the bruise on his hip.

'I dreamed I fell down the stairs and the house was nearly in ruins. I must have bashed into something in my sleep. Maybe that's what made the dream come.'

Mossy, perched on the corner of the table, wondered what exactly Rollo had been experiencing. He hadn't noticed any nightmares about collapsing houses creeping about during the night. In fact, Rollo had slept so deeply that Mossy hadn't been able to feel any of his dreams at all.

As Annie gently rubbed arnica cream onto the swelling, Rollo grabbed a piece of bread and spread it with a thick layer of peanut butter.

'Gotta go, Mum,' he said, taking a bite. 'Or the paper round will be given to someone else, and I've still got Jon's to do as well. See you after school!' Flinging his bag over one shoulder, he headed out of the door.

'Don't overdo it!' Annie called after him, but Rollo just waved a hand and ran to the barn to collect his bike.

In no time Cissy, JJ and Jack had all hurtled through, heading off to school and leaving chaos in their wake. Mossy followed Annie into the barn, settling himself comfortably amongst the tubes of paint, where he could get a good view of the latest work in progress. Annie's exhibition was due to open in a couple of months and she was determined to add this one to it.

Mossy feasted on the energy that filled the room. He

needed a boost after all the troubles with Tannor, and this was the perfect thing to put him back on his feet. He rested his back against a pile of books, stretched out his legs and relaxed. 'Payne's Grey' he read on a tube of paint, which reminded him – how had Rollo hurt himself?

'Dad?'queried Rollo that evening as he carried the empty spaghetti bowl over to the sink.

'Yup?' Jack looked over from the pile of marking he had just dumped on the table.

'The lady we bought the house from, what was she called?' Mossy, perched in his place on the dresser, looked over at him. Why was Rollo asking about Nicky?

'Mrs Rendal. Why?'

'No reason. Just wondered. You don't know her first name, do you?'

'We're doing a poem about Rendal in school,' interrupted Cissy. 'He's a monster that eats people.'

'What, while they're alive?' JJ, looking alarmed, stopped on his way to put a clean saucepan back on the cooker.

'Yeah, 'cos he doesn't like them making a racket, and there's this guy, Be A Wolf, who kills him by ripping his arm off. It's really gruesome,' she explained with a broad grin.

'D'you mean Beowulf?' checked Annie. 'And I think it's Grendel, rather than Rendal. Personally, I don't blame his mother for getting so angry. I'd be furious if anyone hurt any of you.'

'Erm, I think it began with an N... Nicola?' said Jack, picking up a red pen and opening the first book. 'I think that's what was on the papers we had to sign. Why are you so interested?' Mossy stared from one to the other. How did they manage to have all these conversations at once? Cissy started to explain how to rip an arm off, demonstrating on JJ as she talked.

'Did she have a husband?' asked Rollo.

'Not when we met her. She had been married, but I think he died several years before we came.' Nearly ten years, thought Mossy. I had a lot of looking after to do during that time.

'And then you bleed to death,' finished Cissy triumphantly.

Mossy was on Nightwatch by JJ, whose sleeping mind was searching for one-armed monsters, so it was rather later than usual before he stuck his head round Rollo's door. Wondering what had sparked all the questions about past Dwellers, he watched him for a while before shimmering into visibility.

'Oh good, I was hoping you'd come by. I've got lots to ask you,' said Rollo, closing his book and flinging it to the end of his bed. You're not the only one, thought Mossy, maintaining a nonchalant air. 'I had a dream last night,' Rollo continued. 'About falling down the stairs. And you came into it.'

'I did?' Now it was Mossy's turn to look puzzled. Although he regularly sorted out dreams, he'd never imagined that he could be in one.

'What me? Falling down the stairs?'

'No, no, you were far too ill for that…' As Rollo recounted his dream, Mossy's eyes widened in amazement.

'Hang on,' he said, interrupting as Rollo described how he'd helped him down the bank of the stream. 'Where d'you get this story from? And how did you find out about The Travelling Holder? You fell asleep before I told you any of that part!'

'No, no. This was my dream; and what d'you mean by the Travelling Holder?'

'A dream?' Mossy shook his head. 'No.' He paused, struggling to understand it himself. 'This is no dream, it's much more than that.' Despite all the times he wondered about the similarity between Rollo and Tollo, about the suggestions of the Barn Owl and the strange ramblings of the old tortoise, he'd never really believed that it could be true. 'I've wondered before if you might be more than just a Place Reader, what with looking so familiar and with a similar name. And now you seem know too much about things I've never told anyone.'

'What d'you mean 'know too much'? Dreams come out of nowhere, ideas that are just floating about, undecided in your mind.' Hmm, thought Mossy, looking silently at Rollo. I could tell you a thing or two about dreams; floating about in your mind indeed! Sometimes humans just don't have a clue how the world works!

'You know what Tollo said to me,' Mossy explained. 'What I said to him, where we sat…'

'Tollo?' exclaimed Rollo, sitting forward. Now it was his turn to stare in amazement at the Holder. He hadn't mentioned the name. 'That's what you kept calling me in the dream. How come you know that too? I didn't tell you that. I don't understand,' he admitted, frowning. Mossy was confused too.

'What made you ask about the last Dwellers this evening?' he checked, changing the subject slightly. Rollo's face cleared.

'They were in the dream too. But Dad said she was called Mrs Rendal, and I never heard that part. I just heard her husband call her Nicky, and she called him...'

'...Bill.' Mossy finished Rollo's sentence. 'I remember them well.' He paused again, scrutinising Rollo as he weighed up whether to ask the next question or not. He took a breath.

'That bruise on your head, the one on your hip... Have you found the graze on the back of your arm yet?'

'I haven't hurt my arm!' Rollo broke the tension with a laugh. He twisted round, pulling up the sleeve of his pyjamas. 'See!'

'Other arm,' said Mossy calmly, pointing a long finger at Rollo's right side.

'That one's fine too,' laughed Rollo, twisting the other way. 'You're trying to spook me.' He pulled up the other sleeve. 'There's noth...' His voice faded into silence as they both looked at the red graze that was scabbing over just above his elbow. 'How did you know? I couldn't even feel it.'

'I remember seeing it at the time. Back when Tollo, you, saved my life. It **was** you. I've often wondered why you looked so like him, but I've always told myself there was no connection. You're human, a Dweller, and the Travelling Holder is, well...,' he paused, shrugging, 'a Holder, like me, same size, too. So that's why you could tell me there would be more Dwellers coming. You knew, because you know that you are here, now. I'd given up, and if it hadn't been for you coming I'd have died that day, gone, and the house would have been beyond repair, would have fallen down. And then... Then there would have been no Annanbourne for you to come to.' Mossy's voice faltered as he struggled to understand how it all worked.

So this was what the old tortoise had meant when he had told him Rollo was more than he seemed. He hadn't believed it at the time, had convinced himself it was another of the old fellow's crazy stories. Was this what the Barn Owl had hinted at? Goodness knows how the Old Things brought forth such wisdom.

And then he understood that this was what he had to thank Rollo for. For being the friend who saved his life. Well, that would take some doing. But if that was the case...

A broad smile spread across his face. Now all was clear. He lifted his hand upwards, as if to receive a gift. Tollo and Rollo were one and the same. This boy, this Dweller, sitting in front of him, was indeed his oldest and most valued friend. There was no one else like him in the world.

The clouds that fuzzed about his head disappeared. Everything made sense. Now he understood why there had been times in the past when Tollo had looked older. He had come from times yet to come in this boy's life, times when he would be older than he was now. He didn't always travel at the same time. He wasn't always the same age.

'Are you trying to tell me that I was actually there, that my dream wasn't a dream, but real?' Rollo asked. Mossy nodded his head. 'But I fell asleep on the hearthstone, so how come I woke up in my bed, all warm, in my pyjamas? I wasn't wearing pyjamas in my dream.' Mossy shrugged.

'I don't know all the answers, I just know it was you. The odd thing is you've been before. I've met you loads of times over the years. Have you 'dreamed' about Annanbourne before? Dreams with me in them?'

'Never.' Rollo folded his arms. 'See, so that proves it. It was just a dream. And you seeing me there before was just a dream too. Only then it was your dream, not mine.'

'You humans,' muttered Mossy, shaking his head. 'Sometimes you can't see the nose on your own face. And that's not just because it's so short. You don't want to see things unless you're forced to.'

Silence fell in the room.

'Well, Mossy' said Rollo after a while. 'I don't want to argue. After all, in my world you shouldn't exist anyway.' He held out a hand, and Mossy placed his on top, long fingers lying warmly on Rollo's palm.

'No point,' he agreed, smiling. 'But I'm pretty sure I know how it works. It's just the way I was told. You fell asleep while I was telling you about a time when I needed you, a time when I remember you helping. And when you woke up you were there.'

'So **you** say.' Now it was Rollo's turn to mutter under his breath. Mossy wagged a long finger at him.

'You wait. I'll prove it. I'll tell you about a time when I could have done with some help and we'll see what happens. Not now, not tonight, you need a rest. And anyway you still have unfinished business to sort out for Tannor first.'

CHAPTER 31

Hunting

For the next few weeks Mossy kept himself to himself as much as possible. He had no intention of checking his theory about Rollo being Tollo for some while yet, not till Tannor's story was well and truly settled. At night he watched to see if the Place Reader disappeared into visions of his own, but he slept the sleep of the truly tired, and dreamed the dreams of any normal boy.

Life ran chaotically towards the end of term. Mossy was busy keeping Cissy calm before her performance, nudging JJ away from icy surfaces and keeping Jack awake during long, late nights of marking.

'I'm looking forward to the holidays as much as the kids are,' he admitted to Puddle. 'And in the spring we've got Annie's exhibition. Nerves to calm there too.'

The evening before Rollo was due to visit the county archives with his Dad, Mossy clambered onto his bedside table.

'Hello there!' Rollo smiled as he put down his book. 'Just

who I was hoping to see. Can you remind me of anything that will help us work out who the skeleton was?'

'Tannor said the young man was a cousin of the tanner. The only other thing I know is that he was called Josiah.'

'What? The skeleton?'

'No, the tanner.'

'There could be hundreds of Josiahs. Don't you know his last name?'

'Tanner, of course. His family had always been makers of leather. What else would he be called?'

'Well, we're Breezes and I can't think of any job that could be connected to.'

'It wasn't just jobs that gave you your name,' chuckled Mossy. 'There was a family once who lived in the village called Langshanks. You can work that one out for yourself.'

'We're going to go back again after Christmas,' Rollo told him that night. 'It wasn't as easy as I thought.'

Mossy settled himself on the bedside table as Rollo wriggled down further into his duvet.

'They were really interested, and you were right, those papers are a will. And I'm pretty sure I found Josiah Tanner again too. Someone with the same name turned up in Topton at about the time you said the fire burned down the tannery. He made a good business there, had a family, and one of his descendants ended up as Mayor of Topton in 1879. Dead posh they were by then, so maybe getting away from the tannery in the woods and Tannor's 'help' there was no bad thing. I came across all sorts of others too. I found

Widow Knight, and now I know that the Barkers are part of her family too. And Prior Albion was her brother who helped after her husband died, which is why their house is called Prior's Farm. But I couldn't find anything about any more Goodyears. It was as if they completely vanished. How can that happen? Could they have been from somewhere else altogether, nothing to do with round here? If that's the case we'll never find them.'

'Let me have a think,' Mossy suggested. 'For now, I reckon you need to forget all about it and concentrate on holidays and fun. I'm going to keep out of sight too.'

'I still know you're there even if I can't see you, you know,' Rollo reminded him.

'Herfff,' sighed Mossy, frowning. 'You're a tricky one, Tollo.'

'And don't call me Tollo. I'm Rollo. Whatever you may think about your Travelling Holder idea, I'm not Tollo. I'm just me, a boy, even if I can see you sometimes.' Mossy raised an eyebrow and wagged a long, thin finger at him as he slipped quietly out of sight.

'We'll see,' he whispered, his voice fading away with his body.

'Or not,' countered Rollo, shaking his duvet smooth and turning out the light. 'G'night.'

Keeping himself carefully out of sight, out of earshot and hidden in shadows, Mossy made the most of the Christmas season to stock up on energy. Visitors, festivities and the general excitement soon had him fairly bouncing with life, the aches and pains of Tannor's time with them little more than a memory.

On New Year's Eve Annie took the candlestick JJ had given her and placed it in the centre of the table.

'See?' she said as she placed a tall candle in it. 'A new light to start off the New Year, to burn brightly and take us from this year into the next. There's lots to look forward to, but we must remember the past as well.' Cissy gave her a hug and then twirled off round the table to her father.

'It's the middle school plays next year and I'm planning on a starring role. Mr Paul says I did really well in the last one, and the auditions are right at the beginning of term. That's last year and next. I can't wait.'

'Can I light it, Mum?' asked JJ.

Mossy watched the flame of the candle flicker as it caught and remembered the last time he had seen Tannor, curled around the base. He watched the soft glow of the stone as it warmed to the flame and wondered if Rollo could see it too, or whether he only saw such things when he was Tollo. How proud Tannor would have been to know that his Starting Stone was being used to mark good times. And probably surprised, he reflected.

A couple of days later, at the end of a brief Nightwatch, he paused by Rollo's door.

'*Mossy?*' The projection caught him by surprise. He held up his hand. There was the frame of the door, clearly visible through it. He had been so pleased at making it impossible even for Rollo to find him over the past couple of weeks. He shrugged his shoulders. If he had needed proof as to who Rollo was, then this answered his final questions. He stuck his head round the door.

'*What is it?*'

'*I just wanted to ask you a couple of things.*' There was a pause. '*And it would be easier if I could see you,*' Rollo finished.

'Have you ever not known where I was?' Mossy asked quietly once he was sitting crossed legged, his hands resting on his knees, his nose pointing at Rollo.

'I only know when you're close by. Which was why I grabbed that wrapping paper off Cissy when she was about to fling it on the fire. Was it your foot or your arm caught up in it?'

'Foot,' admitted Mossy.

'And I struggled not to laugh when you nearly fell into the soup bowl at supper the other night. But I haven't a clue when you're off somewhere else, just like with anybody.'

'So what are these questions?' Mossy reminded him.

'I'm going back to the county archives with Dad tomorrow, and I wondered if you had any other ideas that might help.'

'Have you tried looking at where Josiah came from?' suggested Mossy. 'Find his parents. Maybe he had brothers and sisters and the Samuel Goodyear is connected with that. If the skeleton was something to do with Josiah, maybe he had a relation who married a Goodyear.'

Mossy didn't have to wait long when Rollo returned. He was bursting with news.

'We found where your skeleton used to live! It's here in

town!' he told Cissy as soon as he arrived home. 'It's just amazing what's recorded in the archives!'

Mossy, who had been sitting on the dresser watching JJ make biscuits, pulled his ears straight to catch every word.

'It turns out that Josiah had an aunt who married someone called Benjamin Goodyear, and it was their son, Samuel, who went missing when he was about seventeen. I think that's who our skeleton was. You see he disappeared just after his grandfather, who was also called Samuel, died. It was all in the archives. You can see he was born, and then he never died, he just disappeared. There's a magistrate's record of the search for him, because, at the same time, his grandfather's will went missing. I think the papers we found are that document. But what's so awful is that, with no will to say that the house was theirs, the family were turned out of their home and ended up in the workhouse, because they had nowhere to live or anything.'

'So my skeleton's called Samuel,' said Cissy, reaching for some uncooked biscuit. 'But we still don't know who his family is now.'

'Well no, because the parents and the other children, all eight of them, died in the workhouse. There's only one brother, Tobias, who isn't marked down as having died. But what's weird is that he disappears too.'

'That's terrible!' said Cissy. 'All those people died just because those papers got lost.' Mossy frowned. Hiding the will had done more damage than simply not letting the dead young man be found and properly buried.

'Still, at least we now have an address of where they lived before Samuel Goodyear went missing.'

'I don't see how that helps,' sighed Cissy. 'A house isn't a family.'

Mossy's nose twitched. If they had the house, then maybe he could help find a way.

'I'm sorry, Mossy. It looks as if we've come to a dead end,' admitted Rollo when they had a chance to speak.

'There's one last thing we could try. You know the house, so we can ask the Holder.'

'It took me ages to find you,' Rollo protested. 'I'm not sure I could find a Holder in someone else's house, and anyway, how do we get in there?'

'Knock on the door, like you do anywhere else. Dwellers open doors, and then I can get in and find out if the Holder can help us.'

'You'd come with me?!' exclaimed Rollo. 'Brilliant! But how?'

They eventually decided that Mossy would travel in the pocket of Rollo's coat when the whole family went shopping for some last bits and pieces for the new term.

'Remember I'm here, please, and don't go stuffing all your usual rubbish in with me,' Mossy reminded him as they got out of the car.

'Is Dragon Street the one with the cinema in it?' asked Rollo, when they emerged from the bookshop.

'Isn't that where you said Samuel Goodyear lived too?' asked JJ.

'Can we go that way back to the car? I'd really like to see the house,' Rollo suggested. Mossy craned his head out of the pocket to peer about.

'43, 41, 39,' JJ read from the doors. 'Why do the numbers

go backwards, and how do we know which one it was anyway?'

'It just said Goodyear House, Dragon Street. I sort of thought the name would be on it.' Mossy could feel Rollo's disappointment stream through him. I should have warned him, he realised, looking at the buildings around them; none of these is more than a hundred years old.

'What's on at the cinema?' asked Cissy, pausing to look at the posters. 'Look!' she pointed at a picture of children swimming through an underwater cave. 'Can we go?'

'We need to finish the shopping first,' Annie told her.

Beyond the glass doors, Mossy spotted a tall, angular Holder with pale, almost white hair, leaning against one of the slender columns inside.

'I'll check what time it's on,' said Jack, pushing open the door.

'*Follow him,*' projected Mossy. '*I need to get in there.*'

Inside, the children examined other posters on the walls.

'I remember that one!' exclaimed JJ. 'When he had to get everything in the right order to be able to escape?'

'*Could you stand by that plant pot?*' Mossy nudged Rollo to get his attention. '*I can see someone who might be able to help us.*' Rollo sauntered across the foyer to a tall palm that grew from a container between the columns. Angels with flattened wings flanked the stairs beyond them. Mossy climbed out onto the soft earth and then dropped to the ground.

'It starts at six thirty,' said Cissy.

Mossy walked across the open space.

'Where did you spring from?' exclaimed the other Holder.

'I didn't see you come in!'

'Edwin Mosstone,' said Mossy, bowing in greeting. 'Usually called Mossy. I'll explain later, but right now I'm looking for some urgent help.'

'Goodun-cum-Kino, but you might as well stick to Goodun; everybody else does. Apologies for not welcoming you properly. It was a bit of a surprise you popping up like that.'

'Cum-Kino?' checked Mossy. 'You mean you weren't always a cinema?'

'Not a bit of it. We rose again back in the 1920s.'

Cissy, JJ and Jack headed out through the door with Annie. Rollo lingered by the ticket desk.

'An end of holiday treat,' Mossy heard Jack tell his wife.

'Were you here long before you were rebuilt?' asked Mossy, edging towards Rollo.

'Since 1623. Why?'

'Perfect!' Mossy stopped in his tracks.

Cissy stuck her head round the door again.

'You staging a sit-in here, Rollo? They've already agreed that we can come if we get everything else done first. Come on, we've got to hurry. It'll be your fault if we miss it.'

Mossy glanced over towards Rollo.

'*You go. I'll find you when you come back.*'

'*OK,*' Rollo fired back. '*I heard what you've been saying. See you later.*'

'Sorry Cissy, in a dream world,' he called, and set off after her.

Goodun was staring around him, searching every corner.

'Is there a third Holder in here?' he hissed, his voice as low as possible. 'Where's he hiding? I can't see anyone, but I heard that projection loud and clear.'

'Ah,' Mossy blushed slightly. 'Right… Well… I said I'd explain… Is there somewhere we can talk properly?'

By the time Mossy had finished telling him at some length about Place Readers and Travelling Holders, Goodun's eyes were almost popping out of his head.

'But I spoke to the Travelling Holder, way back. He said something about 'Watch for Will.' I never understood what he meant. We never had a Will in any of my Dweller families, and these days I hardly know one person from the next, let alone what they're called. They just shoot through for the films.'

'He spoke to you? When?'

'Centuries ago. Back when we were almost a new house, when I looked more like you, though I was never so skinny, but before we became…' he smiled proudly, indicating their surroundings, 'all angles and streamlined, gold-plated and frosted glass.'

'So your Starting Stone survived?'

'It's over there,' said Goodun proudly, leading the way back to the foyer and pointing out a clear panel in the floor, under which lay a worn stone, softly spot-lit. Etched into the glass, and scratched by the passing of many feet, were some words.

Original 17th Century Foundation Stone

'I struck lucky.'

'You did,' Mossy nodded his head. 'But it must have been a scary time.'

'I'll say. It was a close-run thing. Still, none of that explains what you're doing here.'

'I'm trying to find a house that must have been around when you were still quite young. Maybe you knew it? Goodyear House?'

Goodun bowed low, sweeping his arms wide in the formal greeting and welcome.

'We haven't been called by our old name for a long time now, and it's good to hear it.' He grinned as he stood up again.

'Here? Goodyear House was here!' Mossy put an arm round Goodun's shoulder. 'Then maybe you can help us even further.'

'I remember them well.' Goodun nodded his head as Mossy finished explaining. 'And I remember that business of the lost will. Terrible it was. First the grandfather died, then the eldest son went missing, and finally the whole family were forced into the workhouse. I heard the most horrible stories from Weeden, the Holder there. Can you imagine it, trying to look after parents and children separated from each other, sickly and weak, miserable and hopeless? You know, I think Weeden was actually relieved to go when they eventually demolished that place. He'd had a terrible time. They were a good family, the Goodyears, and only one ever came back. Between the workhouse and the tannery that family was as good as destroyed.'

'The tannery? You think it had something to do with the tannery as well?'

'Everything seemed to go wrong for those Dwellers almost as soon as Sam started helping his cousin out at the tannery. It was almost as if Sam was loaded down with trouble each time he returned from there.'

'But you say one of the family **did** come back from the workhouse? Did he stay with you?'

'Well I say, came back, but it was no more than visits. He was only three or four when they were put out on the street, and I didn't see him for several years. When I did I barely recognised him. It was just something about the air around him that had echoes of him as a child. He didn't even know we were his old home. And he'd changed his name.'

'He'd changed his name? Why?'

'I don't really know. He'd taken to calling himself Goodger, Tobias Goodger. He'd been taken on by a sweep from the workhouse, and by the time I saw him again he was running the business. He was a good sweep, worked hard, and later on he was good to the boys who worked for him too. He cleaned our chimneys regularly, but I reckon he didn't want too much of a link to memories of all he'd lost.'

A burst of sound above them made Goodun look towards the stairs.

'Watch out. The film's finished and they'll all be coming out. Step to this side so we're well out of the way.'

'I've got to look for my Dwellers coming back.'

'There's a good viewing spot from the shoulder of that angel. The angels are excellent. They keep still and are really quite comfortable. You can see all the doors from there, and there'll be plenty of time for you to get close while they're buying tickets.'

'Don't you ever worry that they'll rebuild you again here in the town?' Mossy asked as they dangled their legs over the smooth plaster shoulder. 'They keep changing the centres of towns.' He remembered the face of the Holder he'd seen in London and a shudder went through him. Goodun shook his head.

'We've been listed now. Apparently there aren't many Art Deco cinemas like us around these days, so they're going to look after us.' He paused, examining the people passing below them. 'Isn't that your lot there?'

CHAPTER 32

Finders Keepers

Armed with Mossy's information, it only took Rollo one more visit to the archives to find Tobias Goodger.

'You'll never believe it, JJ,' he exclaimed on his return. 'You know your friend Toby at school?' JJ nodded his head. 'I'm pretty sure the skeleton was his great-great, and a whole lot more greats, uncle.'

'And his brother Charlie's in my maths set!' Cissy grinned. 'How weird is that?'

'What? That he's in your maths set?'

'No, dummy. That we should have found his Long Lost Uncle. D'you think he knew he was missing?'

Mossy sat watching them and let his mind wander. Sometimes lost things leave a hole that takes longer to fill than people expect.

'What matters is that we can give them back the will and let them know what we've discovered,' Rollo pointed out. 'And then they'll know that the skeleton we found was from their family.'

'That means it isn't lost any longer,' added Cissy.

Aware that sometimes it could be more than just a name that was handed down through a family, Mossy made sure that he was on hand when Toby, Charlie and their parents arrived. His nose quivered as JJ greeted Toby at the door.

'Hi there, Tobes!'

Mossy started back in surprise, as JJ led his friend through to the kitchen for a drink.

'He's just like him!' he projected in amazement.

'What do you mean?' came Rollo's response.

'Can't you feel it?' Mossy asked silently. Tollo was almost as good at sensing people as Mossy himself. And there was something about the young boy that reminded him of a feeling he'd picked up. As if he were searching for something...

'We read about you finding the skeleton in the paper,' said Mrs Goodger.

'And Charlie mentioned what you'd told him at school,' added Mr Goodger. 'But we never thought it had anything to do with us. I'm as surprised as anyone. How exactly did you find him?' Mossy breathed in the air around the boy's father. There it was again, that same feeling of loss that lingered about his son.

'In the woods.' Cissy waved a hand in the direction of Widow Knight's Wood. 'I thought it might be treasure. Well, I hoped it would be, but this is almost as good.'

'And it's Rollo who's unearthed all this information?' Mrs Goodger smiled at him.

'It's been fun; finding out, I mean. Although it wasn't so

much fun when we realised that someone had died out there.'

'No, I can imagine, but the police forensics people have told us that it looks like it was an accident. There was damage to the skull, and chips of stone in the bone, that make them think he must have bashed his head against the rocks. It's amazing what they can find out from a skeleton these days.'

It was good to know that Tannor was clear of any blame on that front, thought Mossy.

'And without the will we wouldn't have found out any of the rest, or that he was from your family,' Rollo pointed out.

'And you found that out there at the same time?' checked Mr Goodger, tapping the yellowed pages that now lay on his knees.

'Erm…' Rollo paused. All eyes turned to him. Mossy's included.

'Don't land me in this,' he begged.

'I don't remember,' admitted Cissy. 'Where did you find it Rollo?'

'Erm…' repeated Rollo. 'Yeah. It was from there.'

'You mean you went back there without me?' Cissy sounded quite offended.

'When we had told you specifically not to?' Jack was frowning.

'And the police had told you it was out of bounds…' Annie was leaning towards him.

'No, I never went back after you said we shouldn't,' protested Rollo.

'So you kept it secret when we were out there,' Cissy put

her hands on her hips. 'Pwah! Brothers! They never tell you anything!'

'*I'm sorry,*' Mossy apologised. '*I rather landed you in that.*'

Mossy followed behind the families as they walked together to the woods. JJ and Toby ran ahead.

'Just come back safely!' called Mr Goodger.

'It's funny that,' Mrs Goodger confided in Annie. 'He always says it to me whenever I go out, and his father says the same to his mother. Apparently his grandfather did too. It's almost like a family saying.'

Hmm, thought Mossy. So, not just the names and the looks; there's a family worry still about someone being lost. No wonder I could feel something, it must be pretty strong to have lasted all this time. Maybe now at last it can be put to rest.

The police barriers had been removed, though the ground was trampled and muddy. A squirrel threw beech nut husks at them before scampering off, jumping from branch to branch. Two magpies chattered noisily in a tree on the far side of the stream. Mossy spotted prints in the soft earth. It looked like a badger had been inspecting the bank. He smiled. Normal living creatures were returning to the site.

'We think it was a tannery once, and it was Tobias Goodger's cousin, Josiah Tanner, who lived here,' Rollo explained.

'And this was where we found him,' said Cissy, clambering up the bank. Everybody fell silent, and Mossy saw JJ slip his hand quietly into Annie's.

The wall had now been completely demolished and the

stone-lined chamber was open to the air. Mrs Goodger stepped forward and laid a single flower on the smooth earth.

'Found at last,' said her husband.

Back with your family, thought Mossy.

Sun broke through the wintery clouds, and a shaft of sunlight beamed down, pooling on the hard earth floor, washing the surrounding trees with a soft, golden light. The lightest of breezes sifted through the bare branches, and Mossy felt a new clarity open up through the trees.

'I can see why someone wanted to make a house here,' said Annie. 'It's rather lovely with the stream, and the view across the valley is beautiful.'

'And you should try the swing we made,' added JJ. 'It's brilliant.'

'It's good to think of people playing and being happy here,' agreed Mr Goodger. 'It makes up for the sadness of him being lost all this time.'

'The police have said that we can bury him now,' Mrs Goodger added.

A cracking sound made everybody look round to see Mr Barker from Prior's Farm arriving. Mossy spotted Denny sneaking though the trees behind him.

'Thank you for inviting me to join you. It's been quite a business with the police investigation going on,' he said, 'but I thought I ought to let you all know… We've been thinking about the woods, and we've decided to make them a proper conservation woodland with access paths, so they can be enjoyed and appreciated by more people.'

'Sounds like quite a change coming,' Mossy said quietly. Denny nodded.

'And can't you just feel it already? I never dared to come down here in the past, but now it seems like a black cloud has been lifted.'

'But most importantly, we hoped that you children would give us a hand with ideas and plans,' finished Mr Barker.

'Well I've got an idea,' announced JJ, popping his head round from behind the oak tree. 'Rollo says he thinks there used to be a tannery here, so why don't you call this bit Tanner's Wood?'

'That's certainly a good idea, young man. Well worth thinking about,' agreed Mr Barker.

Mossy smiled to himself. Just as Widow Knight would never be forgotten, it looked as if Tannor might be remembered too. It would be good after all his suffering. They had more than fulfilled Tannor's last request. Everything was put to rights and new life was coming to the place. He remembered the hidden glow in Tannor's Starting Stone, that the Holder had never seen until it was almost too late. Now his Holding was set to become a place where visitors would be able to discover the light within themselves. That would be a gift well worth the giving.

'Well done,' Mossy congratulated Rollo later that evening. 'You have done just what you hoped. You haven't changed the past, but you have helped to right a wrong and lifted the sadness from Tannery Cottage.'

Rollo smiled at him, strangely pleased at Mossy's comment.

'You think so?'

'It's one of the things you're good at,' nodded Mossy. 'You may be determined that you aren't a Holder, but this is what Holders do. We look after our Dwellers. There's only one of us who does it at all differently, and that's the The Travelling Holder. He's the one who helps without having any Dwellers of his own. He doesn't seem to need them the way the rest of us do. He simply helps us all. It's quite remarkable, and I've never understood before, but now I do.'

'So you've given up on the idea of me being Tollo?' Rollo raised a questioning eyebrow. 'You agree that it was just a dream I had? Even though it seemed to have all those coincidences?'

'There's absolutely no doubt in my mind any longer.' Mossy folded his arms across his chest as he leaned against Rollo's bookcase and looked up at his friend. There was something about his face that made Rollo wonder what exactly was going through his mind.

Then Mossy reached up a hand to tug at one of his ears, making sure it stood straight. His nose quivered and his eyes sparkled the most brilliant blue.

'But I tell you what. One day I'm going to tell you about when Tollo did come to give me a hand.'

Have you read *The Holder of Annabourne* already?

If not, find it at

www.annanbourne.com

If you enjoyed reading about the Place Reader, find out where, and to when, his special gift took him.

The Travelling Holder

Tiggy Greenwood

Rollo thinks he's just slipping into a dream, but he finds himself pitched into the middle of the English Civil War!

Something extraordinary has happened to him, and to Annanbourne too. Thank goodness Mossy is there to explain, but as Rollo gets to grips with his new situation, it's clear that Annanbourne and its Dwellers are in crisis. Soldiers roaming the countryside are intent on causing trouble. One of the family is so badly injured he loses the ability to speak. And it looks like the only person able to sort things out is a girl. But this is a time when girls are hardly allowed out of the house!

Mossy and Rollo have to team up to defend the family and the farm from the villains who'll stop at nothing to get them out…